Books should be returned or renewed by the
last date stamped above

Awarded for excellence

Kent
County
Council

MURDER CAN BOTCH UP YOUR BIRTHDAY

A DESIREE SHAPIRO MYSTERY

SELMA EICHLER

THORNDIKE
CHIVERS

This Large Print edition is published by Thorndike Press®, Waterville, Maine USA and by BBC Audiobooks, Ltd, Bath, England.

Published in 2004 in the U.S. by arrangement with NAL Signet, a member of Penguin Group (USA) Inc.

Published in 2004 in the U.K. by arrangement with NAL Signet, a division of Penguin Group (USA) Inc.

U.S. Hardcover 0-7862-6403-9 (Mystery)
U.K. Hardcover 0-7540-6979-6 (Chivers Large Print)
U.K. Softcover 0-7540-6980-X (Camden Large Print)

The text of this Large Print edition is unabridged.
Other aspects of the book may vary from the original edition.

Set in 16 pt. Plantin.

Printed in the United States on permanent paper.

British Library Cataloguing-in-Publication Data available

Library of Congress Cataloging-in-Publication Data
Eichler, Selma.
  Murder can botch up your birthday : a Desiree Shapiro mystery / Selma Eichler.
    p. cm.
  ISBN 0-7862-6403-9 (lg. print : hc : alk. paper)
  1. Shapiro, Desiree (Fictitious character) — Fiction.
2. Women private investigators — New York (State) — New York — Fiction.   3. Mistresses — Crimes against — Fiction.   4. Overweight women — Fiction.   5. New York (N.Y.) — Fiction.   6. Teenage girls — Fiction.   7. Large type books.   I. Title.
  PS3555.I226M83 2004
  813'.54—dc22   2004044006

To my husband, Lloyd Eichler,
who makes writing all these Desirees
easier in so many ways

ACKNOWLEDGMENTS

My thanks to —

My editor, Ellen Edwards, for asking the questions that made this a better book.

David Gruber, Esq., of Lehman and Gruber, for once again sharing some of his legal expertise.

My cousin Helen Eichler, for her delicious sweet potato recipe.

Catherine Mendoza of American Airlines, who so graciously provided the information I required on airline practices.

CHAPTER 1

I couldn't help it. One look at the individual shifting from foot to foot in the doorway to my office that Monday morning and my jaw dropped to the vicinity of my midsection.

Vicky Pirrelli was definitely not what I'd expected in a prospective client.

For starters, although I'd gathered from our phone conversation on Friday that she was fairly young, I had no idea she'd turn out to be *this* young. She couldn't have been more than fifteen or sixteen — seventeen, tops. Plus, I could hardly have anticipated the bright green shoulder-length hair, the ends of which were an equally garish shade of orange — and an exact match for my visitor's strapless tube top. Incidentally, that ridiculously meager excuse for apparel — even on an unusually warm October day — stopped far enough above the girl's waist to reveal a pierced and bejeweled navel. (And for the benefit of anyone who might be interested, it also served to establish that Vicky had an inny.) Then there was that blue denim skirt she was wearing. The thing wasn't much bigger than a postage stamp, for crying out loud! I mean, it barely covered the essentials. I shuddered to think of what was displayed to the world when she had occasion to bend down.

"Uh, Miss Shapiro?" The voice was soft, uncertain.

I didn't bother correcting the "Miss," although being a widow, I don't technically qualify. "Call me Desiree," I instructed. "And please come in."

Well, I could say one thing for her. Vicky Pirrelli had better manners than I do. *Her* jaw had remained in place when I verified my identity. And I doubt that I was what she'd been expecting, either. It's been my experience that when people conjure up an image of a female PI, it's almost always the media version. They picture this willowy blonde with legs up to here and breasts out to there who runs around chasing the bad guys in her stiletto heels and a skirt as brief as Vicky's.

None of which applies to me in the least.

I'm short (five-two) and not even *semi*-willowy. Or blond, either. (In fact, I consider my best feature to be my glorious hennaed hair.) What's more, my chest, unfortunately, is the one part of me that Mother Nature neglected to pad. And my skirts are all a respectable length, thank you. As for chasing the bad guys in my stiletto heels, (a) I don't own a single pair, and (b) if I did and could by some miracle manage to run in them, it would be in the opposite direction.

Anyway, I stood up behind my desk, and Vicky walked over to me and extended her hand. (I told you she was polite, didn't I?) Then she sat down alongside the desk on the one available chair in my lilliputian office, positioning herself so close to the edge that I was afraid any minute now the gangly teenager would be picking herself up off the floor.

She seemed to be having trouble opening the conversation, so I started things off with, "You mentioned when you called that you'd gotten my name from the phone book."

"Um, that's right. I . . . um, felt that I'd be more comfortable talking to a woman about . . . about things, you know? I'm not sure why; I just would. And a lot of detective agencies are listed in the Manhattan Yellow Pages with initials. Like XYZ Investigators or whatever, or else they, like, just give last names. So you don't have any idea who you'll be getting, you know? But when I saw 'Desiree Shapiro' " — she giggled nervously

— "well, I didn't figure you'd be a man."

I responded to this with what I hoped was a reassuring smile. "And you were right, too. Listen, Vicky, would you care for a Coke or something?"

"Uh-uh. No thanks."

"All right. Why don't you just tell me why you came to see me, okay?"

She swallowed once or twice, following which she took a couple of breaths. "It's, you know, about my dad."

I waited for her to continue, but after a few seconds of silence it appeared obvious that she'd require some prompting. "Your dad?"

"Everyone thinks he's a murderer. But he never killed that woman; he never killed *anybody*. He didn't!"

"And the police? What do they think?" I inquired gently.

"That he did it," she conceded almost inaudibly. "But they, like, make mistakes, don't they? Plenty of mistakes."

"It's been known to happen. Who was the woman your father's supposed to have murdered?"

"This . . . this person he was having an affair with. Her neighbors heard them arguing, you know? My father never denied that they'd had a terrible fight, but that doesn't mean he, like, stuck a knife in her. Lots of people have terrible fights without murdering each other. He and my mom used to go at it pretty good, too, and *she's* still around. Anyhow, once they were through carrying on like that, my dad, like, wanted things to cool down a little, you know? So after a few minutes he got out of there and went for a walk. It was past eleven o'clock by then, so it's not a big surprise that no one saw him leave Christina's apartment — that was her name, Christina — and that he didn't, like, run into anyone while he was out, either. He got back to Christina's about a half hour later. And as soon as he opened the door he saw her lying there on the living room floor. And there was a knife in her side.

"Well, somebody'd called the police — the person who phoned them didn't give a name — and when the cops walked into the place my dad was, like, kneeling next to the body with the knife in his hand. It was just the way it is in the movies a lot of times. You know, where they catch some poor guy in the act — only it ends up being the wrong guy.

"My father pulled out that knife to *save* Christina. He was about to try and, like, stop the bleeding when the cops arrived.

13

He wasn't the one who stabbed her, Desiree. He swore that he wasn't." Vicky's chin jutted out, and her large blue eyes were blazing. "And I believe him."

"So you're here because you want me to find out who did murder Christina. Is that it?"

"What I really want is, you know, for my dad's name to be cleared, and I guess that's the only way to do it. And don't worry, Miss — I mean, Desiree — I can pay you. I make pretty good money baby-sitting, and also I work at Frank 'n' Burgers, like, four days a week after school. So whatever it is you charge —"

"Let's not be concerned with that now, okay? But speaking of school . . ." Tilting my head, I looked at the girl meaningfully.

"Um, I cut a few classes today," she admitted sheepishly. "I had to."

I nodded. "Look, I'm going to need some additional information from you. Tell me, just when was the woman killed?"

Now, as you're probably aware, the more recent a crime, the better the chance of identifying the perpetrator. In fact, the vast majority of cases are solved within the first day or two. So I was hoping that Vicky's answer would be "yesterday." But I'm a reasonable person. This being Monday, I

14

would have settled for "last week" (although preferably "late last week").

"It was the end of February."

My chest constricted. "That was eight months ago," I protested after a fast count on my fingers.

My new client shook her green-and-orange head. "Oh, no," she corrected airily. "That was in 1992."

CHAPTER 2

This clarification accomplished the almost inconceivable: For a minute there, I was actually at a loss for words. "You want me to solve a murder that's ten years old?" I finally demanded incredulously.

"It *is* possible, isn't it?" Vicky's eyes were pleading with me.

Well, what choice did I have? I mean, I had to level with her. "Yes, it's possible. But I've got to be honest with you; it's highly unlikely. You see, after a while the evidence can get tainted or disappear altogether. Also, memories become hazy, perceptions change, and —"

"Does that mean you're not going to take the case?"

"Well, I —"

"I don't know what I'll do if you say no," she wailed. And with this, the blue eyes filled to overflowing, the tears spilling down the girl's cheeks and onto her chin. My instinct was to lean over and squeeze her hand or something. But I wasn't certain she'd welcome the gesture, so I settled for pushing the box of Kleenex on my desk in her direction. She took time off to wipe her wet face and blow her nose once or twice before pressing on. "My dad had nothing to do with . . . with, you know, what happened to Christina. I swear to God."

"I'm not quarreling with the fact of your father's innocence. It's just that after all these years the chances are very slim that I'll be able to prove it."

Vicky reached for another tissue. "I was, like, hoping that you'd at least *try* to learn what really went on that night." The voice became accusatory. "But you don't sound like you're at all interested in discovering the truth." This statement was punctuated with three noisy honks into a fresh tissue. Then, looking me full in the face, Vicky Pirrelli whispered plaintively, "Please, *please* say you'll help me."

That did it. Tossing my reservations — together with whatever smidgen of common sense I possess — right out the window, I told her what I suppose I knew I'd wind up telling her from the beginning. "Okay, Vicky. I'll see what I can find out."

The girl jumped to her feet and, sprawling across the desk, flung her arms around my neck. "Oh, thank you!"

Then she plopped down on the chair

again, making an absentminded — and totally useless — attempt to bring her tiny skirt somewhere in the neighborhood of her knobby knees.

"Let me ask you something," I said then. "Why did it take so long for you to speak to an investigator about this? I realize you were a small child when the homicide occurred, but why wait until now?"

"Because up until two weeks ago I was just as close minded as the rest of my family." She moistened her lower lip with her tongue. "Before my father was sent away there was always, like, this . . . this *tension* at our house. My parents were, like, forever screaming at each other, you know? I guess that was mainly because my dad used to run around with other women." She colored at the admission. "Me, though, I was pretty crazy about him back then. But later on . . . well, I grew up with the idea that all the fights and everything had been totally his fault."

"You can actually recall this? — that business about the other women, I mean."

Vicky shook her head. "No, but after he went to prison I would, you know, overhear people's conversations. They'd talk about the cheating and about what a terrible husband he'd been. But I realize now that my mom might have been partly to blame for what went wrong with their marriage. She can be a terrible nag sometimes, and she *is*, like, kind of a social climber." At this indictment of her maternal parent, Vicky colored again. "Maybe she kept at him because he never made a whole lot of money or anything — he drove a cab for a living. Her nagging could have been the reason he took up with other women in the first place, you know? Anyhow, because of the way things were between them, my mom must have been ready to believe the worst of my dad. She was, like, positive he was guilty of that murder. Or it could be that she just wanted to think so. What happened, though, was that her attitude about my father — along with just about everyone else's, for that matter — rubbed off on me."

"What occurred two weeks ago to change your mind?"

"I talked to my dad," Vicky said softly. "I didn't have any contact with him at all after he went to prison — not until, you know, that day. He asked me to come and see him then. He told me he didn't want me to go on believing that I was the daughter of a killer. And once I got this chance to, like, hear what he had to say, I realized that everyone had it wrong. My father was no more guilty of stabbing that woman than . . . than I was."

"He must have been very convincing."

"He was," the girl stated firmly.

"Did he, by any chance, mention who he felt might have been responsible for killing this Christina?"

"He wasn't really sure. He said it could have been this tenant in Christina's building — George somebody. The guy used to keep pestering her for a date. My dad said he seemed to be, like, obsessed with her, you know? My dad also told me that Christina had had a problem with one of the women tenants. But he didn't go into details."

"Did he give you the woman's name?"

"He couldn't remember it."

"And these were the only people he spoke about with regard to the murder?"

"Correct. Just those two."

"I have another question for you. Did you inform any of your family members that you were coming to see me?"

"No. I was afraid it would just create a big hassle, you know?"

"And your father? Were any of them aware you were going to visit him?"

"My mom was. She was, like, against it

at first, but then she gave in. I spoke to my grandmom about it, too. You could tell she didn't really approve, either, even though she visited him regularly in prison. Her conscience, probably." Vicky screwed up her face. (Which, having gotten past the two-tone hair and the rest of the distractions, I could now appreciate as being quite pretty — in a waiflike kind of way.) "Well, at least she didn't, you know, try to talk me out of it."

"Wait. This *is* your father's mother you're speaking about?"

"Correct."

"Are you saying she also has doubts about his innocence?"

"Oh, no," the teenager answered dryly. "She doesn't have any doubts. She's convinced he did it."

Well, it appeared that Vicky here was her father's only champion. And this was not particularly encouraging — especially when you took into account the judgment of the woman who'd given birth to him. Listen, most mothers of my acquaintance would be proclaiming their offspring's innocence to anyone within hearing range — even if they'd actually witnessed their darling with the proverbial smoking gun in hand.

"Look, Desiree, my grandmom's very

good to me, and I love her a lot," Vicky hastened to assure me. "But Uncle Tony" — she practically spat out the "Uncle" — "who's her older son, has always been, like, her favorite. He's the good son, the smart son, the one who never gave her any *agita* while he was growing up. Plus, Uncle Tony went to college, and to my grandmom having an education is, like, a really huge deal. Anyhow, he's a lawyer now, making big bucks." She swiped at her left eye with the back of her hand, and for a moment I was afraid she might begin to cry again. But she just shook her head sadly. "I once heard her say that her Antonio — Tony — was the child of her heart."

"You don't sound particularly fond of Uncle Tony."

"I'm not. I suppose I should tell you that after my dad was, you know, incarcerated, my mom didn't wait too long to divorce him. And then — would you believe? — Uncle Tony dumped his girlfriend of six or seven years and married my mother."

I had no idea what to say to this, so I relied on an old standby: "Oh."

"Yeah. My mother was a hottie when she was young — like, really good-looking, you know? She still is, I guess. But so much for what a great guy Uncle Tony is, right?

Moving in on his own brother! Naturally, Grandmom doesn't see it like that, though. She has it in her head that my mother, you know, cast some sort of spell on her precious Antonio and that that's why he married her. But the marriage isn't the only reason I can't stand my uncle. It's mostly because he's such a weasel."

"In what way is he a weasel?"

"In *every* way. He'll, like, talk real sweet to me in front of my mom, play like he's my second daddy, you know? But when she's not around, he treats me like crap most of the time." Vicky's hand flew to her mouth. "I'm sorry."

It took a second or two before I realized that she was apologizing for the word "crap," and I smiled. "No apology necessary. I've heard worse." I didn't add that I'd also *said* worse. "It must be hard for you to live in the same house with someone like that," I commented.

Vicky shrugged. "It's okay. I just try to keep out of his way, which isn't that much of a problem. He's a workaholic, so fortunately he's usually at the office until late."

"To get back to your grandmother, Vicky, did I understand you correctly? Are you saying that even before the homicide she was down on your father?"

23

"That's right. He *was* kinda wild when he was growing up. I heard he, like, drank some and did drugs — they tell me he was really out of control for a while. And then he met my mother. Mom claims she didn't realize he was a user. But she's a sharp lady, so I'm not so sure that's the truth. Anyhow, pretty soon after they connected, my dad started to clean up his act. He checked himself into rehab and all that stuff. Then my mom became pregnant with you-know-who, and they got married. My father took a steady job for the first time in his life so he could support us — that's when he began driving a taxi. And he, like, must have made halfway decent money doing it, too. What I mean is, we had plenty to eat, and I don't remember our apartment being any terrible dump, either. Still, from my grandmom's point of view, with his being a cabby and all, my dad wasn't in the same class as his lawyer brother.

"I was always aware of how she felt, even when I was a kid — she didn't try to hide it. And I never really, like, resented her for it. But I do now."

Pausing here, Vicky glanced at me expectantly. It was plain that at this juncture I was supposed to respond in some way —

perhaps jump in with my own criticism of "Grandmom." Which was something I definitely wanted to avoid. So I took a more positive tack. "It sounds as though your dad tried hard to make a go of things. I bet your mom did, too. But sometimes, in spite of their best efforts, two people just aren't able to make their marriage work."

Vicky nodded her agreement. "They were both only nineteen when they got married. So probably neither of them was, you know, ready for that type of commitment."

"I'm certain that had a lot to do with it," I said, impressed — and not for the first time — with the perceptive quality of the girl's observations.

"Listen, Vicky," I put to her now, "did your father say anything else to you that might help me with my investigation?"

"No, just what I've already told you." An instant later she added almost fearfully, "I hope that's okay."

"Don't worry. I intend to start off by making arrangements to visit him myself."

For a moment Vicky looked astonished. Then her expression cleared, and she murmured sheepishly, "I was, like, positive I told you."

"Told me what?"

"That my father's . . . um . . . dead."

CHAPTER 3

I suppose my bugged-out eyes communicated how rocked I was by this latest tidbit of Vicky's, because she fidgeted in her seat for a few seconds. Then she inquired timidly, "Are you sure I didn't mention that to you — you know, when I first came in here?"

"Very sure."

"My dad died two weeks ago this past Friday," she murmured. "A couple of hours after I left the hospital." A single tear trickled down the teenager's cheek, and she brushed at the wetness with her finger.

"I'm so very sorry, Vicky. Had he . . . uh . . . been ill?"

"No. He'd, like, had this big argument with another inmate the day before, and, well, this man kept some sort of sharp object hidden in his cell — I don't know what it was. Anyhow, the next morning the man walked over to my father and stabbed him in the back with it. Just like that! They rushed my dad to the hospital, but he was, like, hurt really bad."

"And this was the first time you'd had

any contact with your father since he was imprisoned." It wasn't a question; I was looking for confirmation.

A whispered "Correct." A couple of seconds went by before Vicky was able to go on, her voice catching in her throat. "He thought it would be better for me that way, you know? The thing is, as anxious as he was to see me, he was even more anxious to avoid disrupting my life. But he told me he couldn't go to his grave without saying good-bye and at least *trying* to convince me that he wasn't a killer."

"That was truly unselfish of him — to forgo getting in touch with you during all those years, I mean. Your presence at the end must have meant a great deal to him, though. And he finally had the opportunity to set the record straight, too."

Vicky nodded. "He felt that even if he *had* assured me before that he'd been wrongly imprisoned, I probably wouldn't have, like, taken his word for it. No one else did, you know? But now that he was on his . . . his deathbed, he was hoping I'd realize that there was no point in his lying."

An instant later Vicky was crying in earnest. Covering her face with one hand, she reached for a bunch of Kleenex with the other.

Well, hard-nosed private investigator that I am, I was practically at the point of fighting her for the tissue box. But somehow I managed to contain my own tears. Listen, that kind of empathy was the last thing the girl needed just then. (To say nothing of the fact that there are few things more unprofessional than a bawling PI.)

As soon as she'd composed herself, I hurriedly switched to another subject. "Umm, would you happen to have that last address of Christina's?" I was figuring that if I lucked out, this George somebody and the woman the deceased had been feuding with would still be living there.

"I only know that it was, like, someplace in Queens."

Now, I had immediately decided that going to the police about anything like that would be my last resort. After all, can you picture how eager they'd be to help me overturn a ten-year-old murder conviction — especially since the man who was supposedly responsible for the crime was now dead and gone? "Do you think any members of your family would have that information?"

"It's possible my mother does, but she might not want to give it to you. I'm sure she just, you know, wants this whole thing to go away."

"What about Uncle Tony? Or your grandmother?"

"It's the same with them."

Which left me with the police. Not a pleasing prospect.

"I'll, like, work on my mom, though. I think I can persuade her to tell you the address — if she has it." Suddenly Vicky brightened. "Wait. I know the name of my dad's lawyer — it's Blossom Goody. She'd have that address, right?"

"I would imagine so." "Impressed" was hardly an adequate word to describe how I regarded Vicky Pirrelli at that moment. "You can still remember the name of your dad's attorney?"

She laughed. (Actually, it was more of a titter.) "What do you think I am, some kind of Albert Einstein? About six months ago Uncle Tony came home early enough one night to have dinner with mom and me — big thrill. Anyhow, the three of us were, like, sitting at the table when, out of the blue, he said, 'Guess who's interviewing to join the firm?' And then he says to mom, 'Remember Blossom Goody, my brother's defense attorney? It's her son.' Trust me, my memory's no great shakes, only it's pretty hard to forget a Blossom Goody." Vicky grinned. "Sort of like a Desiree Shapiro, you know?"

I grinned back at her. "I guess I do. Have you any idea where Blossom Goody's located?"

"Not exactly. But I think it's Manhattan."

"That's okay. I don't really anticipate any difficulty in tracking her down." I silently added, *That is, if she's still alive,* after which I crossed my fingers. (Well, it couldn't hurt, could it?) "One thing more, though. In order for me to conduct a proper investigation, I'm going to have to question your mother and your grandmother and Uncle Tony. And you did say they want this to go away."

"I plan on, you know, telling my mom tonight that I've, like, hired a PI and explaining why I have to find out the truth. I think I can get her to understand how important this is to me. I'll talk to my grandmom, too. I'm going to let Mom break the news to her sweet, darling mate, though. He won't like it, but there's nothing he can do to stop me. There's nothing any of them can do to stop me."

I refrained from pointing out to Vicky that if her family objected to my poking my nose into the stabbing of her father's mistress, it was doubtful they'd even give me the time of day. And I don't have to mention — do I? — that I needed all the cooperation I could get.

"One thing more."

"You just said that," my brand-new client informed me, giggling.

"I probably did. But I have to be certain you're aware that I might not be able to learn anything at all. And if I do, there's always the chance that what I find out may actually serve to bolster the case against your dad."

"That won't happen; you wait and see," she retorted.

"I want to make sure of the date of the murder. It was in February 1992, you said?"

"Correct. The end of February. My sixth birthday was the very next day — March first. I'm a Pisces," she apprized me for no discernable reason.

Before she could continue I interjected, "I'm a Scorpio" — also for no discernable reason.

"I still, you know, hate thinking about that day. My grandmom was supposed to take all my friends to this restaurant to celebrate — Solly's Pizza Palace, it was called. But the cops had dragged in my dad for questioning right on the spot, so the party was canceled. I had no idea why at the time. I remember I cried that entire afternoon." Vicky smiled poignantly. "Kids are like that, you know?"

"Yes, I do know," I said softly.

A short while after this I decided we could wrap things up. "I imagine we've pretty much covered everything, Vicky. But I'll need some phone numbers and addresses before you go."

She dutifully jotted down the information I requested. Then we both stood up. I had no sooner come out from behind my desk than I found myself on the receiving end of another hug, this one a genuine bone-crusher. Let me tell you, that kid had a lot more muscle than met the eye.

She had already shut the door behind her, and I was checking to see if all my parts were still in working order, when I realized I'd made a slight oversight: I'd never gotten her father's given name.

The intercom buzzed a few minutes later. It was Jackie, my one-third secretary. This fractionalization of her person being the result of my sharing her services with the two wonderful attorneys who lease me my office (okay, cubbyhole) space at an unbelievable-for-New-York rent. Their names are Elliot Gilbert and Pat Sullivan, so guess what the firm is called.

Yep, Gilbert and Sullivan.

Anyhow, Jackie appears to be under the impression that her mission on this earth is to keep everyone around her from lapsing into naughtiness of any variety whatever. I mean, the woman is extremely generous with both her advice and opinions — even if you don't exactly crave her input. She's constantly on my case about *something:* my work habits, my tardiness, my missed dental checkups — even my love life (or, more precisely, lack of it). Sometimes I even forget who's boss, as attested to by the fact that once or twice it actually crossed my mind that she might fire me. On the other hand, though, she's a good and loyal friend, as well as a superefficient secretary, so I try not to fantasize about how lovely it would be if her mouth were occasionally stapled shut.

"*What,* pray tell, was *that?*" Jackie demanded.

"My new client, and she's a really nice young girl — bright, too," I retorted protectively. I mean, so what if Vicky's physical appearance was a little offbeat — or maybe even a little more than a little? And so what if her habit of saying "you know" and "like" had frequently had me teetering on the very edge of a good, loud scream? That was my problem, not hers.

"But the green-and-orange hair! And that getup of hers!"

"This is New York, Jackie, remember? You see teenagers who look like that all the time."

"Yeah, and don't think it doesn't make me want to puke."

"Oh, come on. It wouldn't surprise me if, these days, they had Vicky lookalikes on the streets of . . . of Ashtabula."

"God forbid," Jackie muttered. "What did she want, anyway?"

"For me to prove that her father wasn't guilty of murder. I'll tell you about it later; I have to make a couple of phone calls first."

Locating Blossom Goody was easier than I'd anticipated. Like Vicky, I went straight to the Manhattan Yellow Pages — and there was Pirrelli's lawyer, with an office on the Upper West Side. She answered the phone herself.

I explained that I was a private investigator and that I'd been hired to check into a ten-year-old homicide. "You were the attorney for the man who was convicted of the murder." I was quick to add that the evidence against her client was pretty damning.

"Don't worry about hurting my feelings," Blossom told me in a low, raspy voice. "Lots of my clients wind up in prison. A good thing, too. Most of them belong there. Now, which poor, innocent soul are you referring to?"

"The name's Pirrelli. I don't have the first name, though," I said with an embarrassed little chuckle. "It's a funny thing. I wrote it down, but I can't seem to find my notepad." (Well, it was better than admitting I'd neglected to ask.)

"You're right. That's hilarious."

"Uh, the victim was Christina somebody." Another embarrassed little chuckle. "But I don't have her surname."

Blossom grumbled something under her breath that sounded like, "Figures." After which she told me, "Don't sweat it, kiddo. I'm familiar with the case."

"Uh, I just need some information from you. I wonder if I could stop by — I promise it won't take long. I can make it whenever you say."

"You'll have to wait until Kelly — girl

who works for me — gets back. I moved my offices a coupla years ago, and I can't be certain the Pirrelli file moved with me. Before I let you come over, I'll have Kelly make sure it's kicking around here someplace."

"Thanks very much. When should I call again?"

"Better give it a few hours."

"Okay."

Then, unexpectedly, Blossom elaborated. "Girl's having lunch with her boyfriend. He just returned from Europe — been there almost three months. So who knows when she'll come prancing in. And you can bet they're not wasting their time at some sushi bar, either."

And with this, she gave a lascivious little laugh and hung up in my ear.

CHAPTER 4

I went out for lunch, then tried Blossom Goody at a little after three.

Again, she picked up the phone herself.

"It's Desiree Shapiro," I told her.

"Oh, yeah. I've got the Pirrelli file here."

"Great. Umm, when can we talk?"

"Come over now, if you want. I got time. They haven't exactly been lining up at my door."

"Thanks. I'll leave right this minute."

The phone clicked in my ear.

God! I hate that!

In the taxi on the way to West Ninety-second Street, I began to go over the little that Vicky had been able to tell me about Christina somebody-or-other's murder. And something occurred to me, something disturbing.

Vicky had mentioned that her mother might know the victim's address. Well, suppose she did. What I'm getting at is, suppose she'd known it all along. There was the possibility — God forbid — that during her then-husband's alleged "cooling-off" walk, *she* was the one who'd visited his lady friend. After all, even if her marriage was the pits — in fact, perhaps *because* it was — she might have decided to confront the lovers. I began to weave a scenario in spite of myself.

Mrs. Pirrelli (I had no idea of *her* full name, either) finds "the other woman" alone. Christina, striving for some sort of civility — or simply at a loss about what else to do — invites Mrs. P. in for coffee. But the meeting soon turns sour, with the two exchanging bitter, hurtful words. And Christina tells Mrs. P. that she'll have to leave. Furious at this point, Mrs. Pirrelli grabs a knife from the kitchen counter the instant her rival's back is turned. Then she follows her into the living room — and bye-bye Christina.

I prayed that my imagination was merely galloping away with me as usual. (My imagination being the only part of me that gets any exercise on a regular basis.) I mean, I could just see myself telling Vicky that, yes, she was right, her father was innocent of the crime — but that as a result of her initiating this investigation, her mother could wind up behind bars.

My concern that I might not learn anything new about the case had been replaced with an even greater concern about what it was I *could* learn.

The tiny, sparsely furnished anteroom was in a terrible state of disrepair. The paint was peeling from the scuffed, once-white walls. And the brown-and-cream linoleum floor was badly chipped. What's more, it was partially covered by a multi-colored area rug, the original purpose of which was probably to conceal some of the linoleum's blemishes. Now, however, the once-substantial fabric was frayed and almost threadbare, a worse eyesore than the flooring itself.

A girl I'd place somewhere in her late twenties (listen, that's still a girl to me) was sitting behind a smudged Plexiglas panel to the left of the entrance. "Can I help you?" she inquired, sliding open the panel. I assumed that this must be Kelly. And judging by her positively blissful smile, I decided that Blossom could have been right — about her employee's lunchtime activity, I mean.

"I'm Desiree Shapiro. I believe Mrs. Goody is expecting me."

Picking up the phone, Kelly — or whoever — said a few words into the mouthpiece.

Then she nodded in the direction of the closed door at the rear of the space. "Ms. Goody will see you now."

Rapping lightly on the door, I heard from inside the room, "Don't just stand there; come in."

I walked into an office not much larger than my own — and found myself enveloped by a thick haze. I was about to scream, "Fire!" when I realized that I had entered the lair of a dedicated smoker — a *very* dedicated smoker.

Flailing my arms around for a few seconds, I dispelled enough of the smoke to make out the other occupant here.

The woman seated at the desk looked precisely as you'd picture a Blossom Goody would look. Or anyway, as I'd pictured she'd look.

From what I could see of her from the waist up (she didn't bother to stand when I came in), Blossom appeared to be quite short. And we probably weighed in within a few pounds of each other. She wore her yellow hair tightly curled, Little Orphan Annie style. And she had on a black, short-sleeved top that was stretched to its limits across her ample bosom.

She was, to my distress, in the act of placing a fresh cigarette between her lips and lighting it. Well, as usual when I'm in that kind of situation — and sometimes I get the feeling that I'm a regular magnet for chain smokers — I made a plucky attempt to suffer in silence. But I'd no sooner taken a seat across from her than I began to cough.

"Cigarette bothering you?" Blossom inquired, scowling.

Her manner left no doubt as to the obligatory answer. "No," I got out, burning throat notwithstanding.

"Good." And then my gracious hostess was coughing herself. It was a deep, racking sound that appeared to emanate from her toes and lasted close to a minute. The very instant the cough subsided, however, she was back to her nonstop puffing. "I looked this over for a coupla minutes before you got here," she rasped, waving a manila folder at me. "What do you want to know?"

"Whatever you can tell me that doesn't affect client confidentiality — if that still applies."

"Why wouldn't it?" Blossom snapped.

"Well, being that your client's dead."

"He's *what?*"

And I'd had the nerve to be irritated with Vicky! "I'm sorry. I, uh, should have mentioned that to you on the phone. Mr. Pirrelli died two weeks ago. He was stabbed in prison by another inmate."

"Stabbed, huh?" The words seemed to hang in the fetid air. And while she didn't say it, I had an idea the man's former lawyer was thinking that this was poetic justice. "So if not Victor, who're you working for, then?"

Ahh, so that was his first name: Victor. I managed to respond with, "His teenage daughter," before once more proceeding to hack away.

"Oh, Christ." Blossom shot me a decidedly unfriendly glance prior to grinding out her cigarette.

"Thanks," I said when I could. "I apologize again. I should have told you that, too."

"Never mind; just spit it out. What *exactly* do you want to know?"

"One thing I'm interested in learning is if you think Victor killed Christina, er . . . Christina . . ."

"That's right. You don't have her full name, either. It's Trent."

"Do you believe Victor stabbed Miss Trent?"

"Listen, Shapiro, this is how many innocent clients I represented last year." She held up three fingers, then wiggled one.

42

"And this baby I'm not ready to swear for."

"What makes you so certain Victor was guilty?"

"Did I say 'certain'?" Blossom growled. "But the cops did find him next to the body, holding the murder weapon — the victim's kitchen knife."

"I understand he insisted that he'd just pulled it out of her side."

"So? What would *you* have said?"

"Did the police have any other suspects at the time?"

Blossom shook her Orphan Annie curls and rolled her eyes heavenward. "They caught Pirrelli red-handed, for Christ's sake!"

"Well, in your conversations with Victor, did he ever suggest who else might have committed the crime?"

"Claimed it could have been one of the other tenants in the deceased's apartment house: some older guy who supposedly had the hots for her or this broad she was on the outs with."

"I assume the police at least questioned them."

"Don't assume. They probably didn't bother. Not much doubt in their minds Victor iced the girl. And not only because of the knife or the big fight the two of 'em had that night — heard by half the people in the building, by the by."

"Are you telling me that there was another reason they concluded it was Victor?"

"You got it, Shapiro."

"Does it have anything to do with the trouble he used to get into when he was younger?"

Blossom regarded me with exasperation. "Younger, shmunger. Only six months earlier he'd put his beloved in the hospital. Broken jaw."

"Christina?"

"The same."

Oh, God! That makes everything really ducky! "Uh, getting back to the fight: Did Victor tell you what it was about?"

"According to him, it was just a minor little tiff that got out of hand. Started with Mexican food — supposedly."

"Mexican food?"

"You heard me. It seems that Victor wasn't too crazy about the stuff, while Christina had a thing for it. Being the considerate fellow he was, though, he'd agreed to make this big sacrifice and take her to some Mexican restaurant that night. But then he reneged, and they wound up eating someplace else. Anyhow, when they got back to the girl's

44

apartment, she let him have it. Accused him of being selfish and inconsiderate — that kind of thing. Following which he accused *her* of being a spoiled brat. She countered by pointing out another of his sterling qualities. And he went right back at her. And on and on. And louder and louder. At any rate, that was his version of what happened. But who the hell knows."

"Listen, would you have the victim's last address — and the names of those two neighbors Victor suspected?"

"Must have." And reaching across the desk for the manila folder, Blossom promptly knocked it to the floor.

She got up from her chair to retrieve it, and I saw that she was wearing slacks. I would have cringed even if these hadn't been fire-engine red — and even if she hadn't bent over like that. I mean, while lots of women of my acquaintance don't agree, in my book, pants are a no-no for ladies of a certain width, like Blossom here — and me.

When she was back in her seat, Blossom flipped through the file. Then she tore a piece of paper from a notepad on her desk and jotted down the information I'd requested. "We through now?" she asked impatiently, handing me the paper.

"Uh, can you just tell me if Christina had any relatives?"

The lawyer glowered at me. Nevertheless, she went through the file again. "There was a sister in Pennsylvania." She ripped another sheet from the notepad, scribbled on it, and thrust it at me. After which she leaned forward and placed both hands on the desktop, a clear sign that I was about to be shown the door.

"One more thing," I threw in hastily. "You said it wasn't likely the police followed through on the information they had about those two people in Christina's building."

"That's right."

I put the question to her cautiously. "Uh, but you . . . that is, I was wondering if you brought up their names in some way at the trial? You know, in order to cast some reasonable doubt on Victor's culpability."

"What trial?"

I didn't instantly absorb what I'd heard. "Are you saying Victor wasn't tried for his lover's murder?"

"Guy copped a plea."

"But he swore to his daughter on his deathbed that he wasn't responsible for Christina's death."

"Maybe he was, maybe he wasn't. But he

would have been taking a big risk going to trial."

"So you persuaded him to plead guilty to a lesser charge, is that it?"

"Not me, Shapiro. His brother gets the credit for that."

CHAPTER 5

That last little fact Blossom laid on me before I left her office almost rivaled Vicky's two beauts on the jolt meter.

On the way home in the taxi I came up with a number of appropriate words for Uncle Tony — all of which would have gotten my mouth washed out with soap when I was a kid. I mean, that sleaze was apparently so enamored of his brother's wife that he persuaded Victor to accept a plea bargain so he — Tony — could take up with the woman himself.

And now — wouldn't you know it? — my imagination was off and running again.

And this time Tony was the starring player.

According to my new plot line, Tony is aware of Victor's dalliance with Christina Trent, and he sets off for that lady's apartment determined to remove the one obstacle to his happiness. His plan: to stage a murder/suicide. But once he arrives at Christina's, he finds her alone — and crying.

She tells him his brother went out for a

walk and should be returning shortly. She invites him in. Following which, to explain her tears, she divulges to Tony that she and Victor have just had a world-class argument. It's likely she would also mention that everyone in the entire building must have heard them battling. Or perhaps this is something Tony just assumes. I mean, there are precious few New York apartment buildings that can boast walls solid enough to prevent one from being privy to a neighbor's domestic crisis.

Anyhow, Tony does some fast improvising.

He stabs the girl with her own knife and hurries out to his car. Then he waits, slumped down in his seat, until sometime close to midnight — when he sees Victor about to enter the building. At which point Tony puts in an anonymous call to the police.

But how could he be so sure Victor would pick up the knife? you might well ask.

Obviously, he couldn't. All he could hope for was that the police would arrive in time to find his brother still at the scene. Listen, don't forget that the murder followed a fierce and evidently well-documented altercation between the two lovers. And if, on the heels of that altercation, Victor is discovered alone with the body, well, people have been convicted on circumstantial evidence a lot less compelling than that. But Tony lucks out; Victor is apprehended actually handling the murder weapon. Nevertheless, if the case should go to trial, there is always an outside chance, however small, that he might be acquitted. So, electing to play it safe, Tony pushes him into a plea bargain.

Wait a minute, though . . .

Maybe Tony *wasn't* the one who plunged the knife into Christina. And could be his attraction to his sister-in-law had nothing to do with the legal advice he dispensed. Possibly he truly believed Victor to be guilty of the crime (after all, everyone else seemed to), so he encouraged his brother to take a plea in order to spare him that many more years of jail time.

But on the other hand — I stopped in midthought, willing myself to put an end to all the "maybes" and "could bes" and "possiblies." I mean, as eager as I was to prove that the perpetrator was someone other than Victor Pirrelli, the only thing I seemed to be getting out of all this speculating was a throbbing headache. Besides, at that moment the cab pulled up in front of my apartment house.

Tonight's dinner was to feature leftover

pot roast. And while this was heating, I prepared a humongous salad. I practically emptied the refrigerator, pressing into service just about everything that was still edible — along with a yellow pepper that was a serious question mark.

The phone rang about five minutes after I sat down at the table. It was Nick.

Let me explain about Nick. The man moved into my building some months back, and he's absolutely adorable. This — according to what friends have labeled my weird definition of "adorable" when applied to the male gender — translating into his being short and skinny and appearing to be in dire need of the ministrations of a good woman. (Do I have to say which good woman instantly sprang to mind?) Plus, he's on the pale side, slightly balding, and as a special bonus, his teeth are a little bucked. I mean, it was as if I conjured up Nick Grainger in my fantasies — and he materialized.

For a while, though, the signs that Nick and I would ever share anything other than a creaky elevator were hardly encouraging. When we'd run into each other in the building or at the supermarket, I didn't get much more than a polite "Hello, Desiree. How are you?" Although occasionally — if

I was really fortunate — this might be followed by an "It's nice to see you." Well, I'm not a big fan of unrequited love. So I'd just about concluded that I had no choice but to ditch the guy (something that would, of course, have completely traumatized him) — and this is when he invited me out to dinner.

It turned out that Nick's character — at least, as far as I could tell — was right up there with his bucked teeth. What I'm trying to say is that he seemed to be a genuinely nice person.

I was optimistic about things following our date — particularly after we made plans to see each other again. And then his ex-wife decided to leave their nine-year-old son with him while she jetted off to Las Vegas for a week with her young rocker boyfriend. Only the week has now stretched into months — and still no Tiffany. The truth is, though, that this prolonged stay shouldn't have come as a total surprise to Nick. I mean, quitting her part-time job at the tanning salon just prior to the trip was a pretty good indication of the woman's intentions.

Anyhow, to make a long story even longer, Tiffany had arranged that in her absence Derek's former nanny would pick him up at school and look after him until Nick came home from work. Well, this was fine. Except there was one small glitch. Nick felt that since the boy was in somebody else's care all day, his father should be there for him in case he should awaken during the night. (An eventuality, by the way, that has yet to occur.) So he was averse to leaving Derek with a baby-sitter. A couple of weeks ago, though, Nick — hallelujah! — reconsidered, deciding that hiring a sitter once in a while might not make him such a terrible parent after all.

Which brings me back to tonight's telephone call. . . .

Nick opened with, "I'm not disturbing your dinner, am I?"

"Oh, no, I've already finished," I assured him, a hot potato — literally — in my mouth.

We exchanged pleasantries, and then he said, "I hope you're free Saturday evening. A friend of mine has two tickets to *Proof* that he won't be able to use, and you told me a while back that you'd like to see it."

Now, how many men would remember your mentioning something like that weeks earlier — and only in passing, really?

"I'd *love* to see it! That's great!"

After this Nick asked about my day, and

I was about to give him a quick rundown of my new case when, in the background, I heard Derek calling out to his father. So we hurriedly finalized our arrangements and hung up.

The conversation with Nick diverted my attention from the investigation for a brief time, replacing it with a more immediate concern: what to wear to the theater on Saturday night.

I was sorely tempted to buy something new, something so absolutely stunning that Nick Grainger's eyes would pop right out of his head. But my finances didn't permit. I mean, like Blossom Goody, clients weren't lining up at my door, either. So I had to choose from what had already been paid for. At first I thought the blue A-line might do, but I was soon mentally returning it to my closet in favor of the gray shirtwaist. Then the gray, too, was quickly rejected. I finally settled on a two-piece lavender silk with a coordinating blue-and-lavender scarf. But although it was a good-looking outfit, it was hardly likely to cause Nick's facial features to be displaced.

Having worked out my wardrobe, I was back to wrestling with the murder. A major problem, as you're aware, was that few people — if any — would be able to accurately recount the events of that night. But an equally formidable stumbling block was that, the killer aside, there might be someone out there — or even more than one someone — who, for reasons of his/her own, simply wouldn't want to.

To paraphrase from the Alcoholics Anonymous credo, I prayed for the wisdom to know the difference.

CHAPTER 6

As soon as I was settled in my cubbyhole on Tuesday morning, I tried one of the two Pennsylvania numbers Blossom had given me for Christina's sister.

I told myself that there was really no reason to be nervous about making the call. But I couldn't convince my fingers of that. They were trembling as I dialed. I mean, the woman was under the impression that her sister's killer had been behind bars all these years. And certainly this belief must have afforded her at least some measure of comfort. And now here I was, about to churn things up again.

"Good morning, Cavanaugh Realty," I was informed by one of the perkiest little voices you've ever heard. "How may I help you?"

"Alicia Trent, please," I said, hoping Alicia might still be employed by the same company she was with a decade earlier.

"There's no one here by that name, ma'am." But apparently something occurred to the girl then, because almost immediately afterward she added, "Let me check something for you, though. Hold on a sec, okay?" It was a couple of minutes before she was back on the line. "Sorry to keep you waiting, ma'am, but I had to confirm it. You want Alicia Schnabel; Trent was her name before she got married."

"Thanks, I suppose I do. Is Mrs. Schnabel available, then?"

"Ms. Schnabel is out of the office right now," Perky Little Voice practically chirped. "I expect her in about an hour. Would you care to leave a message?"

"Uh, no, thanks. I'll call her later."

George Gladstone — the obsessed neighbor — was next on my agenda. According to the Queens telephone directory, he was still at his old address. Maybe he worked out of his apartment, I speculated. Or possibly he was retired — the lawyer had referred to him as "some older guy." So I decided to see if I could reach him at home.

"George Gladstone Public Relations," the answering machine apprised me. Well, it looked like George was still in business, anyway. "I'm out on the Coast for a few days. Leave a message, and I'll get back to you."

Naturally, I didn't. Leave a message, that is. But what did the man mean by 'a few days'? Would he be home by Friday? Saturday? And who knows when he'd recorded that message. Could be he'd taped it last week and was due to return any minute. I'd take another shot at him tomorrow, just in case.

On my third try I got lucky.

The listing for Jennifer Whyte revealed that she, too, lived in the same building she'd inhabited ten years ago. And she picked up on the second ring.

"Uh, Ms. Whyte? This is Desiree Shapiro. I'm a private investigator, and I've been retained by the daughter of Victor Pirrelli. Are you familiar with the name?"

For a moment there was silence at the other end of the line. But whether it was the result of the woman's attempting to jog her memory or because she was so stunned by this sudden reminder of that long-past homicide, I couldn't say.

"Sure. I'm familiar with the name. The guy used to have a thing going with Christina Trent, who lived down the hall from me. But they got into this brawl one night, and he picked up a knife and stabbed her to death. That must have been eight, nine years ago, though."

"Well, there's some question now about whether he actually committed that murder."

"Are you serious?"

"Oh, yes. You're probably not aware of it, but Mr. Pirrelli died in prison recently."

"I hadn't heard. How did he die?"

"He had a fight with another inmate, and unfortunately, it proved fatal. Anyway, his sixteen-year-old daughter is convinced of her father's innocence, and she's determined to clear his name."

"That's very commendable of the daughter. But —"

I aborted the protest. "I'm attempting to get in touch with everyone who lived in Miss Trent's building at the time she was killed. Hopefully, someone may be able to shed some light on the crime."

"Sorry, but I'm not that someone. I wasn't even in town then."

"It would still be helpful if you could just fill me in on what you know about the couple — Christina and Victor."

"Him, I never even met. I used to see the guy around sometimes, but that's the extent of it. As for Christina, well, she wasn't one of my favorite people. But she's dead, so let's leave it at that."

"There was some animosity between the two of you?"

"Not enough to induce me to put a knife in her, if that's what's on your mind."

"Believe me, Miss Whyte, it is not. I'd just like your feedback on some things."

"All right," Jennifer said resignedly. "Go ahead. Fire away."

"It would be better if we could do this in person. We can get together at your convenience — wherever you say."

"There's really no purpose in —"

"Look," I cajoled, "you may know something — something important — that you're completely unaware that you know. I can't tell you how many times I've seen that occur." And then to sweeten the pot: "I won't take up more than ten minutes of your time, I promise." Which was a bold-faced lie. Jennifer Whyte could consider herself lucky if I was out of her hair in an hour. But, hey, that fellow Machiavelli wasn't totally off base. I mean, sometimes the ends really do justify the means.

There was a few seconds' worth of hesitation before the woman capitulated. "Okay, you win," she agreed grudgingly. "Why don't you come over here around four. I presume you have the address."

"Yes, I do. And thank you."

She clicked the phone in my ear. But then, it wasn't as if I hadn't expected her to.

★ ★ ★

I had to rev myself up in order to call Alicia Schnabel again. And once I was put through to her, I did something I can't recall ever having done in this kind of situation before: I froze.

"Um, my name is Desiree Shapiro," I managed without too much difficulty. But then, in spite of having planned out exactly how I would approach the victim's sister, I drew a blank.

I was still struggling to get back on track when she finally filled the void with a patient, "Yes? How can I help you?"

"I'm a private investigator, Mrs. Schnabel," I mumbled. After which I just blurted out, "I've been hired to look into your sister's death."

"What are you *talking* about?" the woman demanded, her voice rising to remarkable heights. "Christina was murdered ten years ago. And the police arrested the man responsible right after it happened."

"There's reason to believe they made a tragic mistake."

A whispered, "Oh, God." And then silence.

"Mrs. Schnabel?" I said at last, not even sure she was still on the line.

"You . . . you know this for a fact — that a mistake was made?"

"No, I don't. That's why I'd like to sit down with you."

"Well, naturally, I'm anxious to hear what . . . whatever you have to say. The problem is, though, that I have a pretty tight schedule all this week."

"I could drive down there one evening, if that's better for you."

Alicia let out a harsh, staccato laugh. "I have back-to-back appointments every night, although — Just a moment. Let me check my book." She was on the phone again almost at once. "On Friday I should be through with my last client around six. After that I have a meeting in the office, but I don't imagine that will go much beyond seven. Where are you located — in New York?"

"Yes, in Manhattan."

"Can you be in Philadelphia Friday evening at seven thirty?"

"Absolutely."

"We could meet for coffee before I head home — I live in Merion, one of the suburbs."

She gave me the address of a diner near her workplace, along with explicit instructions on how to get there.

"I really appreciate your seeing me, Mrs. Schnabel. Thank you."

"There isn't any reason to thank me, Ms. Shapiro. I want the bastard who ended Christina's life to pay for what he did — whoever he is." And then so softly, so plaintively that I almost cried: "She was my only sister, you know."

CHAPTER 7

The taxi let me out in front of a small, six-story apartment house in the Briarwood section of Queens.

On discovering that there was no doorman in the building, my initial reaction was disappointment. But I quickly shrugged it off. After all, even if there *were* a doorman and this same individual had been working here at the time of the tragedy — which would have been pretty iffy to begin with — how likely was it that he'd have been able to contribute anything to this cold, *cold* case of mine?

The tenant listing was in the vestibule. I rang the bell to 6D and was immediately buzzed in to the well-kept lobby.

When I stepped out of the elevator, a woman I judged to be in her mid-thirties was waiting for me in the doorway diagonally across the way. For a fleeting moment she reminded me of Jackie. Not that they actually resembled each other facially. But both were tall and large-boned, with short blondish brown hair. Plus, the woman's expression was almost a duplicate of the one Jackie displays when *she's* out of sorts. "Miss Whyte?"

I considered the curt "Come in, Ms. Shapiro" to be an affirmation.

"Call me Desiree," I invited.

"If that's what you want." But I noted that she didn't return the courtesy.

I followed Jennifer Whyte into a good-sized living room that was furnished with old — but what looked to me like quality — pieces. The color scheme of beiges and browns wasn't exactly to my taste, but I had to admit the room had a pleasant, restful feeling.

"Take a seat," Jennifer instructed, indicating a deep, down-filled sofa.

(I can't tell you how much I detest those things! Being somewhat vertically challenged, if I sit back, my feet just kind of dangle there in midair.) I had to position myself on the edge of the cushion in order to make contact with the floor.

"Can I get you something to drink?" Jennifer offered less than wholeheartedly. "You've got a choice: beer, wine, or Coke."

"Are you having anything?"

"I'm not thirsty."

Now, I wasn't either. But I've discovered that there's something . . . well, let's call it *companionable,* about talking over some nibblies or a drink — even the nonalcoholic stuff — that frequently leads people to relax and say more than they'd intended to. Since Jennifer wouldn't be joining me, though, I decided to pass. "Thanks anyway, but I'd better not. Calories," I lied. The truth is that I gave up focusing on my weight years ago. The reason being that after subjecting myself to the most punishing diet ever devised, the slimmer, trimmer edition of me didn't wind up being pursued by anyone remotely resembling Robert Redford — my then big crush. (Listen, I used to be so smitten with the man I was willing to overlook that he wasn't short and skinny. I even closed my eyes to the fact that he had all that great hair on his head.)

"So what is it you want to ask me about?" my reluctant hostess said as she settled into the wing chair at right angles to the couch.

"Well, first, I'd appreciate your telling me a little about the deceased. I know almost nothing about Miss Trent, and her character may very well have had something to do with her murder."

"I wouldn't be surprised," Jennifer responded dryly.

"Would you mind filling me in on why you disliked her?"

"No, I don't mind at all. Actually, we were good friends for a while, in spite of my being a few years older than Christina. But then one day I came home from work early — and guess who I found playing house with my live-in boyfriend."

"Christina," I murmured.

"You got it. Christina. Of course, Aaron swore it didn't mean anything, and Christina cried a whole lot and pleaded with me to forgive her. She promised it would never happen again. Damn right, it wouldn't! I threw them both the hell out of my apartment, and that was the last time I spoke word one to either of them."

"Your former boyfriend, did he take up with Christina after you dumped him?"

Jennifer permitted herself a fleeting smile. Most likely because she was so pleased to hear herself referred to as the dump*er* (as opposed to the dump*ee*). "I doubt that he ever saw her again. He went out to California a week later to visit his brother, and he remained there. He found himself a pretty good job from what I heard."

"Was Victor Pirrelli also in the picture then?"

"No. This happened a couple of months before Christina took up with Pirrelli. And, by the way, do you really believe someone else might have killed her?"

"That's what I'm trying to find out. Did she have any other enemies you're aware of?"

"Other than me, you mean?"

"Oh, I wasn't implying —"

"That's okay. No offense taken. But to answer your question, I really can't think of anyone. Although Pirrelli's wife probably wasn't too crazy about her husband's tootsie — assuming she'd learned about the relationship, that is." There was a pause followed by a mischievous grin. "Of course, Christina waited tables after school at a restaurant a few blocks from here — a little mom-and-pop place. And knowing my old friend Christina, 'mom' couldn't have been too crazy about her, either."

"Can you tell me the name of the restaurant?"

"It was called Vera's. But it went out of business about five, maybe six years ago, right after Vera died."

"And the husband?"

"He moved out West somewhere to live close to his daughter. But I was being facetious when I mentioned the Childers.

Christina was eighteen, and Harold was past fifty. Besides, he was short and fat, and his breath wasn't just bad — it was lethal. As man hungry as Christina was, I'm sure she drew the line at Harold Childer."

"I gather Christina was quite attractive to the opposite sex."

"Very. I always wondered about that, though. She was pretty enough, I suppose, but plenty of prettier girls spend Saturday nights alone in front of the TV. The truth is, Christina was slightly knock-kneed and her eyes were too close together and her complexion wasn't that great. She was kind of flat-chested, too." Involuntarily, I glanced over at Jennifer's own twin peaks, which weren't much to brag about, either. "Not that I'm any Miss America," she conceded — an assessment that, considering the coarseness of the woman's features, I couldn't argue with. "But then, men don't fall all over themselves to get to me."

Suddenly it was as if Jennifer's eyes had caught fire. "Listen, Desiree, it was bad enough that somebody I loved like a sister went to bed with my boyfriend. But Christina's being so popular made it that much worse. Here was a girl who could take her pick of guys, and she has to mess around with mine? Aaron wasn't exactly irresistible, you know. Not unless you're turned on by a big nose and the world's hairiest arms and legs. One of my friends told me a long time afterward that Aaron used to remind her of an orangutan. What I'm saying is that he was no Victor Pirrelli."

"Victor Pirrelli was good-looking?"

"Oh, yeah. He was a *doll* — physically, at least. But to get back to Aaron," she continued, having warmed to her subject, "he was also on the stupid side. An out-of-work high-school dropout."

"So what was it about him that appealed to *you?*"

Jennifer flushed. "For some reason I found Aaron to be the sexiest man I'd ever met. Who can figure out why? It must have been a chemistry thing." Her tone turned defensive. "But even if Christina felt the same way about him — and I don't see how she could have — that still doesn't excuse her. Friends don't do that to friends."

"I couldn't agree more. About the murder, though . . . Isn't there anyone aside from Victor that you can conceive of as Christina's killer?"

Jennifer shook her head.

"I was told that a neighbor of yours, George Gladstone, was obsessed with her."

"I'm not saying George didn't have a thing for Christina, but —"

"He must have been upset about her involvement with Victor Pirrelli."

"Well, naturally, he wasn't too happy about it. But George wouldn't — He's harmless. Believe me. Listen, I feel sorry for the daughter, but my money's still on Pirrelli. The cops even caught him with the knife in his hand."

"He claimed to have pulled it out to try and stop the bleeding."

"Do you really buy that? The guy had a vicious temper. Are you aware that six months before Christina was stabbed they had some sort of argument, and she wound up with a broken jaw? This was only a few weeks after they started seeing each other, too. I was surprised that she didn't press charges against him — or at least point him toward the door. Anyhow, I understand that the night she died, the two of them got into quite a hassle."

"You were out of town that evening, you said on the phone."

"Yes, I was. Sorry to disappoint you, Desiree, but there is absolutely no way you can saddle me with Christina's murder. I'm a practical nurse, and on February twentieth I drove to Lynne, Massachusetts, to look after a new mother and her infant son. I didn't return home until March fifth."

"You remember the exact dates?"

"I was sure this would come up, so I checked an old appointment book before you got here."

"Your cases — are they normally that far from New York?"

"No, but the nurse that this Ms. Gallagher originally hired disappointed her at the last minute. A cousin of mine lives across the street from the Gallaghers, and she called to find out if I was free to go up there for a couple of weeks. It's lucky that I was, too. Otherwise I'd probably be your number-one suspect right now."

"Uh, I hope you won't take this personally. I'm asking everyone who had any sort of a relationship with Christina to —"

"You want the Gallaghers' telephone number, is that it?"

"I'd appreciate it," I responded sheepishly.

Jennifer Whyte was grinning like the Cheshire cat. "Don't worry, Desiree. Actually, I'm very happy to accommodate you."

CHAPTER 8

At six thirty I entered the lobby of my building, turned and retraced my steps, then headed straight for this little coffee shop in my neighborhood.

I deserved a cheeseburger.

As soon as I opened the door to Jerome's, I saw that Felix was working there this evening. Which, if I'd had any other entreé in mind, would have presented a problem. I mean, my option would have been to either switch to the burger or wind up hurting the man's feelings.

You see, Felix, who has to be pushing eighty by now, prides himself on his memory. So he never asks for my order, he replays it for me, rattling off the same choices I'd made the first time he ever waited on me, this being I-don't-know-how-many-years-ago.

"Don't say nuthin', okay?" he instructed tonight. "You want the cheeseburger deluxe, and it's gotta be well-done. Also, the fries should be well-done. And you'll have a Coca-Cola, but I shouldn't serve it before I bring out the rest of the meal." He cocked his head to one side and beamed at me. "So, am I right?"

"You got it, Felix."

Over the food, I thought about my meeting with Jennifer Whyte — in spite of my efforts not to. I mean, I haven't found focusing on a murder investigation to be particularly beneficial to my digestion. But I just wasn't able to banish the woman from my mind.

Once she got started, Jennifer had certainly been up-front about her feelings, I mused. Most likely because she couldn't resist such a golden opportunity to vent about the man and woman — girl, really — who'd betrayed her. I wondered if her claim that she was in Lynne, Massachusetts, at the time of the stabbing would hold up. After all, it was possible that she'd taken a day off from her job there and, seething with bitterness toward her former friend, had returned to Queens to settle the score. On the other hand, though, it was equally possible that soon I'd no longer be regarding Jennifer Whyte as a suspect. Perhaps as early as tonight.

About a second after I put down my fork, Felix materialized alongside the booth. "We got a strawberry pie tonight,

Desiree, like you never ate in your entire life."

Well, I was anxious to get back to the apartment and place that call to Lynne, so I'd planned to skip dessert. (I swear!) But what difference could another few minutes make?

I ordered the strawberry pie. A la mode, of course.

The answering machine was winking at me when I walked into the apartment.

"I have to talk to you, Aunt Dez. It's important," my favorite — and only — niece informed me. "Please call me when you get in. I'm off today" — Ellen's a buyer at Macy's — "so you can reach me at home. It's important," she reiterated, in the event I'd missed it the first time.

Now, Ellen is a nervous Nellie if there ever was one, although she *has* settled down a bit since acquiring Mike Lynton as a fiancé. In fact, for the most part she's been managing to reserve her angst for exceptionally trying circumstances — such as that recent poisoning at her bridal shower. (Which also caused a lot of other people, including yours truly, to start chewing their nails up to their elbows.) The closer it gets to that December wedding date, though, the more trifling the cause of her distress. Still, I phoned her back immediately. After all, *something* was a crisis to *her* — whether anyone else saw it that way or not.

"I'm so-o glad it's you, Aunt Dez," she said in response to my "Ellen?"

"What's wrong?"

"It's about Mike."

My heart just about stopped pumping. "What's about Mike?" I demanded.

"Oh, don't worry; it's nothing like *that*. He's not sick or anything. It has to do with our honeymoon plans. I realize this will probably sound pretty trivial, but I can't help feeling the way I do, can I?" It was evidently a rhetorical question because she hurried on. "We'd already made up our minds to go to the Tropics, right? — maybe to the Virgin Islands or Aruba or someplace in the Bahamas. But then yesterday a friend of Mike's at the hospital — another doctor — mentioned camping to him. Last year this man and his wife went on a camping trip in Upstate New York for *their* honeymoon, and he was raving to Mike about what a terrific time they had. But you know how I am about bugs." I knew. "And there would probably be all kinds of s-s-snakes out there, too." I nodded my head in silent agreement. "And what about b-bears? Plus, how am I supposed to go to the ba— to the b-b-bathroom?" she wailed.

Now, I don't want you to think Ellen is some kind of prima donna. She simply happens to be allergic to anything that crawls, slithers, or roars at you. Something I can readily identify with, despite having once worked on a missing boa constrictor case. (Which should give you an idea of how tough things were back then — professionally speaking, I mean.) Anyway, Ellen's stuttering signaled that she was having a whole lot of trouble coping with the prospect of a week in a pup tent. So I quickly attempted to reassure her. "Did Mike suggest a camping trip to you? And I'm talking about in so many words."

"Well, no, not yet," she admitted meekly.

"Did he give you reason to believe he was even considering one?"

"I'm . . . I'm not sure. Not exactly, I guess."

"Look, he's aware of your feelings about the great outdoors. I'll bet anything he was only making conversation."

"Do you *really* think that's all it was?"

"Yes, I do."

"I hope you're right. I would hate to say

no if that's what Mike wants to do, but —"

"I'm quite certain it isn't."

Ellen sighed. "The fact is, I'm just not the outdoorsy type. I must have inherited your genes, Aunt Dez," she added, giggling. The reason for the giggle being that this wasn't too likely, considering that Ellen and I aren't blood relations. She's actually the niece of my late husband, Ed, may he rest in peace.

"I'll keep you posted," she promised.

I didn't doubt it for a second.

It was going on eight thirty when I dialed the Massachusetts number Jennifer Whyte had supplied me with.

"Hello?"

"Is this the Gallagher residence?" I inquired.

"Yes, it is." The voice belonged to either an extremely hoarse woman or a fairly high-pitched male. The television blaring in the background at an almost ear-splitting volume made it impossible to tell the difference.

"Uh, I'd like to speak to Mr. or Mrs. Paul Gallagher, please."

"Can you hold on a minute?" Obviously, the individual now placed her/his hand over the receiver, because all I heard was some muffled shouting — and then silence. Beautiful, blessed silence.

"Kids," the voice grumbled on return. "This is Mrs. Gallagher. Who's this?"

"My name is Desiree Shapiro," I informed her, "and I'm investigating a criminal matter that occurred in New York City ten years ago. I understand you had someone in your employ at that time — a Miss Whyte."

"Who?"

"She was the nurse who stayed with you for a while after the birth of your baby."

"Oh, you mean *Jennifer*. She wasn't involved in anything illegal, was she?"

I adopted my most official-sounding tone. "We don't believe so, Mrs. Gallagher. This is only a routine call, primarily a matter of updating our records. Would you be able to tell me the exact dates that she was with you?"

There was some slight hesitation. "Are you a police officer?"

Having a God-given talent for equivocating, I didn't find it too difficult to dance around the question. "I'm a detective, actually."

"All right. Well, it should be easy enough to figure out. Let's see, Bobby was born on February seventeenth, and I went home from the hospital three days later. Jennifer was there when I got to the house — on the twentieth — and she was with us for two weeks."

"Would you happen to recall when she took her days off?"

"There weren't any days off. Jennifer said that if it was all the same to us, she'd just as soon work straight through — I gathered she could use the extra money. Anyway, we were only too glad to accommodate her."

At that point the TV began blasting away again. It was so loud this time that I had to hold the receiver at arm's length.

"I'll be right back," Mrs. Gallagher announced, her tone leaving no doubt that this was war. She put the telephone down with a clunk and simultaneously began screaming at her offspring. "Didn't I tell you to turn off that set? I'm . . ." She moved out of earshot, and the rest of the tirade was lost to me. But right apparently triumphed once more, because suddenly there was no further sound from the offending appliance. As she was approaching the phone again, I could hear her delivering that time-honored admonition: "You kids just wait until your father comes home."

The woman got back on the line even more hoarse than she'd been before.

"What else did you want to ask me?"

"I think that about covers it."

"Do you have children, Ms. — ?"

"Shapiro. No, I don't."

"There are some days I wish I could say that," she murmured. And only partially in jest, I'm sure.

I thanked her for her time then, and we hung up.

Immediately after this I dialed Information in order to verify that I'd just been in touch with the genuine article. (Call me suspicious, but that's what a PI is supposed to be, isn't it?) Look, Jennifer was aware that I'd be checking out her alibi. So suppose that in actuality she'd given me the telephone number of her cousin — the one who was the Gallaghers' neighbor. I mean, it was conceivable that Jennifer had alerted this relative to expect to hear from me and had prevailed upon her to pretend to be Mrs. Gallagher. The purpose of this, of course, was to confirm that the nurse had remained in Lynne that entire two weeks.

At any rate, the Massachusetts operator promptly established that the number I'd phoned was registered to a Paul Gallagher.

Satisfied now, I scratched the name of "Jennifer Whyte" from the suspect list in my head.

CHAPTER 9

Only minutes after I arrived at work on Wednesday morning, I tried George Gladstone — and heard a repeat of yesterday's message.

Then I dialed the home of my client, determined to do whatever it took to persuade her mother to meet with me.

A woman answered the phone.

"Mrs. Pirrelli?"

"Speaking."

"My name is Desiree Shapiro," I began, hoping Vicky had already acquainted her mother with the fact that she'd been to see me.

She had. "You're the person my daughter hired to investigate Christina Trent's murder." The tone was accusatory.

"Uh, yes." I didn't point out that "hired" was probably not too accurate a term. I mean, it implies compensation for services rendered, and I really couldn't see myself garnisheeing the teenager's baby-sitting fees. (Although considering that this was the second case in a row that I was handling for free, it crossed my mind — get this! —

that maybe, just maybe, the compensation might come from another source. Like perhaps the powers that be would reward this lack of avarice by providing a way for me to acquire the funds for next month's rent.)

"I have to say, Ms. . . . . Shapiro, isn't it?"

"That's right."

"I consider it highly unethical of you to attempt to take this sort of advantage of a child. Evidently you're not aware that Vicky doesn't have to give you a dime. A verbal contract — or a written one, for that matter — entered into with a minor isn't legally binding."

She could barely wait to enlighten me as to the source of this nugget of information — which was hardly necessary. "My husband's an attorney."

"I know all about contracts with minors, Mrs. Pirrelli. I never had any intention of billing your daughter. She's desperate to establish her father's innocence, and she pleaded with me to help her. I couldn't bring myself to turn her down."

"Oh." There was dead air for a couple of seconds before the woman put to me, "You realize — don't you? — that if by some miracle you do come up with something, it could make things that much worse for

Vicky. For argument's sake, what happens if you uncover positive proof that Victor *did* commit the murder? — which I have no doubt that he did."

"If I can provide Vicky with proof to that effect, at least she'll have the assurance of knowing her father hadn't been falsely convicted. And, hopefully, she'll be able to put all of this behind her. On the other hand, though, there's also a possibility — although granted a remote one — that your ex-husband had nothing to do with that stabbing. And if I can locate any evidence that will support this, think of what it would mean to your daughter."

"I still don't believe —"

"Listen, why don't we get together and talk for a few minutes. I promise not to take up much of your time."

"I can't see —"

"Let me tell Vicky that you were anxious to help."

Mrs. Pirrelli didn't appear to recognize this for the blackmail it was. "I suppose it wouldn't hurt to meet with you," she conceded with obvious reluctance. "You can stop by for a short time today, if you want to. I have no plans for this afternoon."

"When would you like me there?"

"Let's make it at three." She gave me the

address, which was on fancy-schmantzy Sutton Place, no less.

Evidently Tony Pirrelli was doing all right for himself. For himself and his brother's family, that is.

I heard from Vicky at a little past noon. "I was anxious to find out how you're, like, doing. It's okay to call you, isn't it?"

"Of course. You can even contact me at home." I supplied her with the number. "Just do it before one a.m."

"One a.m.! I'm fast asleep by then," she declared, obviously without the slightest clue that I was teasing her. Could be it was the generation gap. "So, um, have you, like, discovered anything?"

"Well, I met with that lawyer, and she gave me the names of those two people in Christina's building that your father mentioned to you. The woman tenant is Jennifer Whyte, and I paid her a visit yesterday. We can forget about her as a suspect, though. She was in Massachusetts at the time of the stabbing."

"Is that for sure?"

"It checked out."

"Oh." Vicky sounded as if I'd just stuck a pin in her balloon, but she recovered pretty quickly. "There's still the guy, the one who was so stuck on Christina, right?"

"Right. He's away for a couple of days, but I'll try to set up something with him as soon as he gets back."

"And there's my uncle Tony, too. I told you he was, like, real hot for my mom, you know? So I wouldn't put it past him to have stabbed Christina and framed my dad for it."

I decided it was best to keep to myself the fact that this same thought had occurred to me. "I'm hoping to persuade your uncle to see me, as well," I said. "In the meantime, I have an appointment with your mother this afternoon. Maybe she's aware of something that could help us."

"Maybe," the teen responded doubtfully.

"Blossom Goody also told me that Christina had a sister in Pennsylvania, and I'll be driving out there Friday evening. Possibly she has some information about Christina that we should know about."

"Do you think?"

"I hope so."

"Uh, listen, Desiree, I forgot to give you the number of my cell phone the other day." She immediately made up for the oversight. "You'll call me if you, like, find out anything, won't you?"

"I will."

"One more thing," Vicky said then. "It dawned on me that sticking your nose into this kind of stuff could be dangerous, you know? So you'll, like, be really careful, won't you?"

I was touched. "Don't worry," I assured her. "I'm always careful."

"Good. I'd hate to have to go and find myself another PI."

Now, I was pretty sure she was joking about the reason for her concern. But I wasn't a hundred percent positive.

Could be it was that generation gap again.

CHAPTER 10

The maid who opened the door to the Pirrellis' sprawling apartment showed me into a living room that was about three times the size of my own and more than ten times as expensively furnished.

As soon as I entered the very modern space, which was done in deep plum, cream, and pale pink — a really striking combination, I thought — a tall woman rose from the modular sofa and came forward to greet me. She wore charcoal slacks and a gray silk V-neck shirt, an outfit that revealed her to be both slender and curvy. (Which is a neat trick, if you can swing it.) "Ms. Shapiro? I'm Mary Pirrelli — Vicky's mother."

I took the hand she extended. "Call me Desiree, won't you?"

"All right. And I'm Mary."

She resumed the seat she'd just vacated, and I plunked myself down on the matching plum chair opposite it. Facing her like this, I determined that Mary Pirrelli was only a step or two away from being genuinely beautiful. I mean, consider those features: almond-shaped dark brown eyes; full, nicely contoured lips; and a short, totally bumpless nose. Plus, her complexion was virtually flawless. And her hair, which she wore pulled straight back and fastened with a gold clip, was such an exceptionally lovely shade of red that only my own glorious hennaed locks could rival it. (Listen, what's true is true.) I have to admit, however, to being ninety-nine percent certain that in Mary's case the color was natural. What's more, Mother Nature had even favored this lady with a widow's peak! There was, however, one slight flaw in her appearance: a couple of overlapping front teeth. In a way, though, they, too, were an asset, taking the edge off all that perfection and making her seem more approachable. If you follow me.

She smiled to reveal a small dimple in both cheeks. (It wasn't fair; I'd have settled for just one of those things.) "What may I offer you? Tea? Coffee? A soft drink? We have some divine cookies, too."

The woman was being surprisingly cordial. But I got the impression her manner was studied. It was as if she'd audited a course in graciousness at some exclusive finishing school.

"A Coke would be nice if you have it, thank you."

Mary nodded in the direction of the doorway, and the maid, who had been standing there awaiting instructions, discretely withdrew from the room.

"You're not having anything yourself?" I asked.

"I had some iced tea shortly before you arrived."

Well, I could forget about getting cozy over our refreshments.

"So my daughter has convinced you to try to whitewash her father's memory," Mary stated matter-of-factly.

"I wouldn't put it like that. As I said on the phone, what she wants me to do is search for evidence that will clear his name."

"Believe me, Desiree, even if this murder had occurred yesterday, you wouldn't find evidence like that. As surely as we're sitting here, my ex-husband killed his —" She broke off, scowling. And it was with a great deal of distaste that she finally got out the word: "mistress."

"How can you be so positive?"

"Let's start with his being found with the knife in his hand. Then there's the fact that the stabbing had been preceded by a vicious argument between the two of them a half hour or so earlier. Also — and this is what clinches things for me — you have to take into account the violent nature of this man. From the time he was a boy, Victor was constantly in some kind of trouble — drinking, drugs, assaults, you name it. This wasn't even the first time he attacked his little girlfriend; he put her in the hospital on one occasion."

"I understood, though, that your former husband had pretty much reformed after the two of you met. Until that incident, I mean."

"Oh, he had. But evidently he slipped back into his old skin. For all I know, he could have been on drugs again."

"Did he ever abuse *you* physically?"

"No, not physically. But he did something far more damaging. He destroyed my confidence, my feeling of self-worth. Victor Pirrelli's middle name was 'cheat'; the man bedded every bimbo he came in contact with. And with Victor driving a cab for a living, there was no point in pressing him to account for his time. Convenient, wasn't it? Still, he certainly brought home enough proof of his . . . er . . . indiscretions. I'd find a lipstick print on his handkerchief one time, a shirt reeking with Obsession the next." Mary shook her head sadly, and when she spoke again her voice was barely above a whisper. "He made me feel as if . . . as if I were . . . a nothing.

"Vicky isn't terribly fond of her stepfather — Victor's brother, Tony." (An understatement if I'd ever heard one.) "I believe that on a subconscious level she's always felt that it would be disloyal to her father to have any affection for Tony. But I'm hoping that one day she'll change her mind and allow herself to appreciate what a fine person he is. I assure you, Desiree, Tony is twice — no, a dozen times — the man Victor was. And he wants nothing more than to have a close relationship with my daughter."

"Perhaps that *will* happen someday," I said encouragingly. "In the meantime, you're now married to somebody you can love and respect. And that counts for a lot."

Mary's long, beautifully manicured fingers absently went to the gold-and-diamond necklace at her throat. "I'm very grateful to have Tony in my life," she murmured, playing with the jewelry. "He —"

It was at this juncture that the maid returned carrying a silver salver. Along with my Coke, which was served in a crystal tumbler filled with ice, was a small porcelain serving dish offering up a tempting assortment of cookies.

The maid placed the refreshments on the end table next to my chair, then turned to her employer for further instructions.

"Thank you. That will be all, Fredda," Mary said in a tone that might have been borrowed from a similar scene in an old forties movie. You know, polite, but patronizing. It was obvious that playing the grande dame was a role Mary Pirrelli reveled in.

Once Fredda had departed, I lifted the plate of goodies and extended it in Mary's direction. She shook her head. "You were saying?" I reminded her — immediately following which I took a few sips of Coke, then began nibbling on a hermit cookie with lemon glaze. (Very tasty.)

"I have no idea. What *was* I saying?"

"You were telling me about your present husband and how fortunate you are to be married to him."

"Yes, that's right. I wanted to point out the difference between Tony and Vicky's father. My ex had no regard whatsoever for either my opinions or my feelings. With Victor, it was all about Victor. Do you know that he refused to so much as consider my looking for part-time employment? —

although we certainly could have used the money. Victor, you see, regarded a wage-earning wife as reflecting adversely on his machismo. Tony, on the other hand, is all for my fulfilling myself. After we were married he even encouraged me to enter college and get my diploma."

Yeah. Probably because he figured that would make you a more suitable mate, I retorted — though not aloud, of course. (Fairly or not, I found I was pretty soured on the woman's second husband without ever having met him.)

"But, listen, if you're thinking that there was anything between us before Victor went to prison" — which is precisely what I *was* thinking — "you're wrong. From the day I became his brother's wife, Tony was an important presence in my life — but only as a friend, nothing more. In fact, he'd been seeing someone steadily for years. I was, however, somewhat dependent on him after Victor's incarceration. I'd taken a sales position at Saks, on their designer floor — I've always loved fashion. But, of course, the bills still mounted up, since I was hardly adequately compensated. Tony insisted on helping out — we were family, he told me. He was there for us — for Vicky and me — in a dozen other ways, too. He drove her to the dentist when I had to work. He took us to the circus. He fixed our leaky faucet. He brought over groceries when I was laid up with pneumonia. . . . At any rate, before long, without ever intending to, we simply fell in love."

"And you divorced Victor," I said, opting for a butterscotch cookie now.

"Yes. But, the truth is, well before the murder I'd just about made up my mind to leave him. Can you blame me, Desiree? Even if I'd been willing, for Vicky's sake, to put up with the shabby way he treated me, I couldn't continue to close my eyes to his dalliances with other women. But, happily, that's all in the past." Her hands made another visit to her throat — and that gold-and-diamond necklace. "I now have a marvelous husband who's faithful to me, and I've got a career I adore — I work for Cecil Baron three days a week."

"Cecil Baron?"

"Don't tell me you've never heard of him." Mary looked at me as if I'd suddenly descended from another solar system. "He's a very well known couturier — his designs are absolutely stunning. Actually, I've been contemplating going in full-time. Not that we're hurting financially," she pointed out smugly, gesturing expansively toward her surroundings. "But I like to keep occupied, and there's very little to do around here, particularly of late. My husband has always worked long hours. And now Vicky isn't home that much anymore, either, what with her extra-curricular activities and these silly after-school jobs of hers — which, incidentally, she's adamant about holding on to. Tony and I talked over the possibility of my putting in the additional days only the other evening, and he doesn't have a problem with it. But I'm rambling on, aren't I? Is there anything else you wanted to ask me?"

"I was wondering if you'd ever met Christina Trent."

"I didn't know she existed — not until she *ceased* to exist." Mary smiled at what she apparently regarded as the cleverness of her own words. "While I was aware that Victor played around a great deal, I had no idea that he was seeing anyone in particular."

I cleared my throat now, mostly in order to delay, if only for an instant, that all-important question I had yet to ask. "Uh, the night of the murder, would you remember what you were doing, say, between eleven and midnight?"

Mary's reaction wasn't unexpected. "You certainly can't think that I —" She laughed harshly, following this up with a blistering glare. "Evidently, you're not prepared to accept that I was ignorant of the fact that there even *was* a Christina Trent."

I slipped into my most placating tone. "It's not that at all, Mary. Honestly. I would just appreciate having the information for my records."

After a moment of staring at me suspiciously, her eyes reduced to mere slits, the woman acquiesced. "All right. I can tell you *exactly* what I was doing: preparing to go to sleep. That was a Saturday, and Sunday was my daughter's birthday. My mother-in-law came over about six o'clock or so and had supper with us. When we finished, Vicky tried on the dress Philomena — my mother-in-law — had made for her to wear the next day; we were taking Vicky and some of her little friends to lunch. At any rate, the dress turned out to be far too large, and by the time Philomena was through with the alterations, it was past eleven, and she was too tired to drive home. So she spent the rest of the night on my sofa. Satisfied?"

"Yes, of course. It's only for my records," I repeated awkwardly. "Uh, when would be the best time to reach your husband? I'd like to —"

"You want to interrogate *Tony?*"

"Well, he was the brother of the alleged killer. And it's incumbent upon me to question everyone who had any connection to the tragedy, no matter how peripheral. You never know. Your husband may be in possession of some crucial information without even being aware of it."

"Please," Mary muttered, not buying into this explanation for a second. Nevertheless, she gave me the man's office number, suggesting I contact him there.

"I appreciate this, Mary," I told her. "And thanks very much for your time this afternoon."

"That's all right. But, Desiree? I hope you're not counting on Tony's agreeing to talk to you."

I responded with an innocent smile. "It's worth a try, isn't it?"

"I suppose so. But just so you understand, my husband is a very busy man. More important, though, I doubt that he'll see any purpose in helping you investigate a murder that's already been solved."

I didn't elect to share with her that — as in her case — if it should become necessary, I had a bit of blackmail in reserve for her precious Tony. A little something that just might persuade him to change his mind.

CHAPTER 11

There was some macaroni and cheese in the freezer (thank God for leftovers), and I intended to enjoy one of my favorite meals to the fullest. So I held off dissecting today's meeting until after supper.

I finally got down to business while I was having a second cup of my infamous coffee. (You haven't tasted bad coffee until you've tasted mine.)

I started off by admitting that I hadn't liked my young client's mother very much — or, anyway, what I'd seen of her so far. (I assure you, however, that my feelings toward Mary Pirrelli had nothing to do with her being such a knockout.) Still, for Vicky's sake I would have been only too glad to eliminate the woman as a suspect. But I just didn't see how, in good conscience, I could do that. Not until I'd at least had a talk with her mother-in-law.

At any rate, right after this I focused on the fact that, à la Jennifer Whyte, Mary had been surprisingly frank with me. Only in Mary's case, this candor was totally at odds with the persona she presented. I'd found the lady to be smug. Even arrogant, at times. Yet there she was, laying bare aspects of her private life that you'd have thought she would have been determined to keep that way — private, I mean. With virtually no prompting, she'd divulged that her first husband's behavior — particularly his nonstop bed hopping — had wrecked her self-confidence. (And why so many members of the male gender persist in leaving clues that prove what hound dogs they are will probably elude me until they put me in my grave.) Naturally, I couldn't help but wonder at her reason for opening up as she had. Listen, those weren't the sort of revelations I'd have made to a complete stranger, would you?

Maybe, I ruminated, this was Mary's way of excusing herself for taking up with her husband's brother — and without wasting a lot of time once Victor was behind bars, either. Or maybe she had been willing to expose the humiliation she'd suffered during her first marriage in order to contrast the character of her ex with that of her current spouse. What I'm getting at is that by offering up Victor as such a despicable human being, she might have figured I shouldn't have much of a problem accepting him as Christina's killer. Whereas, Tony — that saintly fellow — was obviously totally incapable of such an appalling act. Could this have been, I asked myself now, because Mary herself feared (or suspected or *knew*) that Tony was guilty of the crime?

Anyway, I was fairly certain of two things with regard to all of this soul baring: (1) A good portion of what I'd been told was basically, if not entirely, true. (2) The woman was using me as a conduit, hoping that at least some of her observations about the two men would be passed along to her daughter.

And speaking of Vicky, I was amazed Mary hadn't put her foot down about the naval piercing and that green-and-orange hair. (Look, I admit to being from another generation; nevertheless, hideous is hideous.) That rather imperious lady, I mused, seemed to be treading pretty carefully when it came to her offspring. Take another example: the teenager's part-time employment. While Mary had made it clear to me that she didn't approve, she obviously hadn't disallowed it. I got the impression that, in spite of the blissful state of her union with husband number two, Mary Pirrelli had long been doing penance for having foisted a father substitute on her child that the girl so bitterly resented.

I was in the middle of an absolutely spectacular dream in which I was costarring with — get this — Mel Gibson, who some time back had replaced Robert Redford in my affections. (After all, how many years could I be expected to remain faithful to somebody who clearly didn't give a damn about me?) Of course, as with his predecessor, it had been necessary to adjust to some of the man's shortcomings — namely his good looks and athletic build. Anyway, it was Mel's first visit to my slumber land, and I'd just turned down his marriage proposal (although it might have been a proposition — that part is kind of hazy). Immediately afterward, however, he'd extracted my promise to let him know if things didn't work out with this Nick I was so keen on. And now he was asking if he could at least kiss me good-bye. I lifted my face to his, parted my lips, and . . .

. . . the telephone shattered that priceless moment.

Reaching out blindly, I fumbled around on my night table for the offending instrument — and knocked it to the floor. It took a Herculean effort to unglue my eyelids so I could retrieve the damn thing.

I finally muttered a faint hello into the mouthpiece.

"Desiree? It's Vicky," this unbearably cheerful voice announced. Following which — my tone no doubt having belatedly registered on the teenager — she put to me, "I didn't, like, wake you, did I?"

I peered at the alarm clock: *six forty-five, for God's sake!* "It's okay," I told her, yawning. "I have to get up in a couple of hours anyway."

"Oh, good," she said, totally unaware of the sarcasm inherent in the reply. "I wanted to find out how things went with my mom yesterday."

"She was very cooperative."

"Did she, you know, say much about my dad?"

"She mentioned that they hadn't gotten along very well. I think your mother probably had a rough time of it, Vicky." Then I quickly added, "It might not even have been your father's fault. Probably they simply weren't suited to each other. Besides, as you yourself commented, at age nineteen it's unlikely either of them was mature enough for marriage."

"Um," was the extent of the girl's response. "So, like, are you planning to question anyone else before you go to Philadelphia Friday?"

"I hope to. And I promise I'll keep you posted on my progress."

"Thanks. Oh, and Desiree, shouldn't I be sending you a check soon? Like, as a retainer."

In spite of the ridiculously early hour and my frustration at having been robbed of the smooch of a lifetime, I grinned. "Why don't you mail me a dollar. Just to make things legal."

"Sure. But I'm, like, kind of surprised that you didn't think of that yourself."

Imagine. Being reprimanded for my business practices by a kid with a hole in her belly button. Things don't get much more demeaning than that!

I was at the office bright and early that morning. (Bright and early, in this instance, being nine fifteen.) As soon as I showed my face, Jackie said with a smirk, "Having your apartment painted, Dez?"

Well, the first time Jackie had made this remark in recognition of my premature arrival, I laughed. The second, third — and maybe even fourth — times I managed a polite chuckle. But after that the repetition *really* wore thin, with a sickly smile giving way to a frown and then to clenched teeth and finally to well-chosen, if purposely unintelligible curses. None of which deterred her in the least.

Today, however, I did something Jackie just can't deal with: I totally ignored her. *Damn! I wish I'd thought of it sooner!*

"Are you all right, Dez?" she called out after me when I marched past her desk.

"Fine."

"Uh, see you later, okay?"

I didn't waste a minute before attending to what had become my daily mission: attempting to contact George Gladstone. I wound up listening to the same recorded message I'd been listening to for the past two days. And I slammed down the phone in frustration.

Following this I took a crack at Tony Pirrelli. I wasn't under the impression that I'd be getting a warm reception from him, and I was right. In fact, I didn't get any reception from him at all. He refused to take my calls.

On my first try, a snooty secretary asked for my name (which I was certain Tony was already familiar with) and put me on hold. Moments later she was back on the line. "I'm sorry. Mr. Pirrelli is with a client." Only she didn't sound the least bit sorry.

An hour later I dialed Donato, Costello, Pirrelli, and Goldstein again. This time the secretary informed me — without even bothering to check with him — that Mr. Pirrelli was in conference.

I made another attempt after lunch (mine) and was told that Mr. Pirrelli was out to lunch (his — supposedly). *Now* I began to suspect that the guy was avoiding me. (Sometimes I have to be whacked on the head with a brick or two before I can see the light.)

Still, I had this teeny hope I'd be proved wrong. So around four thirty I gave the man one last chance to redeem himself. And guess what? According to his female flunky, Mr. Pirrelli had just left for home.

At this point it was evident that the direct approach wasn't getting me anywhere. If I wanted to reach Victor's devoted brother, I'd have to employ a method that was a little, well, devious. Which was okay with me.

I don't like to toot my own horn or anything, but the fact is, I'm pretty damn good at devious.

CHAPTER 12

I didn't call Tony Pirrelli that evening; I called his wife. "I've been trying to get in touch with your husband," I explained, "but I haven't had any luck."

"I warned you that you could have a problem there. Tony has a thriving practice; some days even I have difficulty getting through to him. Besides — and I'm certain I told you this, too — as far as my husband is concerned, the investigation into that girl's stabbing was successfully concluded more than ten years ago." And then, almost as an afterthought: "As unhappy as he was — as we all were — with the findings, of course."

"For your daughter's sake, though, perhaps you could persuade Mr. Pirrelli to give me a few minutes of his time."

Mary's response was slow in coming. "The fact is, I tried — for Vicky's sake, as you said. Tony just doesn't see any point in revisiting that dreadful incident." It was obvious from her tone that she was embarrassed at having had so little sway over her husband. "Men can be awfully stubborn sometimes, can't they?" she added, attempting a conspiratorial little chuckle.

"They certainly can. But listen, Mary, I really need to speak to him. Just briefly, I promise." (Well, it depends on your definition of "briefly," doesn't it?) "And the thing is, I think he might actually be interested in a meeting, considering what I've learned."

"What have you learned?"

"Well, according to a reliable source, there's been some talk regarding your husband's involvement in Victor's plea bargain. Evidently a few facts were uncovered recently, and questions were raised."

"What are you saying?" Mary demanded, her voice turning shrill. "What facts? What did Tony have to do with that plea bargain? He wasn't even Victor's attorney; my ex was represented by a criminal lawyer — a Blossom somebody."

Was it possible, I asked myself, *that the woman really had been in the dark regarding her spouse's part in his brother's sentencing?* I was just about convinced this was the case. "That's true. But your husband supposedly had some input, as well."

"And this has just come up *now?*"

"It's conceivable that Victor's death

might somehow have brought the matter to light. Anyway, I thought it would also be to your husband's benefit if we got together. I mean, so I could fill him in on things."

"There's evidently been some mistake," Mary maintained, although she appeared to be somewhat shaken. "At any rate, Tony isn't at home, and I don't expect him until quite late. I imagine I could attempt to reach him at the office, though," she offered without much enthusiasm.

"That isn't necessary. Just tell him when he gets in, please, that I'd appreciate his contacting me as soon as possible."

"I will. But even if he agrees to meet with you, Desiree, don't count on seeing him before Monday, at the earliest. Tony expects to be in court all day tomorrow, and we have dinner plans for Friday evening. Then at seven thirty a.m. on Saturday we're flying to the Bahamas for the weekend to attend a wedding — the daughter of one of Tony's most important corporate clients. But I'll try to persuade him to at least phone you tomorrow."

I thanked her and, to be on the safe side, repeated both my office and home numbers — which I'd supplied her with only yesterday.

Putting down the receiver, it occurred to

me that by mentioning Tony's involvement in the plea bargain to Mary, I might have opened up a can of worms. And while this had certainly been inadvertent, I decided it could very well work to my advantage.

My next call was to Vicky's "grandmom."

"Hello?"

"Is this Mrs. Pirrelli?"

"Yes. *Philomena* Pirrelli."

"My name is Desiree Shapiro, Mrs. Pirrelli, and —"

"Victoria's investigator."

"That's right. I wonder if you and I could speak in person for a few minutes — at your convenience, of course."

"What for? What do I know about some stranger's murder? Believe me, if I knew anything that could have helped Vittorio, I would have told it to the police ten years ago, and my youngest child — God rest his soul — would be alive today."

"I'm very sorry for your loss, Mrs. Pirrelli," I mumbled awkwardly.

"Uh, yes, thank you. Listen, you want to talk to somebody about what happened that night? You go talk to the people in that girl's building. Maybe somebody there saw something. Or heard something. But if they did, I doubt it is going to make you happy."

"Why do you say that?"

"Look, Vittorio was not a *bad* boy, Mrs. Shapiro. I swear to you, it was not in his nature to cause harm to anybody — not intentionally. But Vittorio had his father's temper. My Roberto — may he rest in peace — when he got mad, he was like a volcano. What I think is, the night she died, Christina — This was her name?"

"That's right. Christina Trent."

"Well, that night Christina and my son had a very big argument. Victoria told you about the argument?"

"Yes, she did."

"All right. So Vittorio must have taken the knife from the kitchen — but only to threaten the girl. He didn't wish for her to give him any more *agita*. You are familiar with the word *agita?*"

"Oh, yes." It was what I was getting from this case.

"Anyhow, something this Christina said to him made my Vittorio crazy." A pause, then more optimistically: "Or the girl could have tried to grab the knife from his hand, and they fought, the two of them, and there was an accident." Finally, but with very little conviction, she offered, "Maybe *she* was even the one who had the knife, and my son stabbed her in . . . in

111

self-defense. Who knows what really happened, Mrs. Shapiro. I know only the end result: Vittorio killed that girl. And in so doing, he killed himself. You understand what I am saying?"

"I understand."

"And this is all I can tell you."

"Please, Mrs. Pirrelli. Sit down with me anyway. I promise not to keep you long."

"You think I would hesitate for one minute to do this if it would enable you to clear my boy — even now that he is gone?"

"Of course not." And here I went into the usual song and dance. "Nevertheless," I told her, "you may have some important information you're not even aware that you have."

"Believe me, I have no information," Philomena insisted wearily.

Well, it was time to engage in a little blackmail again. "I'm certain it would mean a great deal to your granddaughter to learn that you tried to help her arrive at the truth."

"You believe this truth would make her feel good?" the woman scoffed.

"It's quite possible that it wouldn't. But Victoria won't be satisfied until she finds out, one way or the other, whether her father was responsible for Christina Trent's death."

There was an interval of three or four seconds before the woman muttered, "Okay, okay, Mrs. Shapiro. I need shoes anyhow."

"Shoes?"

"I got a shoe store in Manhattan I go to. They use only the finest Italian leather — like butter, it is. I could come and see you, then go there and pick up a nice pair of black pumps. Your office — where is it located? I hope on the east side, at least."

"Yes, it's on the east side." I gave her the address.

"In the thirties, huh? This is more than twenty blocks from my shoe store. But, all right. I'll be there Saturday morning. Eight o'clock sharp."

Eight a.m. on a Saturday? What is wrong with this family, anyway? Don't they believe in sleep?

I tried to look on the bright side, though. At least my appointment with the Pirrelli matriarch wasn't likely to louse up another chance at a make-out session with Mel (as in Gibson, that is).

After all, how often does lightning strike twice?

113

CHAPTER 13

First thing Friday I got in touch with Jackie to let her know I wouldn't be in that day. Not only because this was both common courtesy and sensible business practice but because I didn't dare not to. Listen, failing to keep that woman apprized of your whereabouts isn't some lousy little misdemeanor. In Jackie's view, it's practically punishable by flogging.

At any rate, her reaction this morning was one of genuine concern. "What's wrong, Dez? Aren't you feeling well?" (I told you — didn't I? — that when she isn't being a pain in the you-know-where, Jackie is a truly caring friend.)

"I'm fine. But I figured it would be easier to work at home than to take my car to the office. I have to drive to Philadelphia later."

"Why would you want to do that?" It crossed my mind now that if it ever came to a competition for "Queen of the Busybodies," Jackie and I would be out in front, running neck and neck. (Although I do like to think that I'm a little more subtle.)

"I have an appointment with Christina Trent's sister — Christina's the girl Vicky's father supposedly murdered."

"I'm aware of the appointment, Desiree — you told me about it on Tuesday," Jackie informed me huffily. "I remembered as soon as you said 'Philadelphia.' What I meant was, why would you want to *drive* down there. You have a worse sense of direction than my uncle Wolfy does — and he's ninety-seven and gets lost going around the block."

"Thanks for the vote of confidence."

I couldn't believe what came out of Jackie's mouth next. Ignoring the snide rejoinder, she said in all sincerity, "I don't have to tell you how much I hate to butt in, Dez" — what was it Robert Burns wrote about seeing ourselves as others see us? — "but the train's also faster and a lot more relaxing. And, of course," she added (gratuitously, I thought), "it knows the way."

It took me a split second to warm to the suggestion. "Actually, it might not be a bad idea to go by train. Thanks, Jackie."

"Anytime," she responded smugly.

I phoned Penn Station for the schedule to Philly, then went on to George Gladstone.

Today there was finally an update to his answering machine message. "George Gladstone Public Relations," it announced. "I'm out of town, but I'll be in the office on Tuesday. Please leave word, and I'll be sure to get back to you."

How do you like that? Either the man had come home for a short while and then left for parts unknown again, or else he'd reprogrammed the machine from wherever the hell he was.

Anyhow, with George out of the way, I directed my attention to the file on Victor Pirrelli. I'd just begun to type up my notes when the telephone rang.

"Hi, Aunt Dez."

The instant I heard Ellen's voice, I felt a stab of guilt. She *had* promised to keep me posted about that camping business, but knowing how concerned she was about it, I should have called her anyway. I was so wrapped up in this case of mine, though, that I'd allowed Ellen — and her anxiety — to fly right out of my head.

"I wanted to tell you that everything's fine. With our honeymoon plans, that is."

"I'm very glad to hear it. What happened?"

"Mike came over last night with a bunch of travel folders — none of which had anything to do with camping, thank God. And we've decided on Bermuda."

"That's great."

"What I mean is, we've *pretty much* decided."

Uh-oh.

"I've been hearing some really nice things about Paradise Island, and of course, there's Aruba and Dorado Beach in Puerto Rico. Also, we haven't entirely ruled out a cruise."

"Well, you want to be sure you can get a reservation. So don't wait too long to nail down your choice."

"Oh, we won't," Ellen said lightly. But it was pretty obvious that she wasn't taking my advice to heart.

I was a bit troubled when I put down the phone. I mean, I had this vision of Ellen and Mike spending their honeymoon in Hoboken, New Jersey, because it was the only place with an available room.

Right after I went back to my typing a second call came in.

"This is Anthony Pirrelli," the man said in a quiet, but somehow menacing, tone. "My wife told me about your conversation with her. It appears, Ms. Shapiro, that you're determined to insinuate yourself into my personal life and the lives of my family."

117

"I wouldn't put it like that," I retorted, bristling. "For starters, your stepdaughter came to *me*. As I believe you're aware, Vicky is convinced that her father — *your brother* — was wrongly imprisoned, and she pleaded with me to conduct an investigation. I was moved to take the case — and without compensation —" I threw in quickly, "because . . . well . . . it was so important to her that I couldn't bring myself to say no."

"You're a regular philanthropist, aren't you?"

It wasn't easy, but I rose above the sarcasm. "Listen, Mr. Pirrelli, I like Vicky; she's a lovely young girl. And I was concerned that if I wasn't willing to look into this, nobody else would be, either."

"I'll let it go at that," Pirrelli said — after which he added ominously, "for now." (I swear, the way he said "for now" made every hair at the back of my neck stand on end.) "But how do you justify telling my wife that I railroaded my brother into accepting a plea bargain?"

"*Railroaded?* I *never* used that word with your wife. All I said was that I'd heard that a couple of . . . uh . . . somewhat troubling facts had recently emerged regarding your contribution to the sentencing agreement."

"Oh, really? And just what are these 'troubling' facts?"

"This isn't something I can go into on the telephone, Mr. Pirrelli."

Tony Pirrelli chuckled, but the sound held no humor. "You're hell-bent on meeting with me, it seems."

"Well, the thing is, I think it might be advantageous to both of us if we could talk in person for a few minutes."

"All right. I'm going to agree to see you. But only to accommodate my family. Let me check my calendar." A few seconds later he announced, "It will have to be next Thursday — in the morning."

For a moment I feared he'd show himself to be a true Pirrelli by suggesting something in the seven to eight a.m. range. But he barked, "Eleven o'clock. My office. Be on time."

What a charming man! No wonder Mary had found him so irresistible.

CHAPTER 14

The train pulled into Philadelphia's Pennsylvania Station at just before seven. To get a taxi, I had to stand in line behind what seemed like a thousand other people (but was more likely closer to fifty) who were queued up in front of the station with the same thing in mind. The line moved with surprising speed, though, and I arrived at the Red Star Diner in time for my appointment — in fact, with a few minutes to spare.

The place wasn't too crowded, so I was quickly able to determine that there was no age-appropriate female sitting alone here. After providing the hostess with my name and notifying her that another woman would be joining me, I was shown to a booth with a red Formica tabletop and well-padded vinyl cushions upholstered, of course, in red. (This was, after all, the *Red Star Diner*.)

I figured I'd have a cup of coffee while I was waiting for Alicia Schnabel. Fortunately, it was pretty good coffee, because before long I was on my second cup. Not because

I wanted it, but just to do *something* until Alicia put in an appearance. When I'd drunk the last drop, I deliberated about whether to go for thirds or just sit there and concentrate on solving world problems. I opted to forego the coffee, since I'd probably have wound up floating away.

By eight fifteen I hadn't come up with a single idea for improving the state of the world. And my patience, never anything to brag about, was on the verge of expiring. Plus, I was starved, and my stomach wasn't exactly shy about letting everyone within hearing distance know that it was being deprived. Well, I would be remedying that situation very shortly, Alicia or no Alicia. But first I'd make an attempt to contact the woman. Which, I lectured myself, was what I should have done about twenty minutes after I got here.

I'd left my cell phone at home, but there was a pay phone at the rear of the diner, right across from the rest rooms. I dialed Alicia's office number — and got a recording. I decided that it might not be a bad idea to try *my* office number to see if she'd left any word on my voice mail. She hadn't. Well, as long as I was in the neighborhood, I made a brief visit to the ladies' room, something I'd been contemplating (but was too lazy to act on) since that second cup of coffee.

When I returned to the booth, it was occupied by a dark-eyed brunette — quite attractive, in an understated kind of way. She was, I noted, smartly dressed in a businesslike gray pinstripe suit. I judged her to be in her early thirties. "Ms. Shapiro?" she inquired.

"Mrs. Schnabel?" I responded. (Don't you hate it when somebody answers your question with a question?)

"Yes. I'm sorry to be so late. I hope you got my message."

"What message?"

"Oh, no! Damn it! I called this place at about twenty to eight to say I was detained and that I'd be here as soon as I could. I suggested that if you were hungry, you might want to have something to eat in the meantime."

"I guess whoever took the call must have been busy around that time and then forgot all about it two seconds later."

"I'm awfully sorry about this."

"No apology necessary, honestly. But I would like to order soon, if you don't mind. My stomach's really giving me what-for now."

Alicia signaled the waitress, who immediately supplied us with menus. They were white with — what else? — a giant red star. After a hasty read-through we both settled on the open roast beef sandwich with mashed potatoes.

The instant we'd passed our choices on to the waitress, Alicia said, "Please. Tell me what you know about Christie's death."

Now, I think I've already mentioned how allergic my digestive system is to the topic of murder. But postponing a discussion of the stabbing until after we'd finished our meal wasn't an option tonight.

"I don't know anything for sure. To start with, though, let me give you some background, Mrs. Schnabel."

"It's Alicia."

"And I'm Desiree. Well, as I stated on the telephone, I'm a private investigator. And on Monday Victor Pirrelli's daughter came to my office. Her father had been gravely wounded in some sort of prison fight a couple of weeks earlier. And after he was taken to the hospital he sent for the girl. Now, she was only six years old when he was arrested, and they hadn't had any contact since then. In view of the seriousness of his condition, however, he wanted to see his only child for what he correctly surmised would be one last time. He was also determined to impress upon her that she was not the daughter of a killer."

"Just a moment. Are you saying that Victor Pirrelli is *dead?*"

"That's right. Didn't I mention it on the phone? He passed away that same night, sometime after his daughter left the hospital."

"And she hired you because — why? Because she wants everyone to know that her father's hands were clean?" Then, before I could respond: "The police found those hands holding the knife that killed my sister, for God's sake! Tell me, why would you give any credence to the story this man fed his daughter?"

"I'm not certain that I do. But I feel it should be investigated. Look, Victor either knew or strongly suspected that he was dying when he proclaimed his innocence to Vicky — that's the girl's name. So he no longer had anything to gain by lying."

"Maybe there was one shred of decency in him, Desiree; maybe he lied to Vicky for *her* sake."

"Naturally, that's a possibility. Still, as I said, his daughter is convinced that he had nothing to do with the murder. And another possibility is that she could be right."

"And the knife?"

"According to Victor, he had gone for a

walk after his argument with your sister —
I suppose you know they had a bitter
quarrel." Alicia nodded. "When he returned, Christina was lying on the living
room floor with a knife in her side. He
maintained that he pulled it out so he could
attempt to stop the bleeding. But before he
got the chance, the police came on the
scene."

"Listen, I'm not sure that you're aware
of this, but Victor Pirrelli was a vile
person, an *animal*. My sister had to go
around with her jaw wired shut for I-don't-
know-how-long because he hauled off and
walloped her. And what business did he
have taking up with an eighteen-year-old,
anyway — him, a married man with a
child? I used to plead with Christie to
break it off," Alicia said plaintively, her
anguish etched on her face. "You can see
how much good it did, though."

At this precise moment, our food was
served. But it went untouched for a time,
because the second the waitress walked
away from the table, Alicia burst into tears,
covering her face with her hands.

It was a good while before she was able
to get hold of herself. And in the meantime,
I sat by helplessly. (Somebody should write
a book about how to handle situations like

this.) I mean, I wanted to console her, but I had no idea how to go about it. Finally, I dealt with the woman's grief in my usual, unenlightened manner: I reached across the table and gave her a few quick pats on the forearm. Which I'm sure didn't provide her with even a thimbleful of comfort. And to make me feel even more ill at ease during this outpouring of emotion, I got the distinct impression that people were glaring at me, damning me as the culprit responsible for my dinner companion's pain.

At last Alicia removed her hands from her tear-stained face, quickly bent her head, and rummaged around blindly in her handbag. After extracting a couple of Kleenex, she wiped her eyes, blew her nose, and then produced a game little smile. "I wouldn't have thought there were that many tears left in me after all these years. I'm terribly embarrassed."

"Don't be silly. You couldn't help it. There are times when giving vent to our feelings like that is just something we need to do."

"Thank you for understanding," she murmured.

After this we sat in silence for a couple of minutes, devoting our undivided attention to what was on our plates. Then I said softly, "What was she like, your sister?"

"Like?"

"It might help me in my investigation if I learned something about Christina's character, the sort of person she was."

"Well, I don't know how much you've heard." Alicia's eyes were making this a question.

"Very little, actually."

She leaned toward me. "Look, Desiree, after our phone conversation, I realized that it wouldn't make sense for us to have this meeting unless I was prepared to be totally honest with you. Frankly, I have a lot of difficulty imagining that Christie's killer was anyone other than Victor Pirrelli. But if I'm mistaken and it *was* someone else, it would mean a great deal to me if I could contribute in some small way to putting that individual behind bars. Which is why you can believe that whatever I tell you about my sister will be the truth. To begin with, she wasn't anything like what some people made her out to be."

"What are you referring to?"

"Well, Christie once told me that there was some gossip about her having loose morals. That is so wrong it's almost laughable. Do you know what Christie *really* was, Desiree? A wide-eyed innocent who believed the best of just about everyone. Maybe that's what got her killed.

"Another thing: People — quite a few of them — assumed she was vain. After all, it almost had to be — didn't it? — with men throwing themselves at her the way they did. And, of course, she *was* very good-looking. But, the fact is, my sister wasn't the least bit conceited. She wasn't even that happy with her appearance."

"What was it she found fault with?"

"She didn't much care for her figure — especially her legs. And she would have preferred a shorter nose. But what troubled Christie most was her complexion; she was prone to breaking out. It didn't happen that often, either — just often enough to be upsetting. I used to assure her that the condition would go away when she got a little older. I was forever reminding her that until I reached my twenties, I had my allotment of zits, too."

I wondered if, at this moment, Alicia and I were sharing the same thought: How tragic it was that Christina had been denied the opportunity to outgrow her teenage affliction!

It's more than likely something of that nature *had* entered the woman's mind, because almost at once she put down her fork and pushed aside her plate, leaving more than half the food untouched.

"Would you, by any chance, have a picture of Christie with you?" I asked gently.

Wordlessly, Alicia pulled a tan lizard wallet from her bag and removed a photograph from one of the plastic sleeves. She smiled poignantly as she passed it across the table. "This was taken only a few months before Christie died. You'll notice that she's resting her hand on her chin. She wanted to conceal the pimple that had erupted only that morning."

The young girl in the photo — it was a head shot — certainly resembled the woman sitting opposite me now. The same dark, silky hair. The same heart-shaped face. Even the features were similar. But Christina Trent had a sort of *allure* that was lacking in her older sibling. Maybe it was the green eyes that made her that much more arresting. (Alicia's were almost black.) Or could be it was the dazzling smile. (Alicia's was pleasant enough, but nothing spectacular.) At any rate, it wasn't hard to understand why men had found the victim so appealing.

"She was lovely," I said, handing the photograph back to Alicia.

"Yes, she was. She was also warm. And generous. And *such* fun to be with."

"Uh, I understand that Christie had a confrontation with one of the other tenants in the building, someone who used to be a close friend of hers."

"You're referring to Jennifer Whyte — I was going to tell you about that. I'm certain those nasty rumors about Christie's morals originated with Jennifer. But let me clarify what occurred there. First of all, the last thing my sister intended was to have *any* sort of physical contact with Jennifer's boyfriend, let alone sleep with him. Apparently, he was unattractive to the point of being repulsive. What's more, you can factor in that until they . . . became intimate, Christie was a virgin. I'll bet no one bothered to inform you of that."

"No, they didn't," I answered, doing my best to hide my skepticism.

I doubt that I was very successful, though, because Alicia responded with a fairly belligerent, "She *was*," before proceeding. "That particular afternoon Christie was in the hall, throwing some trash in the compactor, when along came this boyfriend of Jennifer's — I forget his name. He invited her into Jennifer's apartment — he was living there, too — to listen to his new Bruce Springsteen album. My sister wasn't a big Springsteen fan, but what's-'is-name was very persistent. And Christie, being Christie, didn't want to hurt his feelings, so she agreed to come in for a few minutes. And, by the way, she wasn't aware that Jennifer wasn't home. Anyhow, as soon as he put on the record, he started pouring drinks for them both. And the thing is, Christie didn't drink, so the liquor immediately went to her head. And *then* that snake actually started to cry. Can you stand it? He claimed that his twin brother had recently died of leukemia and that, as a result, his mother went completely to pieces, and he had to have her committed to a mental facility. A story that, from beginning to end, can be attributed to an extremely inventive imagination. Of this, I'm certain. At any rate, between the drinks and the sympathy, Christie wound up in bed with the man. She didn't even know how it happened.

"Well, Jennifer walked in when her boyfriend and Christie were . . . when they were . . . um . . . having relations. The whole thing was a nightmare. As you can appreciate, Jennifer was livid — who can blame the woman? While, for her part, Christie was absolutely devastated by the

131

realization that she'd betrayed her very good friend. She tried to express this to Jennifer and to explain what had led up to . . . what took place. But Jennifer refused to listen. And she never spoke to my sister again." Alicia sighed. "So that was that. Incidentally, this was the first — and last — time Christie had liquor of any kind. After that day, you couldn't even get her to touch a glass of wine."

"Speaking of Christie's neighbors, did she ever mention a George Gladstone to you?"

"George Gladstone . . . George Gladstone," Alicia muttered, drumming her fingers on the tabletop. Suddenly it came to her. "Oh, I remember. He was that older fellow in her building who had such a big crush on Christina."

"What did she tell you about him?"

"Only that he was close to sixty and that he was constantly asking her out to dinner. She also said that sometimes he would look at her in a way that gave her the creeps. You don't think — ?"

"I don't think anything yet. He's been out of town, and I'm going to try to see him next week."

Alicia took a sip of water now. "There's something I'd like you to know."

"What's that?"

"When they met, Christie didn't have any idea that Victor Pirrelli was a married man."

"How *did* they meet?"

"She went to a party in Manhattan, and there he was — my poor little sister's Prince Charming." Alicia pressed her lips together and squeezed her eyes shut for a second before continuing. "Pirrelli attended solo, naturally, and Christie had no reason to suspect that there was a Mrs. Victor Pirrelli in the picture. It wasn't until they'd had their fourth or fifth date that the low-life bothered to mention a wife — who, of course, didn't understand him. His excuse for not leveling with Christie sooner was that he'd been afraid she'd refuse to see him any longer if she learned the truth."

"She wasn't angry at the deception?"

"Certainly she was. But Pirrelli was a smooth operator; also, he was dealing with a gullible young girl. He kept assuring Christie that she had come to mean everything to him. Plus, he gave her that tired old line about planning to ask his wife for a divorce. I don't believe, however, that he ever got around to acknowledging the existence of a child. Just a small oversight, right? At any rate, you can imagine the kind of glib talker Victor Pirrelli was when you consider that he managed to convince Christie to continue going out with him after he'd broken her jaw."

"I heard about that. What caused him to attack her, anyway?"

"Christie said it was an accident," Alicia answered, placing a barely discernible emphasis on the "said." "They were having a heated argument and Pirrelli had intended to punch the wall, but she moved, and his fist wound up connecting with her jaw instead."

"Do you think this was the truth?"

"Obviously, I can't say for sure — I wasn't there. But I tend to doubt it."

"Have you any idea what precipitated that argument?"

"It seems that Christie had invited a neighbor and his girlfriend over for dinner one evening. The phone rang while the girls were busy in the kitchen, so Christie asked the fellow to pick up. It was Victor calling, and when Christie got on the line, he started questioning her. But because he was such a goddam liar himself, Victor didn't accept her explanation. And the following night he came over and accused her of being unfaithful to him. She, of course, denied it, and one thing led to another. Pretty soon my sister's face wound up being a stand-in for a wall."

"Did you ever meet Victor Pirrelli yourself?" I inquired now.

"No. I moved to Pennsylvania when Christie turned eighteen." Alicia hesitated, and I speculated that she might be having a little internal debate as to how much she should elaborate. I could envision her engaging in a mental shrug (sort of an "I might as well" thing) before going on. "A close friend of mine from college had a job with Cavanaugh Realty — the company I'm with to this day — and she told me it was a great company to work for and that a position had just opened up there. I jumped at the opportunity. Frankly, I'd been finding it very difficult to recover from a breakup with a guy who had to be the biggest sleaze in Forest Hills, Queens. We Trent girls sure knew how to pick 'em, didn't we?" A wry smile here, following which Alicia toyed with her napkin for a bit. Then her eyes fastened on my face. "If Christina had only lived," she asserted, "I know that eventually she'd have met the right person, just as I did. *If*," she repeated bitterly, "Christina had only lived.

"Anyhow, I was desperate to get a new start. I wanted Christie to relocate to Pennsylvania with me, but she was crazy about New York. And besides, she was

135

really looking forward to having her own place. So I allowed her to convince me to make the move without her. She'd be perfectly fine, she kept insisting. We did speak on the phone just about every day, though," Alicia hurried to interject, "and it wasn't as if Philadelphia were a million miles away." But the woman's lower lip had begun to tremble, and there was little doubt this last part was offered mostly to justify herself to herself.

Eager to avert what I feared might be another crying jag, I didn't waste a second before putting to her, "Um, the rest of your family still resides in New York?"

"There isn't any 'rest' of our family. Our parents were killed in a train wreck when I was eleven and Christie was only seven. My mother's sister, who was our sole relative, raised us after they were gone. She died about six months before I went out to Philly.

"Oh, who am I kidding?" Alicia demanded at this point. "I had no business going without Christie. May I tell you what haunts me most about all of this, Desiree? The idea that if we'd been sharing an apartment at the time, she might be alive today. After all, a pretty and naïve young girl living alone — that had to be positively irresistible to a Victor Pirrelli."

I groped around for the words that might persuade her to ease up on herself. "Listen, say that when your sister met Pirrelli the two of you *were* rooming together — which, don't forget, was something she didn't even want. Do you really believe that would have made a difference? If Christie and Victor had the desire to be with each other, they'd have found a way. Also, keep in mind that we may discover that Victor actually had nothing to do with Christie's death."

"Still, I should have remained in New York."

"It wouldn't have helped. Honestly."

It took so long to get a reaction that I began to wonder if the woman had heard me. "I'd like to think that's true," she murmured at last.

"Trust me, it is."

"Look, you asked me before if I'd ever met Victor Pirrelli. I hadn't, but the real — the *main* — reason wasn't because I was living out of state. The truth is, I didn't care to get to know him because I already knew him. Or enough others like him. What's more, I used to assure myself that he wouldn't be around that long. Which should have gotten me an 'A' in wishful thinking." And now Alicia took a couple of

137

discreet dabs at her eyes, after which she bent her head and went back to playing with her napkin.

I waited a decent interval before posing my next question. "Can you think of anyone besides Victor who might have wanted to harm Christie?"

"The only other person she ever had any real unpleasantness with was Jennifer."

"Jennifer Whyte was in Massachusetts when Christie was killed."

"Oh."

"Did your sister have any close friends she might have confided in?"

"There was Lainie Hinkle. They'd been *like that*" — Alicia crossed her middle and index fingers — "since grammar school. But anything Christie told Lainie, she would have told me, too."

"I'm sure that's true. But just in case . . ."

Alicia frowned. "All right," she agreed, somewhat perturbed, "I have her phone number in my address book. I'll call and leave a message on your machine when I get back to the house."

"Thanks. I'd appreciate it."

"I haven't spoken to Lainie in years, though, so the number may not be viable anymore."

"I understand."

And then, her voice filled with unshed tears, Alicia said quietly, "I still miss my sister terribly, Desiree. And I'm angry. Sometimes I wake up in the middle of the night and start ticking off all the wonderful things she never got to experience. Like falling in love — I mean, with someone worthy of her love. And getting married. And having children. And teaching. Ever since she was a little girl Christie was determined to be a teacher — she was supposed to start NYU that fall." Alicia shook her head slowly. "She never even met her nephews — I have three boys who would have adored her.

"Promise me that if Victor Pirrelli wasn't the bastard who robbed my baby sister of all of this, you'll find out who was."

I would have liked nothing more than to make that promise. Not only for Vicky's sake, but now for the sake of the victim's sister, as well. But, of course, I couldn't. "I'll do my best," I told her.

"I know you will." And reaching over, Alicia Schnabel squeezed my hand.

CHAPTER 15

Wide-eyed or wild?

I leaned back in my comfortable Amtrak seat, prepared to take full advantage of the train ride. Listen, when I'm on the way home after a meeting like this, it's very rare that I can reflect on the conversation without having to be concerned about making a wrong turn and winding up in Hohokus or someplace equally *not* Manhattan. Which has been known to happen when I don't concentrate all my attention on my driving. Or, to be honest, even when I do.

Anyway, I began to think about Alicia's depiction of Christina as a sweet young innocent — and how diametrically opposed this was to the mantrap Jennifer Whyte had portrayed the dead girl to be. Of course, one version was courtesy of the victim's loving sister; the other, of the once-upon-a-time friend she'd betrayed.

I decided it was more than likely that the real Christina had existed somewhere in between these two conflicting assessments.

I mean, it was possible that Alicia was a hundred percent truthful about Christina's being a sweet and loving person. I was even prepared to accept that she'd been a virgin until she was besmirched by this Aaron — lecherous lout that he was. Still, for Christina — or *anyone* — to be so drunk that she didn't realize she was having intercourse? Pu-leeze!

But then, not being from the big drinkers, maybe I wasn't really capable of making that kind of judgment. Besides, who could be certain that liquor was the only thing our hero had poured into Christina's glass that day?

I had another problem with Alicia's lily-white characterization of her sister, though. Sure, it could be that I was getting cynical in my old age (and I have no intention of telling you just *how* old an age, either). But the thing is, that "My wife doesn't understand me, and I'm going to ask her for a divorce" stuff was pretty stale when *I* was eighteen. (Which I will admit was a couple of years back.) So it was hard to imagine any female over twelve taking as gospel Victor Pirrelli's declarations in that regard. Christina couldn't have been *that* naïve.

I pulled my thoughts up short. On the

other hand, though, maybe she could. She might have believed the man simply because she wanted to believe him. (And we all know what that's like, don't we?)

At any rate, I was hoping to set up an appointment with this Lainie Hinkle, who according to Alicia, had been Christina's closest friend. It would be interesting to get Lainie's perspective on the victim. Doubtless it would be less critical than Jennifer Whyte's. But I wondered if it would be quite as laudatory as Alicia's.

As I recall, the train was just leaving the Metro Park station at this point, and my eyes were tired. I closed them — only for a moment.

I awoke to a fellow passenger's gentle tap on my shoulder. "We're at Penn Station, dear," the elderly woman informed me. "It's the last stop."

I thanked her and quickly gathered my belongings, annoyed with myself for not utilizing this travel time to call up — while they were still fresh in my mind — more of Alicia's characterizations of her dead sibling.

But in the taxi a few minutes later, I was a little less disturbed about my unscheduled excursion to dreamland. I reminded myself that I *had* taken notes, and what's more, that I'd always been able to depend on their accuracy. Besides, to tell you the truth, I had a pretty strong feeling that nothing of any real substance could be culled from my get-together with Alicia Schnabel.

In fact, it looked as if all I'd gotten out of schlepping down to Philly was a pleasant little train trip.

CHAPTER 16

One moment we were just standing there talking. Then suddenly he pulled me close, covering my face with soft, playful little kisses. I was still in a state of shock, trying to grasp what was happening, when his mouth came down hard on mine, bruising my lips. And I responded with a passion born of a long-stagnant love life.

This isn't right, I protested to myself, but I couldn't find the strength to protest to *him.* And now his fingers went to the buttons on my blouse . . .

. . . and the alarm clock went off.

It was hard to believe. But lightning *had* struck twice. What's more — can you imagine? — it was another Pirrelli who was responsible for aborting my second tryst with Mel Gibson. And just when it showed promise of being X-rated, too!

Well, it was probably my own fault, I determined a short while later as I dipped into a bowl of Cheerios and milk. After all, I could have slept another half hour if I had proposed to Philomena that she come here instead of to my workplace. But I'd hesitated to rock the boat. I mean, the office had been her idea, and the woman wasn't too keen on meeting with me to begin with. So even suggesting we get together a few blocks farther away from her favorite shoe store might have wound up being a deal breaker.

It was ten minutes to eight when I got to the office that Saturday. A couple of barely-of-shaving-age law clerks, who were chatting alongside Jackie's unoccupied desk, were the only other people around. One of the young men (boys, really) rubbed his eyes when I came in.

"Yes, Barry, it *is* me," I assured him, stationing myself near the door to await my visitor. Evidently, I was an unwelcome presence, because Barry and his coworker made eye contact with each other, then instantly departed for their respective cubbyholes.

Mrs. Pirrelli showed up at eight on the button.

My initial reaction was one of mild surprise. I hadn't pictured her looking this youthful. But while she could have passed for around fifty, she was almost certainly on the far side of sixty. I also hadn't expected her to be this . . . well . . . *wispy*. A tiny woman, Philomena Pirrelli was beyond slim; she was thin to the extent that her bones protruded.

Something else I hadn't anticipated was that she'd be so fashionable. Although she was dressed entirely in black, right down to her shoes and stockings (remember, she'd just recently lost a son), her clothing was beautifully tailored, and there was little doubt that it was of the finest quality. By the same token, her short dark hair, which was only slightly interspersed with silver strands, was expertly styled.

She wore no makeup except for a touch of lipstick, and a very pale shade, at that — perhaps also in deference to her loss.

There was no way you could call this lady pretty, I concluded after my quick once-over — she had a rather long nose, as well as a prominent mole on her cheek and a really sallow complexion — but her face was intelligent, interesting. And the flashing brown eyes were almost riveting.

"How are you, Mrs. Pirrelli?" I inquired.

"I have been better."

I led the way to my office, and the second she crossed the threshold Philomena made a pronouncement: "Tiny," she sniffed.

"Yes, isn't it?" I managed a smile.

I relieved her of her jacket — fall had put in a chilling reappearance this morning — and she watched with her head tilted to the side as I hung the fur-trimmed black garment on a hanger at the back of the door.

After the matriarch of the Pirrelli clan had declined my offer of coffee, tea, or etcetera, we both took a seat. She was the one to open the conversation. "So what is it that you want of me, Mrs. Shapiro?"

"I hope you'll call me Desiree."

"Mrs. Shapiro," she reiterated firmly. *Boy, was this a tough little cookie!*

"I know the subject must be terribly painful for you, but I have to ask if I'm to do what your granddaughter —"

She waved a bony arm to silence me. "Go ahead. Ask."

"Um, when we spoke on the phone, I gathered you were — that you still *are* — convinced your son was responsible for Christina Trent's death. Although, as you mentioned," I put in hastily, "it's quite possible this wasn't intentional."

"It is true, what you say. The day he died, my son swore to me — just like he swore to Victoria earlier that evening — that he didn't touch the girl." She moistened her lower lip with her tongue before

147

adding in a hushed voice, "I wish with all of my heart that I could have been persuaded of this."

"You were at the hospital after he was injured?"

Philomena nodded.

"I wasn't aware of that."

"Since when is it that I report to you?" Her glance was withering. "I was with him when he passed on," she put in almost grudgingly a moment later. "Listen, Mrs. Shapiro, I loved my Vittorio. But it does not follow that I believed him. All his life he would tell a lie to me — and then he would swear on his father's grave that it was not a lie. Often this was because he was ashamed of the things that he did, and so he would not admit to them."

"I understand he was, uh, sort of wild as a teenager."

"Wild is right. All he knew was drugs, drink, and *puttanas*." She didn't take the trouble to translate, but one of my favorite pasta dishes being *spaghetti alla puttanesca* — "whore's spaghetti" — it wasn't really necessary.

"I couldn't control that child from the day he left my belly," Philomena murmured sadly. After which she removed a black lace-trimmed handkerchief from her

148

handbag and dabbed at her eyes. "I tried; God knows that," she continued, hurriedly crossing herself. "Even as a tiny little one, however, Vittorio did what Vittorio wanted to do. But he was not a bad boy, Mrs. Shapiro. Unfortunately, however, he had this temper, and *that* was bad. I was always afraid that one day it would get him in real trouble."

"Apparently he straightened out after meeting his future wife, though. At least for a while."

My visitor's lips stretched into a thin, straight line. "You think so? Mary O'Hearn was poison for him. A woman with the same given name as the Blessed Mother, too." She crossed herself again. "My daughter-in-law came from trash, and she *is* trash. A fancy house and fancy clothes — they can't change what's in here," Philomena asserted with a couple of vigorous taps to her chest.

I was taken aback both by the words and the vehemence with which they were delivered. And it must have showed. "What I tell you, this is fact. Once they were married, Mary, she was always harping on Vittorio to make more money so he could buy her this and buy her that. All the time she was after him, pestering

149

him to get a better job. But with what, I ask you. With the college education he didn't have because that stupid girl spread her legs and got herself pregnant?"

I didn't see any point in reminding Philomena that Mary didn't *get herself* pregnant.

"Still, he didn't have to remain a taxi driver; he could have been a professional man like his brother. I would gladly have paid his tuition and helped with the rent. But Vittorio said, no, that he liked what he did for a living and that he could take care of his family himself. My son had pride, you see. And I want you to understand that he tried his best to be a good husband. But after a hard day — sometimes twelve hours or more, he worked — all he could look forward to when he came home was nagging and then more nagging. I tell you that if it wasn't for the way he was treated by that wife of his, he would never have looked at somebody else."

"Uh, you must have been very upset when Mary and your other son became involved." I wasn't too happy about bringing this up, but what choice did I have?

"I didn't have any idea they were . . . *involved,* as you say. Not until after they ran off and got married. If I had known what

150

was going on with them, there wouldn't have been any marriage. Of this you can be certain. If it took every penny I have in this world, I would have persuaded that woman to leave my remaining son in peace. But they kept me in the dark, those two. And then one morning, not even one year after Vittorio went to prison, Antonio came to me, and — in the same voice he might have told someone, 'pass the salt' — he said, 'Mary and I got married yesterday, Mama.' If I didn't drop dead then, Mrs. Shapiro, I will probably live forever."

"Antonio had been keeping company with someone else for a long while, from what I heard."

"Six years. And with a wonderful Italian girl, too. Carmela Thomas, she calls herself. Her real name — her family name — it's Tomasso. Her father — who was always a very foolish man — he changed it before she was born."

"They were never engaged or anything, were they?"

"No. But this was because of the other one — Mary." She grimaced when she said the name. "From the very beginning, from the day she came into this family, I could tell that Antonio had the eyes for her — I'm his mother, aren't I? But I didn't let on

I noticed. Who figured anything would ever come of it? Who would even have *dreamed* such a thing?" Philomena shook her head slowly from side to side. "This was *his brother's wife*."

She absently plucked at her skirt before resuming. "It was eight days after they arrested Vittorio that Antonio broke it off with Carmela. *Eight days!* I don't blame Antonio, though. That *strega,* she had him as if under a spell." I didn't get a translation here, either, and this time I really could have used one. (I found out later that *strega* is Italian for "witch.")

"Feeling the way you do, it must be very difficult for you to be in Mary's company. Or don't you see her?"

"See her? Of course I see her," Philomena answered testily. "What can I do? She's married to my Antonio — my sunshine, my heart. And my granddaughter lives with them. Don't let that hair and the silly way she talks fool you. She's a wonderful girl, Victoria. Very good-hearted. Smart, too."

"I wasn't fooled for a minute. I like her a lot."

I had obviously said the right thing, because I was rewarded with a smile — unless the woman was in the throes of a gas pain.

"Is Antonio older or younger than his brother?"

"Older. By six years."

"He was easier to raise, I take it."

"Never did I have a single problem with that child."

"I understand he's quite a successful lawyer."

If Philomena had had any feathers, they would have been plumped up now. "He does pretty good," she said, playing it modest for all of a second or two. But then she couldn't resist the opportunity to gild the man's image a bit. "Antonio could even go into politics one day. The year Vittorio got into his trouble? This was the same year William Clinton was elected president — with the help of my Antonio," she declared, beaming. "Imagine. Helping to elect the President of the United States of America. Antonio worked so hard on that campaign they even invited him to Washington, D.C., for the inauguration."

"Really?" I said, trying to sound suitably impressed before moving on to the point I'd been attempting to reach. "I suppose that with Antonio being an attorney, his brother turned to him for legal advice after the arrest."

"Antonio doesn't do that kind of law,"

Philomena informed me proudly. "But he recommended somebody who specializes in criminal law. A woman. I don't like a woman lawyer. But she did get them to reduce the charge against Vittorio. She arranged for a" — she clicked her tongue — "what do they call it?"

"A plea bargain?"

"Yes, a plea bargain."

Well, it was obvious to me that Tony hadn't clued his mother in on the role he'd played in all of this. If she'd been aware of it, I doubted that Philomena would have been able to resist this opportunity to brag about how clever her firstborn was to have orchestrated a lesser sentence for his brother.

"I have just one more question," I told her then.

She scowled. "What?"

"Do you recall where you were the night Vittorio was arrested?"

"A silly question. A thing like this you don't forget." She was, of course, right. "I was at his apartment altering a dress I made for Victoria. The next day — Sunday — it was her sixth birthday, and she was supposed to wear it to a party."

"Until what time were you there?"

"Eight o'clock I left."

Well, how do you like that? It seemed that Mary Pirrelli's alibi had just been blown to pieces. Before I could speculate on the implications of this, however, Philomena added, "But it could maybe have been a little later, because after breakfast Victoria tried on the dress for me again — just to be sure. And I had to make a minor adjustment."

After breakfast? "You mean you stayed until the following morning?"

"That's what I just said, didn't I?" A moment later, Philomena shook her head sadly. "I asked Mary when we were having breakfast, where was Vittorio that he didn't come home all night. She told me that sometimes he worked double hours. Who could dream that my son was at the police station even as we were speaking and that they were questioning him about a *murder?*"

"What about Mary, Mrs. Pirrelli? Was she home that Saturday evening?"

"Naturally."

"All evening?"

"Listen, I have difficulty falling asleep, and the last time I looked at the clock it was after twelve. So she was home until then, anyhow."

"You're certain?"

A plainly exasperated Philomena frowned.

"I went to bed on the living room couch, and for somebody to get to the door, it would have been necessary to walk right past me. And Mary did not. But why are you asking? Do you suggest that she sneaked out of her apartment in order to go to that girl's house and put a knife into her?"

"Oh, no. I —"

"Because if there was even a possibility she could have done this, wouldn't I have gone to the police? This was my son who was arrested for that terrible thing, do you remember?" She pressed the black handkerchief into service again, patting the expressive brown eyes, which were glistening with tears. Then she checked her watch. "I will be leaving now," she notified me, getting to her feet.

"I really appreciate your seeing me, Mrs. Pirrelli. And I hope you find a pair of shoes you like."

She looked me full in the face. "I don't like very much nowadays, Mrs. Shapiro — not since three weeks ago. But I have a choice: to occupy myself or to go crazy. Look, after Vittorio was murdered, I didn't expect to be doing any shopping — not for a very long time — out of respect for the memory of my son. You understand? I planned to give up going to the movies for a year, as well. And it was my intention not to turn on the radio or the television, either. But I am all alone in a big house, and the walls, they just seemed to close in on me. Call me a selfish old woman, but I finally decided I had to do whatever I could to take my mind away from the death of my child. Getting out and making a visit to a shoe store? It won't help a lot, but it will maybe help a little."

Victor Pirrelli's mother smiled wanly. "For a couple of minutes, anyway."

CHAPTER 17

I could kiss another suspect good-bye.

After all, her detested daughter-in-law was the last person in the world Philomena would have cared to furnish with an alibi. So there wasn't a doubt in my mind that she'd leveled with me about spending that crucial Saturday evening in Mary's company.

Of course, for Vicky's sake, I was happy about being able to finally — and conclusively — remove her mother's name from my candidates-for-killer list. On the other hand, though, that list was getting skimpier and skimpier.

I assured myself I was just getting started.

In fact, true to her word, after Alicia Schnabel had returned home Friday night, she left a message on my answering machine, providing me with Lainie Hinkle's phone number. Or, anyway, with the last number she had for her. And, listen, as a likely confidante of the victim's, Lainie might know something that could be of help to me. It was conceivable she might even provide me with an additional suspect or two.

So as soon as I saw Philomena Pirrelli to the door that morning, I hurried back to my office and made a grab for the phone.

The female who picked up would never win a Miss Congeniality award. "Lainie don't live here no more," she apprized me brusquely.

"Uh, are you a relative?"

"You might say that. I'm her mother."

"Oh, good. Then you can probably tell me how I can contact her."

"Sez you. Me and Lainie aren't even on speakin' terms. Haven't been for years. I got no idea where the little tramp's living now — or with who. What's this about?"

"I'm a private investigator, and I'm looking into the murder of her friend Christina Trent. I —"

"You gotta be kidding me, Miss Whatever-your-name-is. The guy who did that to Christina's been in jail for six or seven years. Maybe more."

"It's true that someone was convicted of the crime, Mrs. Hinkle, but —"

"Murray."

"Excuse me?"

"I'm Mrs. Calvin Murray now."

"Oh, sorry."

"That's okay. I'm not real proud of it."

"Uh, anyway, Mrs. Murray, new evidence came to light recently, and we believe it's possible the police targeted the wrong person."

"No foolin'? Well, how do you like that!" Mrs. Murray took a few seconds to digest this information, following which she demanded suspiciously, "Hey, you don't suspect my girl, do you? Lainie may be a lousy daughter — she's got no respect. Zero. And she don't have the sense of a turnip. But her and Christina, they loved each other — they were like sisters. Besides, Lainie wouldn't kill *nobody;* she hasn't got it in her."

"No one thinks your daughter was responsible for her friend's death. Not for a minute. But she might be able to tell us something that would enable us to establish who was."

"Well, I guess it wouldn't hurt for you to talk to her. Like I said, I don't have no idea where she's living, but you could try her at work. Or, anyways, where she worked last I heard."

Mrs. Murray supplied me with the phone number, and I was about to hang up when she threw in, "But don't bother givin' her my love."

"Nifty Nails Salon, Celeste speaking."

In response to my question, Celeste promptly informed me that "Lainie is no longer with us. She left here four months ago."

"Would you be able to tell me how to reach her?"

"Hea-ther! That place Lainie went to — what was it called?" This was screamed out so loudly that anyone having her cuticles cut at that moment had my profound sympathy.

Two or three seconds later I learned that Lainie Hinkle had taken a job at Lady Fingers. "Did you ever hear of a dumber name for a nail salon?" Celeste put to me.

"Well, I guess it is kind of, uh —"

"You can say that again. Listen, I don't have their number, but it must be in the phone book."

I thanked her, and she told me to have a good day. Then, after wishing her the same, I went to the Yellow Pages. There it was: Lady Fingers. On West Twenty-second Street. Celeste was right, I decided. Lady Fingers *was* a pretty dumb name. At least, for an establishment that didn't sell baked goods.

"Lady Fingers," a bored female voice announced.

"Is Lainie Hinkle available, please?"

The woman didn't quite succeed in suppressing a yawn. "May I inquire as to who wishes to speak with her?"

"You might tell her I'm a private investigator and that it's about Christina."

" 'Christina,' you said?"

"That's right."

I was instructed to hold on, and a short time after this the receptionist relayed a message. "Ms. Hinkle is presently with a client. She requested that you leave your name and telephone number. She'll get back to you in ten minutes."

It was close to a half hour before my office phone rang.

"This is Lainie Hinkle, Ms. Shapiro."

"Thank you for returning my call."

"You left word that you wanted to talk to me about Christina?"

"That's right."

"What *about* Christina?"

I gave my "new evidence" story. And then, without allowing the girl enough time to say "boo," I aborted the anticipated "I wish I could help, but I don't know a thing" protest with the usual counterprotest. I concluded with, "I'd really appreciate it if we could get together for a few minutes."

"I have no problem meeting with you, Ms. Shapiro; just don't count on my having any information that would contribute to your investigation."

"I promise not to. When would it be convenient for you to see me?"

"I could do it right after work. I should be through here around five."

The dozen or so butterflies that must have just infiltrated my stomach fluttered their wings at the thought of tonight's date with Nick. "Um, I'm afraid I can't make it this evening. Is tomorrow possible for you?"

"Oh, that's right, this is Saturday. It must be nice to have a social life," Lainie teased. But I seemed to detect a rueful note in her voice. "Tomorrow's okay, though. Only let's not make it too early. I like to sleep late on my day off."

A girl after my own heart. We settled on one o'clock at a coffee shop around the corner from Lainie's East Third Street apartment.

"You won't have any trouble recognizing me," I was told. "I'll be the one who's still brushing the sleepers from her eyes."

As soon as the conversation ended, I scooped up my attaché case, shoved the

Pirrelli folder into it, and headed out of the office.

Lainie had something there. It *was* nice to have a social life. Take it from someone who'd been without one for far too long.

CHAPTER 18

"Wow!" Nick said when I opened the door to my apartment. "You look delectable."

Now, through the years, on opening that same door, I've been met with a great variety of comments (not all of them welcome) — but *delectable?* The only thing I could figure was that having made a last-minute switch from the lavender outfit to a pink silk shirtwaist, I might have reminded the man of cotton candy or a strawberry soda or something. Still, that was fine with me. Let's say I don't believe in looking a compliment in the mouth.

"Thank you," I murmured almost coquettishly. Then I felt that telltale burn on my cheeks. *Damn! I'll bet Heather Locklear never blushes.* "That's a great jacket," I put in hurriedly — Nick was wearing a really handsome brown tweed. "And I'm not just saying it to return the flattery."

"Okay, then, I won't take it that way," he responded with that melting, slightly bucktoothed grin of his. "Almost ready?"

"*All* ready. I'll get my jacket."

★ ★ ★

I loved *Proof.*

Afterward, Nick and I had a late dinner at a small Italian restaurant not far from the theater. It took only five or six sips of cabernet sauvignon for me to christen myself "theater critic" and laud the performance of the star with such review-type words as "mesmerizing" and "sensitive" and "nuanced."

"The writing wasn't bad, either," Nick reminded me with a grin, *Proof* having won the Pulitzer a couple of years back.

"You're right, of course, but it does require a really terrific actress to do justice to Catherine."

Now, Mary-Louise Parker, who had originated that role, received a Tony for her efforts. And I made the comment that, in spite of this, I couldn't imagine her being any better in the part than Anne Heche — the current lead — was.

"I don't know about *better.* The two interpretations were just different, that's all."

"I suppose that when —" The light suddenly went on in my dim brain. "You saw the show before."

Looking embarrassed, Nick smiled. "Guilty."

"You got the tickets yourself because I

was so anxious to go, didn't you?" I demanded, feeling so pleased — and touched — I was ready to burst. I bet myself he even made certain I was free tonight before making the purchase.

"Not entirely true," Nick told me. "A friend did ask if I wanted the tickets. Actually, you did me a favor, Dez. I thoroughly enjoyed the play that first time, and you gave me an excuse to see it again."

I elected not to believe him and stick to my initial interpretation. But then I cooled down. I was letting that "delectable" business go to my head.

Anyway, over pasta — fettuccine with mushrooms in white wine for me, cannelloni for Nick — I asked how his son was doing.

"He's fine. But, of course, he misses his mother."

"Her boyfriend is still working in Las Vegas?"

"Evidently Choo-choo — that's the boyfriend — and his band turned out to be such a big hit at this club that brought them out there that they keep getting held over. Derek is always asking Tiffany when she's coming home."

"And she says — ?"

" 'Soon.' Whatever that means. You know, Desiree, sometimes Derek's eyes start filling up after she calls. Poor little guy. He can't help but feel abandoned — she's been gone for so damn long now. But then he kind of pulls himself out of it; he doesn't want me to know how hurt he is. I can't decide if that's because he's so anxious to spare me or because he's trying to convince us both how grown-up he is." A sort of half smile here.

"I can see where his mother's absence would be awfully tough on him."

"Believe it," Nick muttered with an accompanying frown so deep that his eyebrows practically touched.

After this we concentrated on our respective pastas for a couple of minutes. Then Nick looked up. "Maybe the three of us could go out one day. I think you'd enjoy Derek's company. He's a really good kid."

I was taken aback. "I'd like that, Nick," I said, not sure whether I meant it or not. Still, it was points — wasn't it? — that he wanted me to meet his son.

"Good." And then glancing down at the breadstick in his hand, Nick seethed, "I could break that woman's neck." And, as if to illustrate, he snapped the breadstick in two — with a vengeance.

We left for home after coffee and a

shared tartuffo. (We'd concurred that it was too late at night to tackle a dessert that rich unless it was a cooperative effort.)

Unexpectedly, in the taxi Nick took my hand and squeezed it. "I had a wonderful time tonight," he told me.

"So did I."

Fifteen minutes later we were standing at my door. I raised my face to his, my lips quivering in anticipation of the kiss they were prepared to receive.

Nick bussed my cheek.

Well, it was better than nothing, I told myself.

That's your story, I responded.

CHAPTER 19

It was about ten thirty when I opened my eyes on Sunday. And — would you believe it? — this person who feels about mornings like she feels about beef liver had a smile on her face. The instant I was fully awake, however, the smile was gone.

My date with Nick, I ruminated, had been almost perfect. But it was a big "almost," since it had to do with the evening's less-than-romantic ending.

Don't get me wrong. It wasn't that I wanted him to go dragging me off to the bedroom or anything. (Not at this point, anyhow.) But a kiss good night — and I'm talking about one delivered to the proper location — would hardly have placed the guy in the caveman category.

I tried giving myself a pep talk.

Listen, he's simply taking things slow.

Unless he doesn't find you attractive, this nasty little voice in my head countered.

Yeah? Then why would he bother asking me out?

Are you familiar with the word f-r-i-e-n-d?

Well, if that's the case, how come he called me "delectable"?

Never mind what he said. People say all sorts of things. It's what the man did — make that, didn't do — that should concern you.

In the end I decided not to place too much stock in the fact that Nick hadn't put some kind of move on me. He was probably waiting for the relationship to develop, that's all.

But the aforementioned nasty little voice I'm saddled with refused to leave it at that. *Face it,* the thing chimed in. *Could be you're just not his type.*

In the taxi, on my way to the East Village, I recognized how fortunate it was that I had an appointment with Lainie Hinkle that afternoon. Focusing on my personal life like this only succeeded in giving me a nervous stomach. It was time I concentrated on the investigation — where there was at least a chance that I might be able to do myself some good.

The cab deposited me in front of the coffee shop Lainie had suggested — a small, dingy establishment in a sorry state of disrepair. It always amazes me how often the most disreputable-looking eateries have the classiest names. (Maybe the ritzy moniker is supposed to blind the customers to their seedy surroundings.) In this instance the sign in the window read GRAND ROYALE COFFEE SHOPPE. (With two *p*'s and a couple of extra *e*'s, no less.)

Once inside, I stood in the doorway hesitating. There were three young women seated alone all appearing to be in their late twenties. And then one of them — a girl with long, frizzed-out brown hair and huge hoop earrings that came close to grazing her shoulders — signaled to me with a tentative wave.

"I'm hoping you're Desiree," she declared when I reached the booth.

"That's exactly who I am."

She half-rose and extended her hand. "Good," she said with a friendly grin. "I'm Lainie; but I presume you've already figured that out."

I shook the outstretched hand, following which I deposited myself opposite her on the peeling brown vinyl seat.

"I hope you haven't eaten breakfast yet — or that if you have, you're ready for a second one," Lainie announced as soon as I was settled in. "This joint — don't let its crappy appearance fool you — has really excellent food. Particularly when it comes to breakfast, which is served until four.

Incidentally, you don't have to worry; they *do* always pass the Board of Health inspections." She handed me a menu. "Here, take a look."

"I gather you don't need one."

"Uh-uh. I'm addicted to their raspberry pancakes."

I put the menu down unopened. "Sounds good to me, too."

Lainie caught the eye of the waiter, a thin, dour man of about fifty, who made his way to the table with a decided lack of enthusiasm.

"What's the matter, Darryl?" she teased, responding to his expression. "Your wife not giving you any lately?"

"You got some mouth on you, Lainie. If you were my kid I'd wash it out good." But he couldn't quite prevent the hint of a smile from turning up the corners of his lips.

"We'll both have the raspberry pancakes, Darryl."

"Surprise, surprise," he mumbled. After which he turned to me. "You want coffee, lady?"

"Yes, please — regular."

"Orange juice?"

"I think I'll skip the juice."

"Okay, two raspberries, two regulars."

As soon as he walked away, Lainie's entire demeanor changed. Leaning toward me, she said, "I'm anxious to hear why the police now think that Victor Pirrelli might not have been the one who stabbed Christie to death after all."

"Um, I may have given you the wrong impression. It isn't that the police are having second thoughts. It's . . . let me tell you what's happened. . . ."

And I proceeded to fill her in on Victor's reunion with his daughter and the man's deathbed protestation of innocence.

When I'd finished, Lainie peered at me intently. "Do you believe what he told his daughter?"

"I'm not sure whether I do or not. But for him to make the claim at that particular time . . . well, in my opinion it warrants serious consideration. Besides, Vicky — his daughter — is absolutely certain her father was telling the truth, and I promised her I'd check into things."

"You know, you don't look like a PI." She laughed. "But I don't suppose I'm the first person to notice that. Back to Victor, though. It's strange, but when I first found out they'd arrested him for the murder, I figured it had to be a mistake. Don't get me wrong. I didn't like the guy one bit. Believe me, Christie could have done a helluva lot better. After all, what did she need with a married man, especially one with that short a fuse? He was such a controlling S.O.B., too. But there's no looking for logic when it comes to *amour*, is there?

"The thing is, though, in spite of everything, I would have sworn that he sincerely loved her. And anyone who felt about someone the way I was sure Victor felt about Christie — well, it was hard for me to accept that he'd have taken her life. Besides, even though Victor had that terrible temper, he and Christie had gotten into it before — and in a big way, too — and it had never turned physical."

"You must be aware that during one of their other fights he broke her jaw."

"She told me it was an accident. Evidently she zigged when she should have zagged."

"You seem to be the only one who accepted that explanation."

"Listen, we were very close. I knew Christina Trent better than anyone else did — even her sister. And she may have been easygoing, but she wasn't stupid. Right after it happened she said that if Victor had actually meant to sock her, she would never have continued to see him, that she'd have been too afraid he might do something like that again."

"How well did you know Victor — or didn't you?"

"I'd been in his company on a couple of occasions, but mostly I knew *about* him — through Christie."

At this point Darryl returned. With a grunt, he none-too-gently deposited our orders on the table in the general vicinity of our respective place mats, apparently concluding that this was close enough. Then he mumbled to Lainie, "You behave yourself, hear me?" And once more unsuccessfully attempting to conceal a smile, he made a fast retreat.

My companion permitted me all of two small bites of pancake (which, I have to tell you, did not disappoint) before remarking, "If he hadn't been caught with the knife, to this day I might have had doubts about Victor's guilt. But as soon as I heard about *that* . . ." Shrugging, Lainie spread her arms and held up her palms. I got in a sip of coffee before she put to me, "You wouldn't happen to know what they fought about that night, would you?"

There was no escaping it. I'd just have to mix the murder in with the raspberries. "According to what Victor told his attorney, it started with his breaking his promise to take Christie for Mexican food, and it escalated from there. But I intend to talk to the tenants in her building next week; it's possible someone might have overheard something."

"Christie had developed this passion for Mexican food," Lainie said, her voice soft with the remembering. "She used to try and bribe me to go to a Mexican restaurant with her. But Victor wasn't the only louse of her acquaintance; I wouldn't accommodate her, either." She eked out a smile. A sad smile. "No excuse, but this was during my sushi period."

I thought it best not to allow the girl to dwell on what my information was now causing her to regard as a breach of friendship. So I was quick to move things along. "Of course, even if that's how the argument started, eventually it turned into quite a battle. Were you aware of any particular problems the two might have been having just then?"

"No, I wasn't. And I spoke to Christie on the day she died, too. I'm positive, Desiree, that she'd have confided in me if there'd been trouble between them."

"You say that until you learned about the knife, you rejected the idea that Victor was the killer. Just who was it you did suspect?"

"No one in particular. But then again, practically everybody. It occurred to me that it might have been this neighbor of Christie's — Jennifer, her name was. Jennifer's boyfriend fixed Christie a drink this one day. And, see, Christie wasn't used to liquor, so she got really high — I mean, she was totally out of it. Maybe there was something besides alcohol in that drink. The —" Lainie made a face. "Oh, I should have mentioned that Jennifer wasn't home at the time. Anyhow, the result was that Christie wound up doing the nasty with that creep. And — wouldn't you know it? — Jennifer caught the two of them going at it. Naturally, she was steamed. Very, *very* steamed.

"It also crossed my mind that it could have been Keith Mackie, Christie's old sweetheart. She ended it with him almost a year before she met Victor because she discovered he'd lied to her about a lot of stuff. Keith wasn't what you'd call pleased about being unloaded like that; he even threatened her."

I pounced. "What did he say? Do you remember?"

"Not exactly. I think it was something like she'd be sorry. But it doesn't make any

178

difference, because I later found out that Keith had gotten married three or four weeks prior to the stabbing. So, obviously, he wasn't still stewing about the breakup with Christie."

"Can you think of anyone else who might have had a motive for killing her? *Any* type of motive."

Lainie wrestled with this for a moment. "There's Victor's wife. Christie said the woman wasn't in love with Victor, but who knows?"

"What about that older man in Christie's building, the one who had such a crush on her?"

"George? He's a possibility, I suppose. He *was* obsessed with her, I guess you could say. And she *did* reject him."

"But you never suspected him of the murder?"

"Maybe I did. To be honest, I can't be sure. It was just so long ago."

And then I had another thought. "Is it possible Christie was seeing somebody on the sly?"

"Christie? Cheat on Victor? Not a chance. She was nuts about him — for whatever reason. Aside from his being such a hunk, that is."

"Listen, would you mind telling me a

little about Christie? It's conceivable that knowing what she was like could help me find out who was responsible for her death."

"Well, she was a wonderful friend — the best. Also, she was smart. She was planning on going to college in the fall — she wanted to be a teacher."

Uh-oh. For the first time since we'd begun our talk, it looked as if Lainie was close to tears. "What else can you tell me about her?" I interjected hurriedly.

"Let's see," she murmured, reflexively brushing at her eyes with her knuckle. "Christie had a soft heart — she was an exceptionally kind person. But that's not to say she was some goody-two-shoes. We did our share of cutting up, the two of us." Lainie grinned impishly. "To be honest, me more than Christie."

"According to Alicia, her sister was a virgin until that awful incident with Jennifer's boyfriend."

"Well, technically that's true; Christie *was* a virgin. She did everything *but,* if you know what I mean. When it came to intercourse, though, she was saving herself for marriage. Or, anyway, that was her intention until Victor came along." Lainie grinned again, more widely this time. "Now, me, I've never been much of a saver." And with this, she revisited her pancakes, and I took the opportunity to do the same.

"Alicia showed me Christie's picture," I brought up a couple of minutes later. "She was very lovely."

"A doll."

"But I understand she wasn't especially happy with her looks."

"True." Lainie shook her head. "Funny, isn't it? I'd have given anything to have a face like that staring back at me from the mirror every morning. But Christina was always finding fault with her appearance. Believe it or not, she was constantly saying how she wished she had my complexion. Can you beat that?"

"It's understandable. You do have great skin."

"Well, I wouldn't call it *great*. And, anyway, Christie had all the rest of it. I guess I'm okay, but nobody's ever accused me of being a raving beauty."

Which was no doubt true enough. While Lainie was, well, *pleasant*-looking, I seriously doubted that anyone (excepting, hopefully, an individual who might someday fall madly in love with her) would regard this girl as beautiful. Her face was large and square. And it sat on a too-short, too-thick neck. She had a wide, rather flat nose. Her pale blue eyes were narrow — almost squinty, really. And I've already mentioned the frizzed-out hair, which was a nondescript shade of brown. On the plus side, however, Lainie had a very engaging smile. It was on her lips quite frequently, too, having the effect of making her appear particularly warm and approachable. Which she was. At any rate, I found that I had this almost urgent need to say something positive again. "You have a wonderful smile, and —"

Lainie cut in, probably to deflect what she deemed to be hollow flattery. "You would have liked Christie."

"I'm sure I would have."

"So who do *you* think killed her?" she asked then. "That is, if it wasn't Victor."

"I don't have a leading candidate. But it was someone who had no qualms about framing Victor for the crime. Evidently this someone put in an anonymous call to the police so that Victor would be discovered in an incriminating position."

"I'm assuming that would eliminate his mother, at least." And in the event I failed to catch on: "Just joking, Desiree. But I don't quite understand. The police were contacted so they'd break up the fight, weren't they?"

"If Victor was telling the truth — and let's go under this assumption for a few minutes — it's likely that call was made well after the fight was over. Victor maintained that once the smoke cleared he went for a long walk. He didn't get back to the apartment until a half hour later. And it was right after this that the cops so conveniently turned up."

And now I gave Lainie more or less the same scenario I'd worked up the previous week when I was casting Uncle Tony as the villain. (A role for which he still seemed to me to be eminently qualified.)

"I'm guessing that Christie told her murderer that Victor would be coming back and that the perpetrator, after stabbing her to death, waited for his return before contacting the police. The hope was that they'd arrive in time to find Victor alone with the body. And, of course, they did. But here's where the killer got a bonus. Victor was such an obliging guy, he even picked up the knife."

"Oh, I don't figure that would have been any big problem."

"What wouldn't?" I asked, confused.

"Sorry. I'm talking about the cops arriving in time. There's a police station nearby — right in the neighborhood." Then, barely pausing for breath, Lainie informed me, "I've been meaning to ask you something."

"What's that?"

"How did you manage to locate me?"

"I tried the number Alicia has for you, and your mother answered the phone. She gave me the Nifty Nails number, and they steered me to Lady Fingers. Lady Fingers," I repeated. "That's quite a name."

"Isn't it? I just love it." I looked closely at the girl to see if she was kidding. She wasn't. "I'm surprised my mother was that cooperative," she commented, wrinkling her brow. "She and I aren't on the best of terms. Which I'm sure you could tell, right?"

"Well, I gathered there might have been some . . . uh . . . misunderstanding between the two of you."

"My mother doesn't approve of me, and I can't say I blame her."

Now, since I'm incurably nosy I had to ask, "Why is that?" But not being a totally insensitive person, I immediately threw in, "Or would you rather not say?"

"It's okay. I don't mind. The fact is, when I was nineteen I started doing drugs, and that caused my mother a lot of grief. It wasn't any picnic for her even when I got clean, though. I still didn't exactly do her proud, considering how boy crazy I was in those days. Not that I'm completely reformed," Lainie added laughingly. "I haven't lost my appreciation for the opposite sex, only I've become a little more selective. Anyway, in spite of that, my mom managed to tolerate me — but just barely. Then a few years ago I had an abortion, and that really tore it. Mom's a practicing Catholic."

Somehow I hadn't pictured Mrs. Hinkle — oops, Murray — as a devout, God-fearing woman. From our brief conversation, I'd imagined her as a little on the fast and loose side herself. Why, I have no idea. At any rate, that shows you how perceptive *I* am.

"When Christina was alive," Lainie mused, "my mother used to refer to us as the odd couple. And, in a way, we were — although Christie wasn't quite as pure and untouched as my mother believed her to be. Still, she was a lot more grounded than I was. Anyhow, my mom thought of her as the sensible one. A major reason for this being that Christie planned on going to college, while I refused to even consider it."

"I gather this mattered to your mother?"

"You can say that again. She was really hung up on my pursuing an education. I imagine a good part of this was due to her not getting past the fifth grade herself — she had to quit school and find a job. At any rate, she almost went ballistic when I told her college wasn't going to happen for me. But, listen, number one: I absolutely hated to study. And number two: I wasn't about to wait four years to start making some decent money."

Unconsciously, I glanced down at Lainie's pale coral fingernails. They looked the way a manicurist's fingernails should look: nice and even and beautifully sculpted. In view of the state of my own nails — which you'd have no problem figuring out that I do myself — I immediately removed my right hand from around my coffee mug and placed it in my lap with its mate. "Uh, about your mother . . . When I told her that Victor might not have been the one who murdered Christie, she became terribly agitated. She was afraid that I wanted to locate you because I considered you a suspect."

"*Me?* You're kidding! But, anyhow, that actually bothered her?"

"You should have heard her leap to your defense."

"Really?"

"Honestly."

Lainie didn't say anything for a couple of seconds. Then, in a small, uncertain voice: "I'd call her, only she'd probably hang up on me." There was another brief interval of silence before she spoke again — with more assurance now. "But nothing ventured, nothing gained, right?" The words were uttered just as I was about to assault her with that same platitude.

"I couldn't have said it better myself," I told her.

In the taxi on the way home, I gave in to the nice, warm feelings that had begun to envelop me the moment I left the coffee shop. My unusually placid state — which must have lasted for a full three or four minutes — had nothing to do with the investigation, of course. That didn't appear to have been advanced one iota. But if this just-concluded meeting should lead to a reconciliation between mother and daughter — well, this would wind up being my most productive day in a long, long time.

CHAPTER 20

That night I concluded that I'd been wrong.

My get-together with Lainie *had* moved the investigation along. In a way, anyhow.

It wasn't that she'd supplied me with so much as the tiniest clue to solving her best friend's murder — not as far as I could determine. And it had nothing to do with her take on the character of the victim, either — one of the primary reasons I'd been so anxious to meet with her. I mean, as anticipated, Lainie had introduced me to yet a third Christina, a girl who was neither the innocent that Alicia had acquainted me with nor the amoral bitch that Jennifer had painted her to be. But, unfortunately, I couldn't see where the latest Christina would be any more apt to aid me in identifying her assailant than the previous two had been.

So what *had* made a difference this afternoon?

For starters, the conversation with Lainie gave added credibility to the theory that that anonymous call to the police was placed well after the warring couple had declared a cease-fire. Think about it: With a station house not far from the victim's building, there was at least a fair chance the police *would* manage to arrive in time to find Victor still hovering over the body of his lover.

What's more, Lainie was virtually positive Victor had been deeply in love with Christina, so much so that she — Lainie — initially disregarded the accusations against him. I was even looking at that broken jaw thing somewhat differently now. There appeared to be the ring of truth in the deceased's statement that she would have split with Victor if he'd struck her intentionally. In fact, it occurred to me that the man might not have been as prone to physical violence as I'd come to believe — not when it came to the women in his life, at any rate. (Listen, in spite of a rather contentious home life, by Mary's own admission he'd never batted her around.) Anyhow, what made Lainie's opinions about Victor so persuasive was, of course, that she'd had absolutely no use for the guy.

And here I played devil's advocate for a minute or two.

Lainie could have been mistaken about

the depth of Victor's devotion to her friend. After all, she hadn't been in his company more than a couple of times, so most of what she knew about the relationship was gleaned from her talks with Christina. By the same token, I couldn't really be sure about the intended target of that jaw-breaking punch, since Lainie wasn't actually *there*. Plus, even if she was a hundred percent right about both these matters, who's to say that one February evening more than a decade ago, Victor Pirrelli didn't just freak out and stab his sweetheart to death?

Wasn't it Oscar Wilde who wrote about each man killing the thing he loves?

In spite of these reservations, however, the result of my meeting with Lainie was that it led to my redoubling my resolve to find Christina's killer. This isn't to say I wasn't already committed to that same end. But, to be honest, I'd been fearful of what I might learn. The thing is, while I wasn't at all certain of Victor's guilt, I was even less certain of the alternative.

Consider the way I'd always presented the various scenarios about his having been set up for the crime. Prior to Lainie's input, I had preceded it — even to myself — with an implied "if," as in, "*If* Victor

190

didn't do this . . ." But from here on in, the "if," while not discarded, would be more like an afterthought.

You see, I was now motivated not only by a desire to keep my promise to Vicky, but by the increasing likelihood that her father was precisely what she'd been insisting all along — an innocent man.

Nick called at around nine thirty.

We spent a few minutes telling each other how much we'd enjoyed last night, and then he said, "Remember my mentioning how nice it would be if the three of us went out one day — you, me, and Derek?"

"Yes, of course," I answered brightly. I wasn't nearly as enthusiastic as I intended to convey, however. The truth is, I had reservations about meeting Nick's son, particularly this early in the relationship. (I preferred to assume that there was going to be a "later" in the relationship.)

Listen, suppose the kid didn't like me? At this point Nick and I weren't so involved that, this being the case, he would even hesitate to bid me sayonara. Especially since he was acting as the boy's sole parent at present — and would continue to fill that role for who-knows-how-much-longer.

There was also the possibility that I might not be crazy about Derek. I mean, I've yet to form an attachment to somebody simply because that person is a head or two shorter than I am and hasn't outgrown the tendency to suck his thumb. And if I *should* have a negative reaction to Derek, it would be something else to be concerned about at a time when Nick and I were still in very nebulous territory.

On the other hand, I might become really fond of the kid, so in the event Nick and I went kaput, it would be almost like a double breakup.

"Can you make it then?" Nick was saying.

Evidently I'd missed something a moment ago. "Um, when is that?"

He chuckled. "I'm glad you're still with me; I had the feeling I might have put you to sleep."

"Oh, it's not you," I assured him. "It's . . . well, I've been kind of preoccupied today."

"I'll take your word for it. Anyhow, I asked if you were free on Friday."

"Yes, I am." *I mean, if I gave him an excuse for that day he'd probably just come up with an alternate.*

"I sort of promised Derek we'd go to his favorite restaurant," Nick informed me sheepishly. "But if you have a problem with it . . ." His voice trailed off.

"Which is his favorite?"

"Serendipity. Ever hear of it?"

"*Hear* of it? I'm in love with the place!" He was talking about a New York institution here — an ice-cream-parlor-cum-restaurant-cum-little-memento-shop. An establishment not only adored by children, but by a whole lot of us aging Peter Pans out there.

A picture of a Serendipity hot fudge sundae (with walnuts and vanilla ice cream) instantly materialized in my head — a gorgeous sight if there ever was one.

"That's great," Nick responded, pleased. "Suppose we ring your doorbell at six. Or is that too early for you?"

"No, no. Six is good."

"All right, see you Friday." His voice softened. "I'm really looking forward to this, Dez. So is Derek."

"I am, too," I responded.

Well, what would you have said?

CHAPTER 21

I had a lot of catching up to do. So I spent most of Monday at the computer transcribing the notes on my most recent interviews.

Now, being a pathetically pokey typist, I'd promised myself — as I always do — that today I wouldn't waste time attempting to analyze the contents until I'd run off the hard copy. But this is one promise I don't seem to have a lot of compunction about breaking. So that's what I did — break it, I mean. The result was that I covered very little ground — and, what was worse, learned absolutely nothing.

I turned off the computer at quarter to five, thoroughly dejected. But I forced myself to snap out of it. They say it's not over until the fat lady sings. And I had no intention of straining my vocal chords just yet.

Listen, I still had a couple of suspects to interview, didn't I? One of whom I was, at that very moment, about to try and contact.

I picked up the receiver and dialed.

George Gladstone's answering machine

had announced that he would be in the office on Tuesday. So it was almost certain he'd be returning sometime on Monday from wherever he'd been all week. Maybe he was even home now.

And he was.

"Gladstone," a male voice asserted.

Hallelujah!

"Uh, Mr. Gladstone, my name is Desiree Shapiro, and I'm investigating the murder of Christina Trent. Some new information has —"

"For God's sake! That poor thing was stabbed to death a good five or six years ago! And the cops *just* managed to come up with whatever the hell you're talking about?"

Well, it's not my fault if, when I mention new evidence, some people take it for granted the police are involved. But, of course, I decided it was best not to correct the man's misconception at this point. I also elected not to contradict him as to how far back the homicide actually dated.

"You *are* with the NYPD — right?"

I was evasive. "I've been assigned to . . . check into things."

"What sort of an answer is that? Look, cupcake, I've been around the block a coupla times, so don't try to feed me that kind of baloney. You're no more a cop than I am. Admit it."

"I'm a private investigator," I conceded timidly.

"Yeah? Who hired you?"

I said that I was employed by Victor Pirrelli's teenage daughter. And then it crossed my mind that if I wanted Gladstone to let me in the door, it might not be a bad idea to pique his curiosity a bit. "The daughter was with him when he died, and what he related to her casts some doubt on his guilt. I'll give you the details in person if you can spare me a few minutes."

"I don't get it. Suppose the guy *didn't* do it. What's that got to do with me?"

"I'm interviewing everyone in your building — everyone who was living there at the time of the murder, that is. Hopefully, someone might have seen or heard something that evening."

"I wasn't even in New York then. I travel a lot on business; I have my own PR firm." After which he added condescendingly, "That's public relations."

"Even so, you may be able to give me some insight into Christina herself that could provide a clue to her killer."

"I'm afraid you're out of luck. I didn't actually know the girl that well."

The words came out mechanically. "It's possible you have some knowledge you're not aware of. I won't take up much of your time, Mr. Gladstone, and I'd really appreciate your help." Then before he could respond: "Particularly since it's obvious that you're a very intelligent person."

"Oh, Christ," he muttered. "You didn't really expect to con me with that one, did you? I know all the tricks. Like I said, I'm in PR."

"I —"

"But what the hell. What have I got to lose? I can fit you in tomorrow about five thirty, cupcake. So why don't you stop by then. Apartment 1C."

Cupcake!

Prior to our conversation I have to admit that I wasn't very kindly disposed toward George Gladstone. It may be a failing on my part, but I seem to have something against letches. Particularly letches of advanced years. And now, after speaking to him, I was even less fond of the man. He was so damn . . . well, "snotty" is the perfect fit for him. But that *cupcake* thing was the clincher.

I mean, doesn't it make you want to throw up?

I had to settle for a bacon-and-tomato sandwich for dinner. Which I'm not claiming was any big catastrophe. The thing is, though, this was also what I'd had for lunch. The only difference being that this evening's sandwich was on rye toast because, among other things, I was out of white bread. Fortunately, there was still some Häagen Dazs macadamia brittle in the refrigerator — all of about three tablespoons.

Well, it served me right for being too lazy to stop in at D'Agostino's on my way home from work tonight. I vowed to get my tush over there in the morning. Look, it's one thing to run out of white bread. But when there's no macadamia brittle in my freezer, I consider myself at the crisis stage.

Anyway, I had just polished off that pathetically meager portion of ice cream and poured myself a refill of the horrendous brew that in my house masquerades as coffee when the phone rang.

"Hi, Desiree. Remember me?"

"I know you won't believe this, Vicky," I got in quickly, "but I was going to call you the minute I finished my coffee." Which, I swear, was the truth.

Apparently I wasn't too convincing, however. "Yeah, yeah." But it was said lightly, without rancor. "You promised to, like, keep me informed," I was reminded.

"Yes, I did. And I realize I've been a little lax about getting back to you. But I have been busy questioning people, and if there'd been anything worth reporting, you'd have heard from me immediately."

"I kinda figured that. You met with my grandmom on Saturday."

"Yes, and she confirmed what your mother told me."

"About what?"

"Your grandmother said she'd spent the evening of the murder with your mother."

"I could have — Wait a minute. Did you . . . You didn't suspect my *mother* of killing that woman, did you?"

"No, I didn't. But I had to make absolutely certain she wasn't the person responsible. Believe me, Vicky, I was just as anxious for your mother to be innocent of this as I am to clear your dad's name."

It took a moment for the girl to respond. "Okay. It's only that, you know, I can't even think what I'd do if my mom turned out to be . . . like, the one."

"Well, you don't have to worry about that; she isn't."

"Mom says you're going to be meeting with my uncle Tony." She spoke the name as if it were a bad taste in her mouth. "Thursday, correct?"

"Yep. Thursday morning. Your mother must have applied a lot of pressure to persuade him to see me."

Vicky giggled. "You bet she did! You should have heard what went on. For a few minutes I thought they might wind up, like, getting divorced over that. But I guess it was wishful thinking, you know? Anyway, she wore him down."

"Listen, Vicky, just to update you, I have plans to see George Gladstone tomorrow. He's the older man in Christina Trent's building."

"You mean the pervert."

"I'm not sure I'd call him a pervert, although I do think it's a little sick for a man who's pushing sixty to pursue an eighteen-year-old girl like that. Incidentally, he claims the two of them were barely acquainted."

"He said that to you?"

"Yes, when I called to make the appointment to meet with him. However, a number of people have already confirmed that he was infatuated with the victim."

"So right off he's, like, a liar."

"That may be. But this doesn't necessarily make him a murderer, too. Could be the man just doesn't want to get involved."

"Well, if he didn't do it, there's, you know, still my stepfather."

"That's true." And now the busybody in me stuck in its two cents' worth. "Um . . . look, Vicky, even from my one telephone conversation with him, I could tell that your stepfather can be a bit difficult at times." (Which is what is called putting it mildly.) "But apparently your mother cares a great deal for him, and she told me that he's eager to make things right with you. So if we should find that he wasn't Christina's killer, well, maybe for her sake, you could cut him some slack."

"Yeah, maybe." But it wasn't more than two or three seconds later that she felt compelled to tag on, "My stepfather wanted my mom real bad, though. He, you know, would probably have done anything to get her — I mean, like, *anything*."

And there was no mistaking the optimism in her voice.

CHAPTER 22

The door to 1C was opened by a short, thin man in a white shirt liberally splattered with red. "*Scaloppini alla pizzaiola* — my lunch," he explained, following my eyes. "I've been too busy to change."

Now, after paying that long overdue visit to D'Agostino's first thing Tuesday morning (or my idea of "first thing," anyway), I'd gone into work. But anticipating my meeting with George, I'd found it almost impossible to concentrate. At this moment, however, I wasn't quite sure that the gentleman facing me was, in fact, George Gladstone.

True, he was slightly stooped and had his share of wrinkles. Nevertheless, he somehow managed to convey a sort of youthful energy. If this fellow was near seventy, he carried his years pretty well; I would have put him in his late fifties. And I wasn't influenced by his bright auburn hair, either — what few strands he'd managed to hold onto, that is. I mean, it was apparent that this was not the color the guy was born with.

"Mr. Gladstone?" I inquired uncertainly. "I'm Desiree Shapiro."

"Obviously." He took the hand I was holding out to him and gave it a perfunctory shake. "Well, don't just stand there. We don't want to give the neighbors anything to talk about, do we? Come in. Come in."

I followed him down a narrow hall into a small, cramped room.

"I assume you won't mind if we have our little discussion in my office."

"No, of course not."

"Good. I haven't had the chance to straighten up the living room yet. I was away more than a week; got back only yesterday."

I couldn't believe it! Considering the mess in here, I had to wonder about the state of the living room. There were papers strewn all over the place — on the desk, the floor, on one of the chairs. There was even a crumpled Baby Ruth wrapper lying next to the wastebasket, illustrating that my host was no Michael Jordan. What's more, anything not hidden by papers was covered with dust.

"Well, what are you waiting for? Sit down," George instructed, brushing a couple of folders from a sturdy ladder-back chair, then patting the seat cushion to reinforce the command.

I obliged, and he took the chair opposite me, behind the desk.

"You really aroused my curiosity on the phone, cupcake. But that was the intention, wasn't it? Anyway, let's have it. What was it Pirrelli told his kid?"

"It isn't so much *what* he told her as *when*."

"Would you mind giving that to me in English?"

"He was on his deathbed at the time — I think I mentioned that. Which means he had nothing to gain by lying. And he swore to Vicky — his daughter — that he was an innocent man."

"And — ?"

I began to squirm. "Well, as I said, Pirrelli was dying, and he —"

"That's it? This is your new information?" George fumed. Then addressing the room itself: "She lets me think she'll be imparting some juicy revelations. So being the inquisitive fellow I am, I invite her into my home. And what does she have to tell me? Nada, that's what! The woman has the notion that I'm some goddam patsy!" And now he glared at me. "If I weren't in one of my rare benevolent moods, Ms. Shapiro, I'd drag you straight to the door by that hennaed hair of yours." *(Look who's casting aspersions on* my *hair!)* "But, as I said, you're in luck today. You can leave under your own steam."

"I'm really sorry about being misleading," I put in quickly, "but I was very anxious to meet with you. You see, I believe there's a good chance that Victor Pirrelli told his daughter the truth, and I could use your help." I reached for my most heart-tugging expression. "If you would be willing to answer just a couple of questions for me . . ."

George pursed his lips, tilted his chair back, and stretched his arms over his head. Then, righting the chair, he sighed. "It appears that I *am* a patsy, after all. As long as you're here, you might as well tell me what you want to know. But make it fast."

The words came out in a rush. "Uh, how well acquainted were you with the deceased?"

"I answered that one for you yesterday," he responded impatiently. "Not well at all."

"I was informed by a number of people that you asked her out on several occasions."

"So?"

"Well, that would tend to, uh, indicate that you at least had a few conversations with her."

The telephone rang at this juncture, and George picked up without so much as an "excuse me."

"Sylvia, darling," he crooned into the mouthpiece. This was soon followed by an unctuous, "Of course you're still my favorite client. How can you even ask me that?" A pause. "I had every intention of getting back to you last night, but I fell asleep at eight o'clock — imagine! I was completely done in, though. That entire trip was nothing but work, work, work. And, as you're aware, I've had some health problems lately." After this George listened intently for a while. Then in a soft, mellifluous tone he assured the caller, "Don't you worry; I'll handle it. That's what I'm here for, darling."

Replacing the receiver in its cradle, he jotted something on a notepad, grousing as he wrote. "I should have dumped that old biddy years ago. But who else would put up with her nonsense?" He glanced over at me. "Well, let's get this done with. Where were we?"

"I was saying that I understood you'd attempted to date the victim."

"*Date?* What *date?* I asked her out to dinner a few times. Sue me, but I just don't enjoy eating alone. My *braciole* even seems to taste better when there's a pretty lady seated across the table from me. However, Christina Trent declined my invitations — and that, Ms. Shapiro, was the end of that."

"Uh, please call me Desiree."

"Fine. And, to you, I'm George." He made it sound as if he were bestowing some kind of singular honor on me.

"So, um, you're saying you had no romantic interest in the dead girl?"

"How am I supposed to answer that? I thought it would be pleasant to have her join me at some of our finer restaurants. But I'm not totally lacking in testosterone. So I won't claim that I'd have been unhappy if, *had* we shared an intimate little supper, anything developed as a result of it."

This seemed to be as much of an admission as I was going to get from the man, so I moved on.

"Would you have any idea if there was somebody with a grudge against Miss Trent?"

"You think the only thing I have to do all day is pay attention to a bunch of gossiping old ladies? I've got a business to run, cupcake, remember?"

"So you're not aware of any unpleasantness the victim might have been involved in?"

"No, I'm not."

The phone rang again.

This time it was "Nelson, baby" whose minor award for something-or-other George would be communicating to the media first thing in the morning.

"You mentioned yesterday that you were out of town the night Christina was killed," I said when the call ended. "Would you mind telling me where you were? It's just for my records."

"You're joking, right? That happened so long ago I can't even be certain what year it was. All I know is that I returned the day after the murder from whatever trip I'd been on. And the neighbors were all talking about how Christina and this Mr. Wonderful of hers had had a very nasty fight, during the course of which he stabbed her to death."

"The murder occurred in 1992," I provided.

"Jee-sus! I didn't realize it was *that* far back."

"It was in February."

George's forehead pleated up like an accordion. "February, huh?"

"The twenty-eighth."

He shook his head. "Sorry. But I'm not able to account for my time a decade ago — who the hell could? I've already told

208

you everything I can, so you might as well toddle on home. There are a number of people anxiously waiting for me to return their calls." He started to rise, then evidently struck by a thought, sat back down abruptly. "Wait a minute. Maybe I *can* assist you with . . . Why did you say you want the information? No, don't tell me," he commanded, his voice heavy with sarcasm. "I remember. It was just for your records, wasn't it?"

Fishing in one of the desk drawers now, George extracted a set of keys. After which he got up and walked over to two tall filing cabinets a few feet from his desk. He inserted a small key into one of the cabinets. "Tax returns," he apprized me, pulling open the bottom drawer. "I keep 'em for ten years."

Judging by the disarray in the man's office, I was prepared to pitch a tent there while I waited for him to lay hands on the object of his search. But he quickly removed a large manila envelope marked February 1992. And in less than five minutes he extracted an American Express receipt from a place called Di Carlo's Restaurant.

The address was Hollywood, California. The date was February twenty-eighth. And the time stamped on the slip was *22:50*. I did the math in my head (with a little help from my fingers): *ten fifty p.m.*

"Now, don't forget to mark this down for your records, huh, cupcake?" And George Gladstone smiled complacently.

CHAPTER 23

When I left George I was torn between letting loose with a piercing scream or a good, long cry.

But I convinced myself that being a grown-up (at least chronologically), it would be unseemly for me to allow myself the luxury of either one. I settled for kicking the inside of the elevator car, where no one would be privy to my childish behavior. But, to be honest, it didn't actually provide much of a release.

The possibilities on my suspect list now added up to a grand total of one. And the way things were going, I could expect that Tony Pirrelli, too, would produce the perfect alibi. It was practically predestined.

The elevator took its sweet, creaky time before delivering me to the basement. I walked down the hall to the superintendent's apartment and rang the bell.

The thirty-something person who opened the door could certainly have been a man. But a woman wasn't out of the question, either. The individual had to be close to six feet tall and lean, with long, light brown hair that was pulled straight back and secured with an elastic. He (she?) showed no noticeable facial stubble. Wore an androgynous pair of fly-front pants. And had a chest that was even flatter than mine.

"I'm Desiree Shapiro," I said.

Naturally, I figured that the sex of this somebody standing on the other side of the threshold would be established once we were through with the introductions.

"I'm Jamie Bracken," I was told. We shook hands.

Well, the voice that imparted this information — sort of quiet and midrange — could have gone either way. Plus, I'd only met two Jamies in my life. And one was male, the other female.

"What can I do for you?" he asked amiably. (I decided that, unless I learned otherwise, in my mind I'd start referring to this individual as a "he," since I was leaning — be it ever so slightly — in that direction.)

I stated that as a result of some new facts having recently been uncovered, I was investigating a homicide that had occurred in the building ten years earlier.

"I assume you're referring to Christina Trent." I thought I detected a degree of skepticism when he followed this with, "Are you a PI?"

"Guilty," I admitted. "You're aware of the tragedy, I see. Does that mean you've been the super here all this time?"

"No, but in those days, that was my pop's job. I've been living in this apartment most of my life. Is there something special you wanted to know?"

"I wonder if you could possibly tell me which of the present residents were also tenants back then."

"No problem. Step inside for a few minutes, and I'll get you the information."

Jamie led me into a small kitchen, where a plateful of food, which was yet to be touched, sat on the counter.

I checked my watch. It was just before seven. "Oh, I'm so sorry; you were about to have dinner. I, um, could come back later." But the offer was halfhearted — and the fingers of both hands tightly crossed.

"I'm not the least bit hungry. Have a seat, and I'll be back in a couple of minutes."

He returned with a ledger and a lined yellow pad. Sitting across from me, Jamie proceeded to quickly transfer some information from the ledger onto the pad. And a short time afterward he handed me a sheet of paper that listed eighteen units, along with the names of the occupants.

"Thanks. I really appreciate this," I told him. "One more thing: Did you yourself see or hear anything that night that might in any way relate to the crime?"

"I was at the movies with a friend, I remember. And then we went for something to eat. I didn't get home until almost one. Pop was in all evening, though, and he wasn't aware there was anything wrong. But Christina lived on the top floor, so no matter how loud the shouting got, the voices wouldn't have traveled all the way to the basement."

"Can you tell me anything about Christina? — as a person, I mean."

"I'm afraid not — other than that she was a very pretty girl. We'd occasionally bump into each other, but our conversations never went much beyond, 'Hi, how are you?' "

At the door I reiterated my thanks.

"No problem. Listen, *I* should be thanking *you*. After all, you got me a reprieve."

"A reprieve?"

Jamie turned toward the dish on the counter. "You've never tasted my aunt Charlotte's pot roast."

I started on six — Christina's floor —

and worked my way down, managing, in the course of my canvassing, to interrupt about a dozen suppers.

The Corey twins' apartment was adjacent to the victim's. Tiny, twittering little ladies, they appeared to be well into their eighties and had this disconcerting habit of completing each other's sentences.

Sandwiched between them on a faded chintz-covered sofa, I outlined the reason for my visit. Then I asked what they could tell me about the evening their neighbor was killed.

Rachel was the first to respond. (Or was it Rosamond? No, it was Rachel, all right; she was the one in the pink housedress with the yellow flowers.) "It was awful, that argument. You —"

". . . never heard anything like it," her sister finished for her.

"We would have called the police —" Rachel said.

". . . but they'd argued before, so we had no idea —"

Back to Rachel again. ". . . that something so terrible was happening. Besides, he was such a nice-looking young man that —"

". . . we never dreamed —"

". . . he might *harm* her."

"He did punch that sweet child in the

face once, though. Cracked her jaw, too," Rachel's sibling reminded her.

"Christie said it wasn't his fault, that it was an accident, but —"

". . . she could have been fibbing —"

Rachel nodded. ". . . to protect him."

"It was wrong of us not to have picked up the phone," Rosamond concluded.

Another nod from Rachel. "Very. But we just took it for granted this was like those other times we'd heard them quarrel —"

". . . only louder."

"You didn't happen to make out anything that was said, did you?" I asked.

The ladies' "No" was simultaneous.

Now, it was apparent that both sisters were extremely agitated at this juncture. Evidently my questions had resurrected the guilt they'd saddled themselves with all those years ago — and had eventually managed to suppress. "Listen, if I'm right about what actually transpired, your call wouldn't have prevented the murder," I assured them. "The police would have come and left by then. You see, there's a very good possibility Christie was killed *after* the fight, when her boyfriend was out for a walk."

"Oh, I do hope that's true," Rosamond murmured gratefully.

216

"I honestly believe that it is."

"Will you have a bite with us?" a relieved Rachel invited.

"Yes, do." Rosamond seconded.

"We have our dinner late on Tuesdays — when we've finished our exercise class."

"My sister makes the most delicious Southern-fried —"

". . . chicken. It's my specialty," Rachel informed me proudly.

Well, it was getting late and I hadn't had much of a lunch and the chicken smelled absolutely wonderful. I had no choice, however, but to decline the offer. Inducing myself to say the words wasn't easy, though.

At any rate, after learning that neither twin had heard a third voice coming from next door that night, I went on to determine they had nothing else of relevance to share with me. And following this I prepared to leave.

But I pointed my nose in the direction of the kitchen for one last whiff before getting back to my bell ringing.

The majority of the people I spoke to after that insisted they hadn't heard a thing all evening.

In some instances, it would have been

surprising if they had, of course, since their apartments weren't in very close proximity to the dead girl's. And of those who were most likely to be within shouting distance of Christina's flat, a youngish man maintained that he'd spent the night at his fiancée's. An overly friendly middle-aged fellow — "call me Roger, Dezzie" — told me his kids used to play the TV so loudly you wouldn't have heard a sonic boom. While Hannah De Witt — a plump, elderly lady who was missing her upper dental plate — declared that she was always fast asleep by eight thirty.

There were a few residents, though, who did admit to being aware of the battle going on at Christina's.

A tight-lipped couple took the position that it wasn't any of their business to interfere in what they chose to regard as a domestic dispute.

Another tenant, her eyes moist (thanks to me, she, too, appeared to be in the throes of reawakened guilt), confided that she'd been terribly concerned about the possibility of violence. In fact, she was on the verge of dialing 9-1-1 when her then-husband prevailed upon her to "butt out."

I finally came across someone who actually got on the line to the local station house.

Just before eleven the yelling upstairs reached the point where Mrs. Gottlieb, in 5A, felt compelled to make the call. "It wasn't that I could barely hear myself think — honestly," she stressed, "although that was certainly the case. The reason I decided to take action, though, was because I was becoming increasingly afraid that somebody could get hurt — physically, I mean."

As it turned out, however, Mrs. Gottlieb was put on hold, and she hung up when her infant son began to cry. And only moments after this the racket ended.

"I figured it had all blown over," the petite blonde said, her tone filled with self-recrimination. "But on Sunday, a neighbor told me about the stabbing and how, at around midnight, these two officers found the boyfriend right next to the body. So I concluded that the altercation must have either continued or resumed, but at a much lower volume.

"You know, even if it wasn't . . . even if, as you suggest, it was someone else who stabbed that poor thing, everything might have turned out differently if only I hadn't taken anything for granted and had just kept trying to contact the police." And now Mrs. Gottlieb's eyes were also filling up. It seems I'd struck again.

★ ★ ★

Naturally, I was frustrated, but not surprised, that no one I spoke to could (or would) shed much light on what had transpired that night — or provide any substantive information regarding the victim. I was about ready to call it quits when I remembered that there was one person on Jamie's list who hadn't responded when I'd rung the bell earlier. I went back up to the sixth floor for another try.

This time, only seconds after I pressed the buzzer to 6F, a tall, angular female of about fifty opened the door. She hadn't heard any loud voices coming from her neighbor's apartment, she said. Not a sound.

Well, she was hardly the first of the building's occupants to give me that same story. But by now the repetition had really gotten to me. Plus, in the present instance, I was talking to someone who'd lived directly across the hall from Christina.

I was on the verge of challenging this contention when I took a better look at Miss Penelope Sweeney — and closed my mouth.

The woman was wearing a hearing aid.

CHAPTER 24

It was bad enough that I was discouraged and depressed. But I refused to subject myself to starvation, as well. So when I got back to Manhattan, I stopped off at Jerome's.

I was hoping Felix wouldn't be working at the restaurant tonight, since I was sort of leaning toward a steak sandwich. But who was the first person I set eyes on when I slid into the booth?

Naturally.

"You want the cheeseburger deluxe," Felix recited, "only it should be well-done. . . ."

Now, you probably figured this would wind up being my order. And you'd be right, too — wuss that I am.

Anyhow, I managed, to my own surprise, to banish any thoughts of today's disappointing interviews and enjoy the meal. Even if it wasn't a steak sandwich.

Later, at the apartment, I couldn't delay the postmortem any longer. I started off by attempting to put a positive spin on George Gladstone's airtight alibi. After all, with George removed from my incredible shrinking suspect list, I could focus all my attention on the one name that remained, right?

Well, maybe not.

I wasn't able to shake the fear that had gripped me earlier in the day: that Tony Pirrelli would come up with proof of *his* innocence — a proof as convincing as everyone else's. The conclusion to be drawn from this being that the *real* killer of Christina Trent had never made it onto my list in the first place.

And in this horrible, unthinkable eventuality — what then?

My questioning of the occupants of Christina's building certainly hadn't uncovered any new possibilities. In fact, her former neighbors hadn't enlightened me in the slightest — or had they?

Actually, there *were* some bright spots. The responses I'd gotten made my theory concerning the events of that night more feasible than ever. You see, if none of the dead girl's fellow tenants had alerted the police to the altercation taking place, this increased the likelihood that the call had been made later on. And for the specific purpose of setting up Victor for the crime.

I also carried two other substantial

pieces of information home with me from Queens. (1) The victim had lived on the sixth floor. (2) The building's only elevator was practically a relic. Listen, talk about S-L-O-W — that contraption was as close to immobile as you can get. It was highly doubtful that the thing had had the energy to go zipping up and down even ten years earlier.

What I'm getting at is that it would have taken Victor Pirrelli a good few minutes to make it upstairs to his lover's apartment. So if somebody had been on the lookout for his return before putting through that crucial phone call, the odds of the police arriving in time to find Victor still at the murder site appeared to be better than I'd initially speculated.

My (partially) sunny outlook was short-lived, however. While I was becoming increasingly comfortable with the idea of Victor's innocence, I was feeling less and less confident that I'd be able prove it.

How's that for irony?

On Wednesday I astonished myself by accomplishing much more at the office than I expected I could — and this would have been true even if I hadn't been so dispirited. Sitting at the computer, though, I almost mechanically transcribed a very decent portion of my notes. The explanation for this unnatural productivity is that I'd somehow managed to make my mind a total blank. (Which probably should have been a lot harder to do than it actually was.)

I spent most of that evening with my eyes fixed on the television set. But without really seeing what I was looking at. I kept thinking ahead to tomorrow — and the moment of truth.

This was when Uncle Tony would — or would not — manage to produce a solid alibi for himself. And I hadn't the slightest conception of how to proceed if he did. Or, for that matter, if he didn't.

By the time I was ready for bed I had dry mouth, an Extra-Strength Tylenol headache, and a left arm that was flame red and even bleeding in a couple of spots — my jangled nerves having dictated that I scratch it for the better part of three hours.

Believe it or not, though, I was able to get a good night's sleep.

You see, I have this kind of . . . I guess you could call it a built-in escape hatch. On rare occasions, when I'm disturbed about something, it enables me to drop off in minutes, providing a temporary refuge from whatever it is that's currently driving me up a wall.

I was grateful that this turned out to be one of those rare occasions.

Listen, I *had* to be well rested and on my toes Thursday morning — that, or risk being eaten alive by the formidable Uncle Tony.

CHAPTER 25

I was at the law offices of Donato, Costello, Pirrelli, and Goldstein five minutes before the appointed hour. I didn't dare show up late. I had the feeling that if I arrived even two seconds past the mandated eleven a.m., Anthony Pirrelli, Esq. would deny me access to his illustrious self.

I'll say one thing for him, though: He didn't leave me cooling my heels in the posh waiting room. Within five minutes after I arrived, a silver-haired woman with a frosty smile showed me into Pirrelli's inner sanctum.

The place was impressive, all right. A king-sized space, with gleaming wood furnishings and carpeting so thick it practically reached my ankles.

"Ms. Shapiro, sir," my escort announced.

The man seated at a massive mahogany desk at the far end of the office didn't lift his eyes from his papers.

"Have a seat, Ms. Shapiro." His arm shot out and gestured toward a small, beige tweed sofa that sat against the wall, six or seven feet to the right of the desk. It was only after I'd obediently placed my derriere where indicated that he deigned to raise his head and swivel around in his chair to face me.

Tony Pirrelli had a large, well-padded frame, but he wasn't what you'd call heavy — I put him at maybe ten pounds over his ideal weight. He had a full head of wavy brown hair and decent features (if you were willing to ignore the disdainful expression on his face, that is). Still, it was pretty safe to assume that Tony here had been no match for his younger sibling in the looks department.

"I have an important meeting to attend in a few minutes," he announced, "so let's get right to it, shall we? Just what is that bilge you fed my wife concerning my participation in my brother's plea bargain?"

He wasn't asking me; he was challenging me. And it took a second or two before I was able to compose myself. (Listen, compared to this character, George Gladstone was a goddam honeybun.) "All I said to Mrs. Pirrelli was that some questions had been raised in this regard."

"Is that a fact." A sneer accompanied the words.

"Um, most likely this renewed interest in the matter came about as a result of your brother's passing."

"And what exactly *were* these questions you're referring to? And who was raising them?"

I'd anticipated this, of course. Nevertheless, at that instant I'd have been delighted to bury myself in Tony Pirrelli's carpeting. "I, er, was given the impression it was someone in law enforcement. But I got all of this secondhand — I wasn't actually privy to any discussions. So, I really don't have an answer for you."

"Why is it I'm not at all surprised to hear you say that? Look, I will tell you this just once. Ten years ago I believed — and I still *do* believe — that Victor was responsible for that girl's death, his denial to Vicky notwithstanding. Even if you choose to downplay his having been apprehended with the murder weapon in his hand — and I don't see how any thinking person can give something like that short shrift — it's impossible not to factor in that my brother was a very volatile person. Are you aware that he'd physically attacked this same young woman less than a year before she was killed?"

He didn't pause long enough for a response.

"So understand this. My certitude with regard to his guilt is the reason — the *only* reason — I urged Victor to agree to a reduced sentence rather than risk a trial. And not merely for his sake — although whether you accept this or not, I did love my brother — but for the sake of the entire family, my mother in particular."

And now there was a strange look on Tony's face. (Could it actually have been sadness?) "Under the terms of the arrangement worked out with the district attorney, Victor could have been a free man this year, Ms. Shapiro. Unfortunately, however, he was involved in a few incidents during his incarceration that negated an early release."

Tony absently rubbed his finger along the side of his nose before continuing. "A moment ago I mentioned 'family,' to you. I'm going to mention it again. You would be doing my family a great service if you terminated your investigation. Thus far, your efforts on behalf of my stepdaughter have succeeded only in opening old wounds. And, trust me, that's the extent of what you can expect to accomplish. You have no hope of presenting Vicky with an alternate villain because none exists. And, obviously, the longer this thing drags on, the more profound her unhappiness when you finally tire of getting nowhere."

"But I —"

His rising voice stepped on my protest. "Frankly, I can't see any reason you'd *want* to continue with this. My wife informs me that she impressed upon you that a contract entered into with a minor isn't legally binding. But even if Vicky has every intention of compensating you for your services — and I'm sure she does — she simply doesn't have the wherewithal. As for the rest of us — Mary, my mother, and I — we're anxious to see this entire business put to rest. So we're not inclined to pick up the tab for her — not unless you should agree to call a halt to all of this fruitless poking around here and now."

He was apparently waiting for a response — but not the one he got. "Look, Mr. Pirrelli," I said as if I hadn't heard the offer (or — to be accurate — *bribe*,) "I knew all about contracts with minors before I got involved with this case. I told you before that I took it for only one reason: I didn't have the heart to say no."

"If I were you," Tony Pirrelli said very deliberately, "I'd reevaluate that decision."

And with this, he swiveled around in his chair, after which he placed both palms on the desk, preparatory to getting to his feet. "Now, if you'll excuse me."

"Uh, I have just one question, Mr. Pirrelli." He turned toward me again, a black look on his face. I managed to ignore it.

"Was Mrs. Pirrelli — your wife, I mean — aware of your involvement in the plea bargain? I'm talking about at the beginning."

"What my wife was — or was not — aware of is, if you'll pardon my bluntness, absolutely none of your business."

Well, I pretty much knew the answer to that anyhow. Unless the woman was the second coming of Meryl Streep, she was truly staggered when I laid that little fact on her last week. Plus, at this stage, it didn't seem to be a pertinent factor — just something my pesky curiosity had demanded I try to clarify.

At any rate, it was now time to *really* push my luck. "Will you answer one other thing for me, then?"

At this point the man regarded me as if I were a specimen that belonged under a microscope. But at least he was still in his chair, so I forged ahead. "Uh, this is just for my records, Mr. Pirrelli. Would you mind telling me where you were the night Christina Trent was killed?"

"Mind? Certainly I mind! That, too, Ms. Shapiro, is none of your business." And on this agreeable note, he rose.

It didn't take a Rhodes scholar to determine that the interview was over.

CHAPTER 26

I ran from the building. (Well, walked really fast, anyhow.) The greater the distance I put between myself and Tony Pirrelli, the happier I'd be.

This morning's meeting had to rank right up there with the most aggravating I'd ever had. *Meeting*, my foot! The man didn't *talk* to me — he reamed me out. Even when — just before leaving — I finally managed to get in a couple of questions, they went unanswered. I mean, talk about an attitude!

Listen, if there were any perks for Victor in being sent to prison, it was not having to be in the good counselor's company all that often.

At any rate, after the browbeating I'd just taken, I desperately needed a nice, warm hug. And few things elicit that kind of feeling in me the way Little Angie's pizza does. Take my word for it, this is absolutely the best pizza in New York, if not on the entire planet — its thin, crispy crust playing host to your choice of a slew of unbelievably delectable toppings. So before heading for the office, I stopped in at Little Angie's for a slice or three of comfort.

"Well? How did it go — your get-together with the brother?" Jackie demanded the second I walked in the door.

"He was in fine voice."

"What does that mean?"

"I'll tell you about it later," I muttered.

Pondering today's little session in my cubbyhole a few minutes after this, I had to caution myself. It would be a mistake to jump to the conclusion that Tony was Christina's assassin merely because, by not presenting an alibi, he was the only one of my suspects still standing. (Or because the prospect of nailing him for the crime did not exactly cause me to weep buckets.)

It was conceivable, I conceded with extreme reluctance, that the killer was someone out in left field somewhere. Like an individual from Christina's past. (Although at her age how much of a past could the poor thing have accumulated?)

Anyhow, going on the presumption that it *wasn't* Tony who'd plunged that knife into the victim, I realized it was quite possible that at this juncture he'd *want* Victor to be guilty of the murder. What I'm getting at is that Tony might very well be reluctant to accept that he'd actually convinced an innocent person to go to jail. Especially when that innocent person was his own brother. Could be, I mused, this was the main reason he was so anxious for me to drop the investigation.

I also acknowledged that Tony's keeping his involvement in the plea bargain a secret from both Mary and Philomena wasn't necessarily indicative of his guilt. It was just as likely his silence on this subject stemmed from a concern that they might attribute his motive to something other than filial devotion.

Nevertheless, there was a big stumbling block to accepting that Tony's hands were clean. *Why,* I put to myself, *if he wasn't responsible for Christina's death, did the man refuse to reveal his whereabouts that night?*

Are you serious? I shot back. If there was one thing I could swear to, it was that Tony Pirrelli had this enormous sense of privilege. It would simply have gone against his nature to explain himself to me.

All of this said, however, my money was still on Tony. Particularly when, just then, I replayed in my head a certain piece of advice he'd favored me with that morning.

After I'd found it necessary to once again state my reason for taking the case, Tony had countered with — and I'm repeating this verbatim: "If I were you, I'd reevaluate that decision."

Well, from where I sat, this sounded an awful lot like a threat. And, brave creature that I am, it scared the bejesus out of me.

But while I might have been quaking from the top of my glorious hennaed head straight down to my toes, I wasn't a quitter. Threat or not, I had no intention of breaking faith with Vicky.

I determined that the logical course of action now would be to have a talk with Tony's former girlfriend. After all, the homicide had taken place at some point in the hour before midnight on a Saturday — a "date night," if you'll pardon the expression. So there was a better than even chance that either the girlfriend had spent that evening with her lawyer beau or that he'd come up with an excuse of some kind for not being available. I made a quick search of my notes for the woman's identity. "Carmela Thomas, she calls herself," Philomena had told me.

From a strictly selfish point of view, I was hoping Carmela hadn't married in the last ten years. If she had, though, I really had no objection — providing she'd been thoughtful enough to retain her maiden name. Anyway, it was one of those two, because I found a listing in the White Pages for a Carmela Thomas with an address in the East Seventies.

I scribbled down the phone number and shoved it into my handbag for later.

I had a light supper, dawdling over my coffee — two cups of it — for quite a while. Then I made an effort to kill some more time by taking a third crack at last Sunday's *New York Times* crossword puzzle — with predictable results. (Listen, I'm not alone in my opinion that the people responsible for creating those things have more than a trace of sadism in their natures.) At seven forty-five, I put down the puzzle (in disgust) and was about to try to reach Tony's ex, when I received a crisis call from my friend Harriet Gould, who lives across the hall.

It seems that this afternoon the Goulds' retarded and terrible-tempered Pekinese, Baby, had alienated their every-other-Thursday cleaning lady by giving her a "playful little nip" (Harriet's words) on the ankle. Following which Mrs. Bauer stated her intention of finding substitute employment unless Baby was either muzzled or gassed. The latter alternative was, of course, unthinkable — even to me, Baby's sworn enemy. And Harriet didn't give the muzzle idea very high marks, either. I finally convinced her that once Baby got used to the contraption, she'd hardly be aware that it was there. It was a lie, but once you pee on my brand-new faux crocodile Italian pumps, you've got to expect a payback.

It was after eight when I finished dispensing advice to Harriet, and I immediately dialed Carmela Thomas, figuring that there was a good chance she'd be home by now. But her answering machine let me know I was wrong. I continued to call the number at approximately fifteen-minute intervals until, at just past nine thirty, a woman answered the phone.

"Miss Thomas?"

"Yes, this is Ms. Thomas." The voice was low and pleasant.

"My name is Desiree Shapiro, and I'm investigating the murder of Christina Trent."

"Christina who?"

"Trent. Um, I realize it was a long time ago, but Christina was the young girl Victor Pirrelli supposedly stabbed to death."

"Oh, my," she murmured. "How could I have forgotten her name?" And then: "But did I hear you correctly? Did you say '*supposedly* stabbed to death'?"

"That's right. We're looking into the possibility that Victor was wrongly incarcerated."

"The 'we' being — ?"

"I'm a private investigator, and I've agreed to check into this for Victor's daughter — she's a teenager now."

"Already? I can hardly believe it! How is Victor holding up, by the way?"

"He was killed in a prison fight a few weeks ago."

"*Killed?* Oh, my God. How awful! I didn't exactly approve of the man, but for anything like that to occur . . . Tell me, though, why are you calling me regarding what happened to that unfortunate girl?"

"I understand that you and Tony Pirrelli were . . . seeing each other in those days, and I wanted to touch base with you about something. I wonder if we could sit down and talk for a few minutes — whenever it's convenient for you and anywhere you say."

"I don't want to be uncooperative Ms. — ? I apologize; I seem to have forgotten your name."

"Shapiro. Desiree Shapiro."

"Listen, Ms. Shapiro, I can't for the life

of me imagine how I could be of any help to you. I didn't know the victim at all. In fact, I didn't know Victor that well, either."

"Even so," I persisted, "you might be able to clarify a couple of things. I'd really appreciate your meeting with me — I won't keep you long, I promise."

"Unfortunately, that's just about impossible. I'm working to launch a new magazine, and I don't even have time to get myself a haircut. Tonight's the earliest I've made it home in over three weeks. Whatever it is you want to ask me about, why don't you ask me now?"

Well, from the finality of her tone, I figured I had maybe a hundred-thousand-to-one shot of persuading the woman to do this in person. Plus, considering that there was only a single piece of information I actually needed from her, I supposed there wasn't any real necessity for a face-to-face visit.

"All right. Would you, uh, mind telling me where you were the evening of the tragedy? I realize this goes back a decade, but I'm hoping the events that took place at the time will have fixed that night in your memory."

"Let me be certain I have this straight. Am I considered a suspect?"

"Oh, no. I'm afraid I put that badly. My purpose in inquiring about this is to establish whether you and Tony Pirrelli were together when the girl was murdered."

"You believe *he* stabbed her?"

"He's only one of a half-dozen possibles," I responded. Which, while it might not have been truthful, seemed like the wise thing to say.

"But why would —" Carmela stopped abruptly, evidently having arrived at the answer to her own unfinished question. "You think he set Victor up, don't you? That he wanted his brother out of the way because he was in love with that social-climbing wife of his?"

"I don't really think anything. I'm just not ready to eliminate anyone who might conceivably have a motive, that's all."

"I see." And now the woman inquired cautiously, "Did Tony claim we were together that evening?"

"He refused to tell me anything at all regarding his whereabouts."

Three or four very long seconds went by. Then, just as I was wondering if Carmela, too, would fail to shed any light on the matter, she said something under her breath that I took to be, "Sounds like him." Another couple of seconds elapsed before she added, "Look, I wound up having to cancel our date — a bad cold. I'm sorry, but I have no idea where Tony was that night — or with whom."

There was a smile on my face when I hung up the phone.

For the present, I refused to concern myself with the details about how to gather evidence against Tony. Or to revisit the possibility that someone else — someone I either didn't know or hadn't considered — was the perpetrator here.

At this moment, it was enough for me that *suspect* Tony Pirrelli still lived.

CHAPTER 27

The second I awoke on Friday I asked myself what in God's name I'd been so happy about last night.

If I failed to discover evidence linking Tony Pirrelli to the crime, I'd have to start all over again. And how would I even begin to hunt up another could-be murderer?

I mean, when you put it in perspective, this was a homicide dating back to an era when hardly anyone had ever heard of feng shui, TV's *Frasier* was still occupying a barstool at *Cheers,* and I was experimenting with becoming a blonde (don't ask!).

Still, I conceded that for now at least, there was no reason to saddle myself with a whole lot of anxiety about digging up alternative suspects. I'd concentrate on the one I already had and hope for the best or — depending on how you looked at it — the worst.

Once at the office, I spent the better part of the morning trying to figure out how to proceed. The only thing I could come up with was to have another talk with Mary and Philomena. Persuading either of those ladies to see me again, however, could be even more of a problem than determining exactly what it was I hoped to learn from them.

I finally had to postpone mapping out any plans in that regard — although it was extremely iffy that I'd have devised anything worthwhile anyway — because my concerns about tonight's date with Nick and son kept pushing their way into my head.

I knew I was being silly. Chances were that Derek and I would get along just dandy. I'd certainly do everything I could to ingratiate myself with the kid — even if he had two heads and breathed fire on me. But if, in spite of my heroic efforts, young Derek still had the poor taste to wind up hating my guts, this didn't necessarily mean the end of my relationship with his father.

Or did it?

The bell rang promptly at six.

I opened the door to a smiling Nick and a surprisingly handsome nine-year-old. (Listen, as much as I myself found Nick's looks quite irresistible, I had to concede that Derek here must resemble his mother.)

"What a great outfit! It's terrific on you, too," Nick said appreciatively as the pair entered my living room.

I was wearing a favorite of mine — a lightweight blue wool suit that was a particularly good fit in addition to making my rather nondescript blue eyes actually seem *blue* blue, if you know what I mean. "Thank you," I simpered. I guess I must have beamed a little, too. Then Nick made the introductions, following which a solemn Derek held out his hand. *Isn't that cute?* I thought as, just as solemnly, I shook the proffered appendage.

Moments later I grabbed my coat, and then we were off to Serendipity.

We were seated on the ground floor, toward the rear, at a white, marble-topped table, a colorful Tiffany-style lampshade overhead. As usual, the restaurant was packed with children in excellent voice, accompanied by their overly indulgent parents. Plus, there was a decent smattering of mature diners who, to satisfy their sweet tooths, had bravely entered this kiddie mecca sans any visible offspring — and with whom I readily identified.

A cheerful waiter almost immediately presented us with menus. And after deliberating very briefly, we made our selections: one of those foot-long hot dogs with all the trimmings for both Nick and me and a hamburger for Derek. It goes without saying that these dishes were accompanied by a round of Cokes and a large side order of French fries (well done, naturally).

During dinner I began to relax about Derek. I suppose it didn't hurt that he told me how much he loved my red hair. ("It's really *beautiful*," he said.) Or that he was so polite in responding to my questions about school. (His favorite subject, he informed me, was math.)

"Do you have any idea what you'd like to do when you're older?" I inquired.

"Well, when I was young, I wanted to be a cop — my uncle Arnie, my mom's brother, is a police sergeant. But now I'm not too sure anymore. My dad says you're a private investigator, and that sounds kind of interesting. Do you like it?"

"Most of the time."

"How come not all of the time?"

"Well, when things aren't going the way you want them to, when you either can't find out who committed the crime or can't prove that the guilty person *is* guilty, you're apt to get pretty discouraged."

"So then what do you do?"

"You keep plugging away and hope it will all turn out okay in the end."

"And does it?"

"With any luck, it does."

"What —"

"Why don't you save the rest of those questions until Desiree's finished her hot dog," Nick admonished mildly.

The boy nodded, his face turning red. "I'm sorry," he mumbled to me, his lower lip quivering.

"No problem." I smiled at him. "I've certainly been doing my part to keep you from eating, too."

Derek smiled back — gratefully, I thought — and shifted his complete attention to his hamburger.

Before long we were ready for the highlight of the meal.

Father and son opted for Serendipity's famous frozen hot chocolate — prepared with fourteen varieties of chocolate! — while I never deviate from their hot fudge sundae with vanilla ice cream and walnuts. (They don't serve macadamia brittle there. Besides, I've always regarded hot fudge and vanilla ice cream as being made for each other. Think Mickey and Minnie. And bacon and eggs.)

At any rate, after the waiter took our

order, Nick excused himself to go to the men's room.

The instant he left, I was in the company of an entirely new Derek.

"Are you in love with my dad?" He made it an accusation.

"Um, we haven't known each other long enough for me to even think along those lines," I answered, taken aback.

"Well, I want you to understand that he's never going to marry you. My dad likes brunette hair, like my mom has. Not yucky red hair, like yours." *Why, that incredible little phony! Only a short while ago this "yucky red hair" of mine was "beautiful" — and he'd spoken with such wide-eyed sincerity, too!* "My dad also prefers somebody who's thin, same as her," he went on. And to ensure that I was receiving the message, he peered sideways at the seat of my chair, his eyes lingering audaciously on my ample bottom for a couple of seconds.

Now, at first I had an almost overwhelming desire to give Nick's pride and joy a good, swift kick in the you-know-where. But apart from the fact that his sitting down precluded anything of that nature, I quickly reminded myself that Derek had had it rough lately. He wouldn't be lashing out like this, I determined, if he weren't still traumatized by his parents' breakup and, of course, his mother's temporary (let's hope) abandonment.

Just then our desserts arrived. I merely sat and stared at my sundae, waiting for Nick to rejoin us. Besides, I was too shaken to even lift the spoon.

Derek, meanwhile, blithely devoted himself to his chocolate confection. He let at least a minute go by before looking up to announce, "They're going to get married again — my mom and dad — you wait and see."

"I know how much you want that," I responded gently (after reminding myself once more that the boy was in pain), "but it's not something you can count on. There are —"

"They *will* get married again, I told you! And don't you dare say any different!" And with this, a wild look came into his eyes, followed by a smile I can only describe as "diabolical." (I swear!) And now, his cup of frozen hot chocolate in hand, Derek leaned over and very deliberately poured the entire contents in my lap!

"Why you little bastard!" I screeched, jumping up.

Predictably, at this precise moment Nick returned to the table.

"What happened?" he demanded, grabbing a napkin and starting to blot me off as best he could.

I'll say this for the kid, he gave quite a performance. "I . . . I spilled my dessert all over Desiree. It was an accident, Dad, honest." And to me: "Please don't be mad; I'm so sorry." Then he dissolved in tears.

"There's nothing to cry about, Derek. I'm sure Desiree realizes it wasn't intentional," Nick assured his son. "She didn't mean to yell at you. But after getting soaked like that, well, her response was like a reflex. You know what that is, don't you?"

Still snuffling, the lousy little brat nodded.

Now, all this time I'd simply been standing where I was, more or less in shock, while Nick continued to minister to me and servers from all over the room hurried forward bearing fresh napkins. It suddenly dawned on me that if I contradicted Derek's version of how I'd acquired a lapful of the house specialty, I'd be playing right into his hands. I mean, who could I expect this doting father to believe — his beloved son or some casual date he didn't even have a desire to kiss?

"I apologize for screaming at you and for the terrible name I called you," I said to Derek. "I don't know what could have come over me. Can you ever forgive me? Please tell me we can be friends again."

"Derek?" Nick put in.

"Uh, yeah, I guess so," the kid replied, obviously thrown by what, to this day, I regard as a truly inspired strategy.

"I can't even believe I reacted that way," I murmured, addressing Nick. "It's no excuse, but the investigation I'm involved in has been going badly, and I've been getting these terrible headaches, and my nerves are shot, and I can't sleep. I don't know. I just haven't been myself for the last few days." And now it was my turn to squeeze out a few false tears.

"Don't worry, Desiree. We all lose it on occasion. None of us are saints — none of us here, at any rate. Right, Derek?" Nick glanced over his shoulder at his progeny while lightly patting my arm.

"Yeah, sure," was the grudging response.

Anyone who noticed me on my way to the ladies' room a few minutes later must have been mystified.

There I was, covered in this sticky brown gunk — and unable to keep from grinning. But trust me, there's an enormous sense of satisfaction in managing to foil the plans of somebody so . . . so Machiavellian. Even if that somebody is nine years old.

CHAPTER 28

Nick — Derek in tow — saw me to my door.

I had just extracted the key from my bag when Derek suddenly clutched his stomach. "I don't feel so good, Dad," he announced, pulling at Nick's sleeve with his free hand. "I think I'm going to throw up."

I would probably have burst into applause at the kid's discomfort — in my head, that is — if I'd given this complaint any credence. But I wouldn't have believed anything Derek said if he were standing at the Pearly Gates, answering to St. Peter. (As you can see, while I may not practice the religion of my birth, every once in a while the Catholic in me still comes shining through.)

"Do you mind, Dez?" Nick asked, already half-turned in the direction of the elevator. "You'll be okay, won't you?"

"Of course I will; I'm right in front of my door. So get going." And to Derek's retreating back — and in my sweetest voice: "I hope you feel better, honey." (I know. That "honey" almost made me gag. But I figured it would still be a lot easier for me to say it than for the kid to hear it.)

I watched the two of them hurry down the hall, after which I put my key in the lock and turned it. I heard a click, but the door remained shut. I tried again — and now it swung open.

Was I so non compos mentis that I'd forgotten to secure the apartment? I wondered. I confess that it had happened before — and more than once — but not too recently. I vaguely remembered locking up when I went out, though, only I really couldn't swear to it. After all, I'd been preoccupied with my concerns about what the evening — and Master Derek — might have in store for me.

But surely Nick would have noticed such an oversight. An instant later, however, I recalled that as soon as we'd made our exit, Nick had gotten busy fiddling with his son's scarf.

At any rate, being slightly spooked, I momentarily considered heading across the hall to commandeer Steve Gould, Harriet's husband. But I instantly nixed the idea. I mean, was I a bona fide private investigator — or a mouse? Then I thought that maybe I could appropriate a heavy object of some sort from the Goulds: a baseball bat, say, or how about a rolling pin? But I vetoed this option, as well. Given my previous record in the door-locking department, the chances were excellent that the only person responsible for precipitating my attack of nerves was me.

Fortunately, I didn't actually have to walk into the apartment to turn on the living room lights, since the switch is only a few inches to the left of the entrance. What I did was *lean* into the room, so that if the circumstances warranted, I could make a run for it — while screaming at the top of my lungs, naturally. But as far as I could tell, nothing had been disturbed. And there was no sign of any fiend eagerly waiting to inflict pain on me.

Having established these things, I finally gathered the courage to cross the threshold. Following which I took a fast peek into the other rooms. I quickly verified that they were also just as I'd left them.

When I'd finished lecturing myself on my inexcusable negligence, I shed my pitiful-looking blue suit — something I was extremely eager to do. Then I got into pajamas and plopped down on the sofa with *Towards Zero*, my favorite book by my favorite author. It didn't much matter that I'd read this same Agatha Christie dozens of times before. I still enjoyed it. Plus, it was nice to revisit a mystery I'd managed to solve — at least, by the second go-around.

But it wasn't long before Nick wormed his way into my head — Nick and that awful son of his. Talk about formidable opponents! Listen, I'd take my chances and go up against another woman any day, rather than mind wrestle with a kid like that.

But maybe I no longer had to worry about Derek. For all I knew, tonight's unpleasantness had put the kibosh on my relationship with Nick (such as it was). I mean, while the man seemed to have taken my "little bastard" outburst in stride, it could be that he'd simply been trying to make the best of a very uncomfortable situation. Even if the incident hadn't caused him to sour on me, though, one thing was obvious: Derek was out to disappear me from his father's life.

And now, as at the restaurant, I took a stab at being charitable. I really did make an attempt to consider the kid's unhappy circumstances — honest. But it would have required a more generous heart than mine to overlook his behavior that evening. Especially when you factored in my fear that in the event his father and I weren't already kaput, little Derek would devise a way of making it happen.

It took a while, but I was finally able to tear myself away from the Nick/Derek subject and get back to Agatha Christie.

Only a few minutes later, however, I was reminding myself that if I had any hope of tying my friend Tony to the death of Christina Trent, I was going to have to do some inspired plotting of my own. But it had been an exhausting day. It was getting late. And I was in no condition to engage in any mental exercises at the moment, my brain having turned to mush hours ago. I'd be better able to deal with the problem after (hopefully) a good night's rest.

Picking up the book again, I read until midnight, at which point my eyes lowered to half-mast and the print began to blur.

It was time to try to get some sleep.

I was standing in front of the night table — my hand poised to turn off the light — when my glance fell on the bed less than six inches away.

A sheet of white paper was pinned to the pillow. It contained a one-sentence message, neatly hand-printed in large block letters:

DROP THE TRENT INVESTIGATION
OR IT'S YOUR LAST!!

CHAPTER 29

I admit it. I looked under the bed.

Even while I was conducting a thorough search of the apartment, though, I was aware of how silly this was. Whoever had been here — and I really had no doubt as to the identity of the "whoever" — was long gone by now.

Still, I was uneasy. Suppose that, in retrospect, my visitor — Tony Pirrelli, of course; who else? — decided that I might ignore the advice with which he'd so thoughtfully provided me today. The man could then elect to pay another house call, this time to make a thousand percent sure I'd drop the investigation. But while I kept telling myself this was highly unlikely, the thing is, I don't always listen to what I have to say.

So before crawling into bed that night, I removed my .32-caliber security blanket from the lingerie drawer (which has been home to it for many years) and placed it on the night table — within easy reach. Although if it had ever come down to my actually having to pull the trigger — and for the first time ever, incidentally — I would probably have wound up shooting off my own big toe.

Sleep didn't come easily. It must have been past five before I finally dropped off. The escape hatch that had served me so well yesterday had evidently left the premises again.

I was brought back to consciousness by the telephone, on the other end of which was a disgustingly chipper Ellen.

"I didn't wake you, did I?"

I glanced at the clock: eleven ten. "That's okay. It's time to get up anyway."

"I'm really sorry, Aunt Dez. Go back to sleep; I'll talk to you later."

"I *said* it was time to get up, didn't I?" I retorted irritably. (I believe I've already mentioned that I'm not what you'd call a morning person.) Naturally, the instant the words were out, I regretted my tone.

But if Ellen was offended, it didn't show. "Barbados," she stated.

"Come again?"

"Barbados. That's where we'll be going on our honeymoon." And now she went on to tell me that these cousins of her friend Ginger's (a girl my niece almost unfailingly refers to as "Ginger, who lives in my building") had recently spent *their* honeymoon on Barbados and raved about the island. "Also, a nurse Mike works with vacationed there last year, and she absolutely loved the place," Ellen continued. "From what she told Mike, it sounds wonderful. Our travel agent thought we'd made a perfect choice."

"Whew! I'm glad that's settled. I was afraid that by the time you decided where you wanted to go, you wouldn't be able to get in anymore."

"Well, Mike and I just wanted to explore all the possibilities," a slightly defensive Ellen responded.

"*Mike* and I?"

She let loose with one of her inimitable giggles. "Okay, *me*. But it's a big decision, right? How many honeymoons does a person get to go on?" And here, without so much as a second's pause, she switched topics. "What's been happening at work? Any new cases lately?"

Now, normally when I take on an investigation Ellen's among the first to hear about it. Lately, though, she'd been so caught up in her wedding plans — and, more specifically, the honeymoon arrangements — that the subject just never came up.

"Nothing too interesting," I responded. I mean, how would I even begin to fill her in on my latest undertaking?

I didn't dare tell her about the note, of course. And only partially to spare her the worry. Listen, Ellen being Ellen, it was a virtual certainty that she would have badgered me mercilessly to come and stay with her until the killer was removed from society. And if, in my weakened mental state, I was persuaded to bunk with her for awhile, she'd have clucked over me to the point where, in a matter of days, I would have been certifiable. Even if I was able to impress upon her my need to stay in my own home, at the very least I could expect her to monitor me by phone every few hours to assure herself that I was still drawing a breath. Also not exactly easy on the nerves.

At any rate, as soon as Ellen and I said our good-byes, I threw on some clothes and shoveled down a bowl of Cheerios. Then I got out the Yellow Pages, where I found a listing for a locksmith located only a few blocks from my building. I told him my apartment had been broken into and that I needed him to install a new lock for me as soon as possible.

"No problem. I'll be there Monday morning, eight a.m. sharp."

"But in the meantime the intruder could decide to come back," I whined.

"Nah, I don't think so. But if you wanna feel more secure, stick something heavy up against the door."

"Look, I'm terribly nervous about this. Could you possibly make it sometime today?"

"*Today?* You gotta be kiddin'. You wouldn't even ask if you knew how busy I am. And tonight's the wife's birthday — she just turned fifty." (I was sure the woman would be delighted to know how reticent he was about sharing this information.) "Anyway, I gotta get home on time. I'm taking her to dinner at this Eyetalian restaurant called Felidia's — the wife loves Eyetalian food. You ever been?"

"No, but I hear it's terrific."

"It better be, at those prices," he grumbled.

"Listen, if you could possibly find a way to get here this afternoon, I would really appreciate it." And then I hurriedly added, "I'd be happy to pay you extra for your trouble."

It seems I'd said the magic words. "We-ll, seein' you're so upset and all, I suppose I *could* postpone my two o'clock appointment until Monday. That one didn't sound like no emergency to me."

★ ★ ★

The phone rang at a few minutes past two. "Hi, Desiree. It's Vicky. I'm just, like, checking in again, you know?"

She didn't have to identify herself. If the voice hadn't told me who it was — which it did — the "like" and "you know" would have done the trick.

"Anything, like, happening with the investigation?"

For all of a second or two I wondered how much I should reveal at this juncture. I certainly had no intention of telling her about the threatening note, and I concluded that it might not be such a great idea to pass along her stepfather's lack of an alibi, either. I didn't want to give her any reason for a premature celebration. Besides, I thought it best to keep this fact to myself until I nailed down precisely what my next step would be. So I responded with a simple, "I'm afraid not."

"Well, then, why don't *you* ask *me* if there's anything's new?" She was suspiciously upbeat.

"Okay, Vicky, I'm asking."

"For starters, my mom's totally furious with her precious husband — things have been pretty weird between them for over a week now. Anyhow, the other night I heard them yelling at each other. She wanted to know why, if his intentions were so honorable, Uncle Tony never said anything about his being the one who got my dad to, like, take a plea." There was a moment's hesitation before she put to me, a bit of an edge to her tone now, "I found out you were the one who told her about that, Desiree. Why didn't you ever mention it to me?"

"Because the man might actually have had your father's welfare at heart, but I was positive there was no way you'd allow for that. As for giving your mother the information, I was under the mistaken impression she was already aware of it."

"Well, I still don't think it was right. After all, I *am* your client. But, anyhow, Uncle Tony claimed that he'd had it with, you know, going over the same thing with my mom day after day but that he'd say it once more: He did what he considered to be best for his brother. He insisted that the reason he kept it to himself was because he was, like, concerned she'd misinterpret things, that she might take it as an attempt to get rid of the competition. Those weren't the exact words, but that was the gist of it. And then *she* said she didn't know *what* to think anymore. That was all

I heard, because Uncle Tony told mom to lower her voice, and they, like, started to talk more quietly from then on.

"But listen to this. The next morning, while we were, you know, having breakfast, my grandmom telephoned Uncle Tony. And guess what. Grandmom knew about the sentencing thing, too." Again, it was obvious the girl felt that I'd left her out of the loop.

"She didn't learn about it from me, Vicky," I interjected hurriedly.

A pause. "Okay. Maybe my mom said something to her. Anyhow, Uncle Tony picked up in the kitchen, and I, like, gathered from his side of the conversation that this was what it was about. Grandmom must have laced into him pretty good — you know? — because for a while there he could hardly get in a single word. And then he finally, like, semi-whispered into the phone that his only purpose in becoming involved with my dad's sentencing was to help him. 'That's something I shouldn't have to say — not to you,' I heard him tell Grandmom. Then, right after that, he decided to take the rest of the call in the den, and he asked my mom to hang up the kitchen phone. But when he came back about five minutes later, he was, like, all

263

red in the face, and he was carrying his briefcase. He glared at me and mumbled, 'You and that damned idiot you got yourself tied up with.' Uh, sorry, Desiree. Please don't let it bother you; he is *such* a jackass.

"Well, anyhow, he must have *really* been upset, because he left for work without finishing his breakfast. And the man's an absolute porker."

"How unusual was it for your grandmother to ream your stepfather out like that?"

"Oh, very." Vicky sounded positively gleeful. "I can't remember her even raising her voice to him before. He's always been, like, her favorite person in the whole universe."

It occurred to me then that, as things presently stood, it might not be too smart for Vicky to continue living in that house. After all, as a result of my investigation, Uncle Tony was now coming under attack by his nearest and dearest. And while I considered it highly improbable, I couldn't ignore the off chance that he might attempt to vent his anger on the person who had sicced me on him in the first place. "Listen, Vicky, is there any possibility of your moving in with a friend or relative for a while?"

"As of this morning I'm staying at Grandmom's — my mom insisted."

"Did she tell you why?"

"Oh, sure. She said she was going to have my bedroom painted."

"But you didn't believe her."

"My room had a paint job, like, a year and a half ago. She'll have it done again, though — you know? — just so I'll accept that this was the reason.

"But I don't really mind. Maybe it means that my mom is finally, like, wising up. Besides, Grandmom makes the best osso buco you've ever tasted."

"Well, it was probably wise for your mother to get you out of the house, Vicky. Not that I can say one way or the other whether your stepfather killed that girl. Or that, even if he did, you're in any danger. But why take chances?"

"Then you'd better be careful, too," Vicky responded soberly. "Uncle Tony's not, like, overly fond of you, you know?"

"Don't worry. I'll be fine." I managed to say it with conviction — while simultaneously checking my watch.

Where the hell is that locksmith anyway?

CHAPTER 30

I won't say I was nervous. But whenever I heard footsteps in the hall, my heart took a nosedive to my ankles.

That day — as I do every so often — I decided I never should have been a PI to begin with.

So how did it come about? you might ask. The truth is, I often ask myself the same question.

I suppose it was because when I was very young and very dopey this struck me as being a really exciting profession. Also, it gave me a kick just thinking about the reactions I'd provoke when I told people what I did for a living. To appreciate all the dropped jaws and bulging eyes my career choice inspired, you have to consider that this was back in the Dark Ages. (I was, of course, barely out of infancy.) And at the time, there weren't a whole lot of female private investigators around, not even celluloid versions. Plus, you have to take into account the short, round, and multidimpled torso I walk around in and then consider what the wonders of

Egyptian henna did for my hair. (All of which is not to say that I don't still generate those same "I can't believe it" looks today. Only maybe not as frequently.)

Anyway, for quite a while I handled mostly divorce and insurance cases, stuff like that. Plus, I tracked down my share of missing pets. So in those days pretty much the worst I had to fear was that some individual named Rover might be tempted to sample a chunk of my ankle, which never happened, or that some dyspeptic cat could elect to sharpen its claws on me, which did happen. Twice, in fact.

The closest I got to any real danger came through association. This was after I met my late husband, Ed, who was also a PI. You see, Ed was involved in the kind of investigations that — if you weren't careful — could land you face down in a dark alley one night. Not that this ever occurred. Maybe because, unfortunately, Ed wasn't around that long. We were married for only five years when he choked on a chicken bone and died. Sounds like a joke, doesn't it? But, believe me, there was nothing funny about it.

Anyway, somewhere along the line — this was a number of years after Ed was gone — I took on a murder case myself.

Then after that, another. And another . . .

But back to the afternoon following the break-in.

I reminded myself, rather unkindly, that I could be shopping up a storm at Bloomingdale's on this beautiful, sunshiny Saturday — if only I'd had the sense to stick to randy spouses and lousy drivers and furry little fugitives, none of whom actually intended me serious bodily harm. (In retrospect, both cat scratches were extremely superficial.) But no, I had to go and get the idea I was another Sam Spade. So here I sat on the living room sofa, dry-mouthed and all but immobile as I awaited my savior — a locksmith named Benny.

I deliberated whether to try to reach the man — it was already after three — but figured I'd hold off for a while. Then, just to assure myself that my limbs were still in working order, I got up and went into the kitchen for a glass of water. As soon as I plopped back down on the sofa, I lit into myself again.

Considering my profession, you'd assume I would know enough to properly secure my own apartment, wouldn't you? Listen, I have this acquaintance — also in my line of work — who's a whiz at breaking into places with his American Express card.

And more than once I myself had employed a hairpin to gain entry to someplace I hadn't been invited. Evidently, my own lock was, if you'll excuse the pun, similarly easy pickings.

Benny showed up for our two o'clock appointment at ten after four. But I was so grateful he showed up at all that I had to restrain myself from planting one right on his beefy, stubble-studded cheek.

He took one look at what I'd been relying on to safeguard myself and my property and began to cluck. Then he wagged a finger at me. "This here's a piece of garbage, lady. No wonder somebody got in. My three-year-old grandson wouldn't have no problem bustin' in here."

He recommended what he termed "the best," a lock he swore was absolutely pickproof, and I told him to go ahead and install it. After this he replaced the chain on the inside of the door with something shorter and stronger. When he left, my checking account was $306.45 lighter. But for the first time since spotting that warning on my pillow, so was my breathing.

Nick phoned at a little after five. *Damn! I should have called him today to find out how Derek was.* (I had to play the game, didn't I?)

"I wanted to say hi," he told me, "and to let you know that Derek feels really terrible about getting that mess all over you last night."

Yeah, I'll bet the little stinker's all broken up about it, I said to myself. What I said to Nick, however, was heavily edited. "I was just about to dial *your* number, honestly; I came home only a few minutes ago. How's Derek's upset stomach?"

"Gone. I fixed him some tea as soon as we got upstairs, and apparently it helped."

"Oh, that's good. Look, please tell him not to give the accident another thought; those things happen. And will you let him know again how sorry I am about losing my temper that way? I still can't believe I —"

Nick spared me any more helpings of crow. "Hey," he said, chuckling, "I'm not so sure that if Derek had christened my clothes like that, I wouldn't have called him a little bastard, too. And he's my own son. Seriously, though, I hope you've already brought that suit to the cleaners."

"Not yet."

"Well, don't wait too long, okay? You wouldn't want the stains to set."

"I'll take it in sometime this week." I

270

didn't add that since around midnight yesterday I'd been too preoccupied with the state of my own mortality to give much thought to the condition of my apparel. I mean, things with Nick were already complicated enough without laying that intruder business on him, too. Besides, I wasn't in a big hurry to have the dry cleaner verify something I was pretty certain of already: that little Derek had done irreparable harm to one of my favorite outfits.

"I expect you to give me the cleaning bill, of course," Nick said then.

"Absolutely not."

"I insist. Listen, he's my child, and it's my responsibility."

"We'll talk about it another time."

"I mean it, Dez, so don't argue. Anyway, there's another reason I called. I'd like to take you to dinner Wednesday evening, if you're free."

"It so happens you're in luck."

"Eight fifteen okay?"

"Perfect."

"Oh, by the way, it won't be necessary for you to wear overalls or anything. Derek won't be joining us."

Replacing the receiver in its cradle, I felt really, *really* good.

It wasn't merely because I wouldn't have to put up with Derek on Wednesday. (Although had I occupied a more athletic body I would have turned cartwheels over this alone.) Similarly, my mood had little to do with Nick's concern about my defiled clothing. (Although, clearly, this was another indication of the man's considerate and caring nature.) The main reason I was now bordering on euphoric was that Nick evidently hadn't had any second thoughts with regard to my cursing out his beloved offspring.

Maybe we stood a chance of developing a solid relationship after all. That is, if there was some way I could avoid being in Derek's company again — at least for the foreseeable future.

I made a silent plea: *Please, Tiffany. Come home and retrieve your kid.*

CHAPTER 31

I had no intention of tossing away my shingle. If I'd had a shingle to toss, that is. After all, what kind of a PI would I be if the instant somebody pinned a threat on my pillow, I threw in the towel and got a job at Taco Bell?

A living one, my inner voice retorted.

I ignored it.

I also didn't have the slightest desire to return to the type of practice I used to have — this afternoon's bellyaching to the contrary. To be honest, it's very satisfying to be instrumental in bringing one of the bad guys to justice — a feeling I just didn't experience when, say, I located Elvin Blaustein's pet boa constrictor. And it wouldn't have made any difference, either, if that case had had a happier ending. (Unfortunately, the creature had crawled into the radiator and ended up in the building's heating system. By the time I located him — her? — the thing had gone to its Maker.)

Aside from the personal gratification I

derive from solving serious crimes, though, I had taken on this particular job in order to help a young girl clear her father's name — hopefully. And I had an obligation to fulfill.

At any rate, thanks to Benny's pickproof lock, I no longer considered making a dash for the closet at the smallest sound. And right after dinner I was even composed enough to tackle the enormous dilemma of how to move along my investigation into the death of Christina Trent.

In spite of Tony's little love note, I hadn't deviated from my intention of inducing his wife and mother to meet with me again. (Actually, it was about all I had to work with.)

But even if they agreed to see me — what then?

Let's say I asked if they knew how Tony had spent the evening of the murder. To begin with, the very fact that I had the effrontery (from their point of view) to make that sort of inquiry could result in my head's being handed to me. Sure, right now the two Mrs. Pirrellis were furious at the man's secrecy with respect to his role in the plea bargain, and apparently they had grave doubts as to his motive. Maybe, too — especially in the mother's case —

Victor's death was attributed to his incarceration. (Although he almost certainly would have wound up behind bars even without his brother's assistance.) Nevertheless, it didn't figure that either Mary or Philomena would be very tolerant of some stranger's insinuating that their Tony could be a killer. Regardless of whether, deep down, one or both of them harbored this same suspicion herself.

On the other hand, however, suppose one of the ladies was willing — and able — to account for Tony's whereabouts. Wouldn't *that* be just dandy? I mean, I'd have to go and dig up another likely murderer. No problem, right?

Still, I couldn't *not* attempt to determine, once and for all, whether there was any possibility that Tony Pirrelli had committed the crime.

The sticking point, though, was that it wasn't enough to hope that he wouldn't be furnished with an alibi. I had to also hope that in the course of our talk — and how's this for pie in the sky thinking? — one of the women would inadvertently provide me with some small but crucial piece of information. Information that would enable me to establish that Tony had done away with his brother's lover. Hell, at this juncture

I couldn't swear that Tony had even been aware that this lover existed.

Well, I'd have to figure out a way to get these ladies to open up — and then cross my fingers that they had something worth opening up *about*. And right now my mind was a complete blank. I tried to keep from feeling discouraged, reminding myself that I'd been in this kind of situation before and that I usually managed to devise a strategy that enabled me to get to the bottom of whatever mess I was faced with. But this time I wasn't exactly optimistic.

At any rate, all I'd accomplished tonight was to saddle myself with another one of my Extra-Strength Tylenol headaches. And at around ten o'clock I pulled a Scarlet O'Hara.

I'd think about it tomorrow.

The one thing you can be sure of is that you can never be sure of anything.

The following day — Sunday — I made no attempt to come up with that strategy for interviewing Mary and Philomena. Because, as it turned out, there was no longer any reason for it.

It was a couple of minutes past eleven a.m., as I was buttering my corn muffin, that the phone rang.

"Ms. Shapiro?" a woman inquired tentatively.

"Speaking."

"This is Carmela Thomas. I hope you don't mind my contacting you at home."

"No, not at all," I assured her.

"I just didn't feel I could wait until Monday to unburden my conscience, so I looked up your residence in the telephone book. You see, I lied to you the other evening."

I'd been standing at the kitchen counter when the call came in, and now I had to grab a chair before my knees gave out completely. "You lied?" I said in a voice that sounded strange to my ears. (Maybe this was because my tongue seemed to be malfunctioning.)

There was an embarrassed little titter. "They say that hell hath no fury like a woman scorned. And they're absolutely right — whoever *they* are. At any rate, Tony and I were together at the time of the murder."

I was so devastated that for two or three seconds I had difficulty getting the words out. "Would you mind telling me where the two of you were that night?" I finally put to her.

"At a dinner in Manhattan. A presidential

fund-raiser. There were probably any number of people at the affair who would be able to vouch for Tony's presence. I can provide you with a few names, so you can check it out if you like."

I didn't doubt her truthfulness. But I felt I'd be remiss if I neglected to confirm the information. "I suppose it would be a good idea to have them — for my records."

Carmela mentioned a well-known society couple and some banker from New Jersey. "Oh, and there was also the poor woman who became Victor's defense lawyer. She'd certainly remember Tony's being there. That was where they first met. Now, what was her name again . . . ?"

"Blossom Goody."

"Yes, that's it."

"Why did you refer to her as 'the poor woman'?"

"Did I say that? I suppose it just slipped out. She was there with her then-husband — he's also an attorney. I called her a 'poor woman' because, from what I understand, the husband ran off with his twenty-five-year-old secretary a few months later, and it took quite a toll on Blossom."

"The bastard." As in Carmela's case, it just slipped out.

"Amen. But from what I saw of him,

Blossom didn't lose very much — although she evidently didn't perceive it that way. The fact of the matter, however, is that the man was a real loudmouth. Even worse, he was an outrageous flirt — to the extent where it had to be terribly humiliating for Blossom. He behaved as if he thought no female could resist him, and take my word for it, he was no Mel Gibson."

Well, in spite of her having fallen for someone like Tony Pirrelli — something that was pretty difficult for me to comprehend — it appeared that Carmela wasn't totally devoid of taste after all. "And the breakup really affected Blossom?"

"A mutual acquaintance told me that she went to pieces afterward. She started to drink. Eventually she even had to give up her job — and it was at a very prestigious law firm, too."

Of course! It should have occurred to me before. It just wasn't feasible that someone like Tony would want someone like Blossom to represent a member of his family. I mean, forget about how he might have felt toward his brother. The real issue was, what would people think? But since the Blossom I met with wasn't the same Blossom Tony chose as Victor's counsel, it made some sense. "That's too bad.

Blossom seems to be doing okay now, though," I informed Carmela. "She has her own practice."

"I'm glad to hear it."

"I appreciate your coming forward like this," I said then. (But I can't claim that, at this moment, I actually meant it.)

"I had no choice. I haven't been able to sleep since denying to you that I'd been with Tony when that girl was killed. But your call presented me with an opportunity, and . . . well . . . I'm afraid I took it. I cringe at admitting this, but the truth is, I still haven't forgiven him for . . . um . . . I can't seem to find a euphemism for it . . . for dumping me for another woman. And his brother's wife, at that! Not even five minutes after you and I hung up, however, I realized how foolishly — how *inexcusably* — I'd acted. I should have gotten back to you at once, but I was so ashamed of myself that it took a while for me to work up to it."

Carmela seemed to be waiting for me to say something now, so I did. "I can appreciate why you were . . . less than truthful. I can't swear that, given the same circumstances, I wouldn't have done the same thing myself."

"Don't misunderstand me," she was

quick to assert. "It's not that I've continued to carry a torch for Tony — I got past that long ago. It's just that he brought a great deal of pain into my life, and I was suddenly in a position to perhaps disrupt *his* life a little."

It was at this point that I rallied. I wouldn't — I *couldn't* — let my only surviving suspect be wrenched from my grasp like this. Not until I determined positively that I had no choice. "Just one question, if you don't mind, Ms. Thomas."

"Please. Go ahead."

"You were with Mr. Pirrelli that entire evening?"

"He wasn't out of my sight for more than ten or fifteen minutes at a clip."

"And you left — when?"

"It must have been a little after midnight." Then, anticipating what might come next: "We went home together, Ms. Shapiro. Tony spent the night at my place."

So that was that.

"I thank you for getting in touch with me and straightening things out," I said with as much sincerity as I was able to muster.

"No thanks are required. It occurred to me that my lie could conceivably lead to Tony's being arrested for murder. Well, maybe that's somewhat far-fetched. But, at the very least, it might cause him some serious trouble. And I certainly didn't want to be responsible for anything like that."

Which, being I'm a true Scorpio, I considered very charitable of her.

CHAPTER 32

Of course, I'd call Blossom Goody tomorrow to verify Carmela Thomas's devastating information. But I held out almost no hope that I'd wind up with a smile on my face.

In the meantime, I spent most of Sunday alternating between an attempt to conjure up a few entries for my blank suspect list and just moping around. For a while, though, the former wasn't any more productive than the latter. I mean, the guilty party could be someone I didn't even know existed. And how do you deal with a thing like that?

At last I latched onto some new, less nebulous candidates. (Which, I suppose, is what happens when you've got desperation spurring you on.)

Anyhow, would you believe Christina's sister? How about her best friend? Listen, who could say for sure that those relationships were as loving as I'd been led to believe?

But the thing is, if Christina Trent had been having a problem with one of those two, it would no doubt have been very much on her mind. And it's likely she would have confided in someone else who was close to her. If the difficulty was with Alicia, for example, wouldn't she have unloaded to Lainie — who was practically a *second* sister to her? And this would hold true in reverse — I mean, if it was Lainie who was in disfavor. Yet neither of these ladies appeared to be aware of any rift concerning Christina and the other one.

It's also likely the victim would have disclosed the falling out to her boyfriend. But Victor didn't mention either name to his daughter when she asked him to speculate about who might have murdered his lover.

Still, I could come up with a couple of explanations as to why something of this nature — if it did occur — never came to light. Possibly the deceased had been really tight-lipped. Or if she did unburden herself to someone, her confidante could have failed to appreciate the seriousness of the breach and, therefore, neglected to pass it on.

In spite of this rationale, however, I have to concede that it was a strain to picture Christina Trent's sibling or her best buddy wielding the knife that killed her.

Then, for some reason, Jamie Bracken — who was the super's son in those days — popped into my head. And I immediately began to prime him for what had been George Gladstone's starring role in my crime of passion theory. After all, I had only Jamie's word that he'd been out that night.

Look, suppose he was aware of the commotion upstairs and went to Christina's apartment to check things out. By the time he gets up there, though, the girl is alone. Now, Jamie's had this terrible crush on Christina all along (according to my scenario, anyway), and he makes a pass at her. And — Breaking off, I had to laugh at myself — only it really wasn't funny. I wasn't even sure Jamie was a "he," for God's sake!

Why don't you just drag people in off the streets and accuse them of the crime? I thought disgustedly. I mean, talk about grasping at straws! But then my more practical side provided me with a reminder: What else did I have?

I'd phone Alicia tomorrow to find out if she was aware of any ill feelings between her sister and Lainie. After which I'd ask Lainie the same thing about Christina and Alicia. And regardless of how these conversations panned out, I'd pay another visit to Jamie. Plus, I'd start re-interviewing Christina Trent's fellow tenants. Perhaps some of them had held out on me, and I could manage to be more persuasive when I spoke to them again. Or perhaps I simply hadn't posed the right questions. I could also try to locate some of the people who'd moved out of the building in the ten years following the killing.

Forget whether any of the avenues I was preparing to explore were likely to yield results. For now it was enough to know that — as unpromising as they were — they were *there*.

Ellen called around ten o'clock that evening.

"Are you free for dinner tomorrow night?"

I hesitated. On the one hand, I was anxious to pursue the new activities I'd mapped out for myself earlier. On the other, I could use some stress-free time with loved ones.

Stress-free won out.

"Let me check my social calendar," I said. It didn't take long. "Yes, I am. It seems that Nan Kempner was forced to cancel our reservation at the Four Seasons."

"Who?" Obviously, my niece does not read the society columns.

"Never mind," I told her.

"Oh, okay. What time? Mike and I both have the day off, so whenever you can make it is fine."

"How is seven thirty?"

"Perfect. And by the way, Aunt Dez, don't expect Chinese food this time."

I should explain a couple of things. Ellen manages to prepare a very tasty breakfast. But for some reason that I will never be able to fathom, this is the extent of her culinary talents. I mean, once evening rolls around, my niece's kitchen skills are pretty much restricted to the speed with which she opens the takeout containers from her favorite restaurant. Anyhow, I couldn't believe that those little white Mandarin Joy cartons wouldn't be decorating her kitchen counter on Monday. I mean, I've always been in terrible fear that Ellen would starve if that place should ever move out of the neighborhood — or, God forbid, go belly-up. At any rate, my curiosity refused to allow me to wait a day to be satisfied. "Can you give me a clue as to what kind of menu you've planned?"

"Oh, sure. We're having roast turkey and green beans with almonds and pecan pie and . . . well, you'll see tomorrow." She said this off-handedly, as if it were the most natural thing in the world for her to serve something other than Chinese takeout.

"You ordered from a deli," I accused.

"You'd better hope Helen and Li Chang don't find out. They might never forgive you."

Ellen laughed. "I did not order from a deli — or anyplace else."

I almost fell off the couch. "What can I bring?"

"That sweet potato thingy you make would be lovely," Ellen said timidly.

"You've got it."

"Great. But, listen, if you're too busy, we'll just bake a couple of potatoes and —"

"It's no problem," I assured her.

"Are you positive?"

"I'm positive."

"Because if there *is* a problem —"

Now, as much as I love my niece, on occasion I could be tempted to place my hands around that swanlike neck of hers and squeeze. "I'll be bringing the 'sweet potato thingy,' " I practically hissed.

"All right. If you're sure." And then: "How's work?"

"You don't want to know," I grumbled.

"Yes, I do. Tell me. Are you involved in a difficult case?"

"I'll fill you in when I come over."

"Well . . . okay. But, listen, Aunt Dez. Whatever the problem is, you'll handle it," Ellen pronounced firmly. "I know you will."

Her faith in me was so touching that I hated myself for that impulse to strangle her only a minute earlier.

But then, before hanging up, she added, "Are you *really* sure you have time to make that casserole?"

And my hands started itching again.

CHAPTER 33

It was exactly 9:33 (according to the digital clock on my nightstand) when I phoned Jackie Monday morning to tell her not to expect me that day.

"Are you feeling okay?" she said sharply.

"I'm fine. It's just that I have a couple of things to take care of at home, so I thought I might as well stay put and work here."

"Is that the truth?"

It was as if I were being interrogated by Ellen all over again. (And Ellen and Jackie really have nothing in common — except for the fact that they're both top-notch practitioners of the not-so-gentle art of nagging.) I gritted my teeth.

Jackie, however, was unperturbed by this lack of a verbal response. "I noticed that you haven't been looking too good lately, Dez," she was considerate enough to let me know.

I kept the "thanks a lot" to myself.

"Could be you're coming down with something — you do catch cold pretty often. And going all the way out to Pennsylvania probably didn't help."

I couldn't believe it! That was more than a week ago! Besides, this was a pleasant, two-hour train ride to Philadelphia she was talking about. I mean, it wasn't as if I'd dragged my butt halfway across the world to, say, Uzbekistan. Plus, I do *not* catch cold very often at all. "Please take my word for it. I'm perfectly okay," I maintained with the last scrap of patience I could dredge up.

"Really?" But, once again, Jackie didn't hold out for a reply. "Well, if you're sure . . ." she added, thus sparing her eardrums from the shrill scream that was, at that moment, poised to leave my throat.

At just before ten I attempted to contact Blossom Goody.

"I'm sorry, but Ms. Goody was . . . um . . . detained this morning. She'll be in around noon."

Detained, my patootie! Blossom needed to find herself a secretary who could lie with more conviction.

"May I take a message for her?" the woman inquired hopefully.

"That's okay, thanks. I'll call later."

I hung up, saddened. Poor Blossom. She might have sobered up, but as she herself had put it, they (meaning clients) weren't exactly lining up at her door. Evidently she hadn't even rebuilt her practice to the extent that it warranted her showing up at the office during normal business hours. "Men," I muttered in honor of the person responsible for Blossom's decline — the louse who'd thrown her over for some chippy who was barely out of diapers.

At any rate, I had my breakfast, after which I got into some clothes and smeared on a little lipstick so as not to frighten children and other living things. Then I went shopping for the few items I needed for what Ellen refers to as the "sweet potato thingy."

As soon as I came home I put the potatoes up to bake, and while they were in the oven I tried Alicia Schnabel's office. I was informed that Ms. Schnabel was with a client and wouldn't be returning that day. It was suggested I contact her the following morning.

Well, I'd speak to Lainie first, then. I checked my file for the phone number of Lady Fingers and had actually dialed the first two digits when I changed my mind. Lainie, too, could hold until tomorrow.

At twelve thirty I figured it was time to take another stab at Blossom Goody.

Blossom herself picked up the telephone. "Goody speaking."

"This is Desiree Shapiro, Mrs. Goody. I'm —"

"For Christ's sake, hold your water until I get out of my coat." And she slammed the receiver down on something hard, most likely her desk.

"So what's up, Shapiro?" she asked about two minutes later. "You find the *real* killer yet?"

I ignored the question — along with the sarcasm. "Uh, I'm preparing a report on my investigation, Mrs. Goody — for my files. And I want to make certain I have everything straight. I wonder if you'd mind verifying a couple of points for me."

"Depends. What do you" — a pause — "want to know?" I was reasonably certain Blossom was at that instant popping one of her ever-present cigarettes into her mouth. Almost at once this was pretty much confirmed by a slight scraping sound — like a match being struck.

"You were brought in as Victor Pirrelli's attorney by his brother?" I began.

"Yeah, that's right." And she snorted. (Apparently this was her version of a laugh.) "Met Tony the night of the murder, as a matter of fact — how's that for timing?"

"Um, where exactly was this?"

There was a hint of suspicion in Blossom's voice. "What the hell difference does it make?"

"I'm just curious, that's all."

"At a dinner, if you must know. A fundraiser."

"Uh, Mr. Pirrelli . . . he was at this fundraiser the entire evening?"

Blossom didn't respond immediately. And when she did, her tone was even more disagreeable than usual. (And perky she'd never been.) "Listen, Shapiro, I don't like being jerked around, got it? If you're under the impression Tony might've had something to do with what happened to that girl and you want to find out if I can alibi him, why the hell can't you say so?" And now she began to cough. It was a cough so wrenching that, listening to her gasp like that, I had some momentary trouble with my own breathing.

"You're absolutely right," I agreed when she was all coughed out. "And I'm really sorry; I should have leveled with you. But I was concerned about what your reaction might be."

"Would you like me to tell you? I'd have thought your brain was off on vacation. Which is what I think now. I can't, for the life of me, figure out how you could suspect that Tony Pirrelli had any part in the death of his brother's little side dish. What's more, I can vouch for his being at that dinner at the time of the stabbing — we were at the same table. In other words, Shapiro, I'm in a position to *know* that your theory's a load of crap."

Now, while I'm practically an expert at controlling myself when I'm probing for information, I had reached my limit. I mean, there is only so much Blossom a person can take. "Listen," I shot back, seething, "even if Tony didn't kill Christina Trent, this doesn't rule out the fact that he had a damn good motive for —"

My retort actually seemed to chasten the woman. "Oh, don't go getting all sensitive on me," she protested, interrupting the outburst. (And I was just warming up, too.) "I was under the impression you realized I was harmless, that I have a tendency to . . . to . . . Let's put it that what I lack in stature I make up for in mouth."

This being as close to an apology as I could expect from Blossom, I figured it might be safe to try another question. "You, uh, wouldn't have any idea when Tony left the affair, would you?"

"Christ, Shapiro!" she groused, but good-naturedly for once. "You don't give up, do you? But as it happens, I can answer that one for you, too. I noticed him and his girlfriend at the door, just as my husb— just as I was saying my good-byes. Which was around twelve, maybe a couple of minutes past."

I was in the process of digesting this when she inquired, "Anything else on your mind?" I didn't detect so much as a trace of sarcasm, either.

"I guess that about does it. Thanks a lot, Mrs. Goody," I said, trying to sound grateful to her for telling me what I'd been dreading to hear. "You've been a big help."

"Yeah, well, that's me all over: mother's little helper."

CHAPTER 34

I was close to a half hour late in getting to Ellen's. For this, I could thank a cheerful young taxi driver who was probably from somewhere in the Middle East and whose familiarity with the English language was apparently too limited to include the words "I don't understand." Or "How do I get there?" Or any variation thereof. And the thing is, since I was kind of preoccupied, it took a while before I realized we weren't headed in the right direction. Then it required another few minutes to communicate that West Nineteenth Street is *down*town from East Eighty-second. And even when we were finally southbound, the man proceeded to make two more wrong turns.

But what really set my teeth on edge was that every so often he'd look back over his shoulder and, with this beaming smile, attempt to engage me in a little pleasant conversation. One time it was "Is nice night, huh, lady?" And not long afterward: "Your hair, she is *beyootiful*," (I cringed at this reminder of my nine-year-old nemesis.) "Is natural — the color?" It was only two or three minutes later that he came out with "You got huzbond?" — on this occasion barely missing a parked car.

I still consider it a minor miracle that I reached Ellen's place with all my parts intact.

Mike — Ellen's almost-husband — opened the door to the apartment and promptly bent his six-feet-plus frame in half to enable me to plant a kiss on his cheek. Then I put the sweet potato casserole on the coffee table so my niece and I could exchange hugs. Which we did with so much enthusiasm you'd have thought we hadn't gotten together in years. And, actually, not more than two and a half weeks ago we'd met for lunch about midway between Macy's, where Ellen works — which is on Manhattan's west side — and my office — which is across town, on the east side.

Anyway, seeing those two together, I was all smiles. They are *such* an attractive couple.

Ellen is five-six and slender — about the width of a pencil. She has large, dark eyes, silky brown hair, and a positively dazzling smile. In case you're interested, the girl happens to be the spitting image of the late Audrey Hepburn. Okay, maybe I'm exaggerating a bit. But no one can tell me there isn't a definite resemblance.

As for Mike, he's a very nice-looking guy. I've already mentioned that he didn't get cheated in the height department. Well, to fill in the picture a little, there's also a lean physique, sandy hair, and clear blue eyes — all of which go together very nicely.

They were both in jeans tonight, with my niece also wearing an extremely becoming yellow knit tunic.

Anyway, while Ellen went to heat up my contribution to tonight's dinner, Mike poured the merlot. Then the three of us sat around for a while, sipping our wine and making selections from a cheese board that offered Brie and Jarlsberg, along with a good-sized wedge flavored with jalapeño peppers and another that was studded with pistachio nuts (this last becoming an instant weakness of mine). Grapes, slices of apple, and a variety of crackers surrounded the cheeses.

We talked for a time about how much Mike loved being at St. Gregory's and how fortunate he felt to be working under the hospital's top cardiovascular surgeon. "I can't tell you how much I admire that man," he said. "Not just for his technical skills, but for the way he is with his patients;

Dr. Beaver sincerely cares about them."

"Mike's like that himself — people matter to him, too," Ellen apprized me (as she had countless times before). In response to which her fiancé flushed.

"By the way, Dez," he brought up then, "has your niece informed you we've finally made our honeymoon plans?"

"I phoned her about that the other day," Ellen answered for me.

"Bet you didn't think we'd ever get around to it," Mike joked.

"Bet you're right."

He grinned. "Fooled ya!"

After this we discussed *The Sopranos*, *Sex and the City*, and cable TV in general. Ellen had just begun to sound off about a problem she'd had with a customer that week when the timer rang, and my two hosts hurried into the kitchen.

Mike was back first, carrying a large platter of sliced turkey, which he placed in the center of the folding table that had been set up in the living room. Ellen marched in right behind him with a green-bean-and-almond casserole. And before long these two items were joined by cranberry sauce, gravy, mushroom stuffing, and cucumber salad.

"Good Lord, Ellen, this is a real feast!" I

exclaimed. Immediately following which I took my turn in the kitchen so I could put the finishing touches to the sweet potato casserole. (Ellen's kitchen, like my own, won't accommodate three people at once — not unless you're willing to knock down a couple of walls.)

"I can't get over this," I marveled about five minutes later, as I added my dish to the rest of the bounty. "Everything looks wonderful, too."

"Thank you," Ellen murmured modestly.

"And you honestly didn't order in?" It was difficult for me to accept that my niece's two little hands were responsible for a spread like this.

"Gee, thanks. You have a lot of faith in me, don't you?" she snapped.

I would gladly have kicked myself — if something like that were humanly possible. The apology was already on my lips when Ellen began to giggle — as only she *can* giggle. I glanced at Mike, who was smiling broadly.

"We were at my parents' house for dinner on Friday," he explained. "It was my dad's birthday, and this is his favorite meal." He chuckled. "It's like they have two Thanksgivings there every year. Anyway, as usual, Mom kind of overdid it

— she really cooked up a storm. Believe me, there was enough to feed a dozen sumo wrestlers. So I let her twist my arm and send a good portion of what was left home with us."

"The only thing is," Ellen interjected, "his mom couldn't give us any of the candied yams — we polished them off that night." And now she quickly added — as befits a loyal niece — "but your sweet potato thingy is even better than her yams."

"Well, I'm not so sure of that," I said with what seemed to me the proper amount of humility. "Anyway, I thank you both for inviting me tonight."

"You always feed *us* so well that Ellen and I wanted to share our little banquet with you," said my nephew-to-be.

At this point Ellen giggled again. "I have a feeling you were really starting to believe that I prepared all of this. Am I right, Aunt Dez?"

"If a man can walk on the moon, anything is possible."

Happily, the subject of murder wasn't broached before the end of what was truly a marvelous dinner. In fact, not until we'd consumed the very last pecan in our scrumptious pecan pie (topped with your choice of Häagan Dazs Belgian chocolate or vanilla ice cream, no less).

"I only took a tiny sliver on Friday so there'd be some left over for now," Ellen had announced virtuously as she was serving the pie.

At any rate, it was Mike who finally brought up my investigation. "Ellen has the idea you've taken on a very difficult case."

"It's beyond *difficult,* Mike," I said disgustedly. "I'm looking into a homicide that took place a decade ago."

Mike whistled. And Ellen squealed, "A *decade* ago?"

"Yup. And I just learned that I'll have to backtrack and start almost from the beginning again. I'm not all that optimistic about getting anywhere, either."

"Care to tell us about it?" Mike asked tentatively.

"Actually, I do. Maybe it'll help me gain some perspective."

And so I launched into a synopsis of what had transpired over the last couple of weeks. In deference to Ellen's loving — and nervous — nature, however, I omitted any mention of the note and its consequence. And by consequence I mean that since receiving that tender little epistle, I made sure my .32 was never much farther than an arm's length away. (Tonight, for example, the weapon was nestled in my handbag, in the event that I should have an unfriendly encounter before returning to the sanctuary of my apartment — and Benny's pickproof lock.)

I concluded my soliloquy with the information that all four of my original suspects had airtight alibis for the time of the stabbing.

"Wow," Mike said, "that's quite an undertaking — investigating a crime that dates back so many years. But listen, Dez, are you that positive Victor Pirrelli didn't commit the murder?"

"I'm not comfortable using the word 'positive.' But the more I checked, the more likely it appeared that Victor Pirrelli had paid for another person's deed. Just consider this: Somebody waited about *a half hour* after all the shouting was over — waited, in fact, until Victor returned from that walk he took — before contacting the police. Why?"

"So he'd be found with the body," Ellen answered firmly.

"That's how I see it."

And from Mike: "But how could the killer know Victor would even be coming back?"

"Probably because Christina told him so."

Mike nodded. "And you're convinced the alibis of the four suspects are legitimate?"

"You be the judge.

"Jennifer Whyte — she's the one with the smarmy boyfriend — wasn't even around at the end of February, when Christina Trent was killed. She's a practical nurse, and she was in Lynne, Massachusetts, caring for a newborn child from February twentieth until sometime in early March — I don't remember the exact date."

"What about days off?" Mike inquired.

"I checked with the woman Jennifer worked for. She didn't *have* any days off."

"And the elderly man downstairs — what's his story?" This from Ellen.

"George Gladstone, too, was out of state then; he was on the West Coast. He showed me a receipt from a restaurant in Hollywood, California, stamped February twenty-eighth — the night of the murder. The time was also stamped on the slip. It was ten fifty p.m. out there, which would make it ten minutes to two in New York. And Christina was stabbed sometime between eleven and midnight."

Tilting her head to one side, Ellen looked at me quizzically. "The man kept this receipt for a *decade?*"

"For tax purposes — he's in public relations. He said he retains all that stuff for ten years — I understand a lot of people do."

"Oh."

"Which brings me to Mary, Victor's wife. Well, Philomena Pirrelli — she's Victor's mother — spent that night at Mary's home. She slept there. And she swears the woman never left the apartment."

"I don't suppose she could have been lying to protect her," Mike threw out.

"That's the last thing she would have done. After all, if she'd been able to implicate Mary, it could have absolved her son. Plus, Philomena absolutely despises her daughter-in-law, who, incidentally, is still her daughter-in-law — or maybe I should say is her daughter-in-law again. You see, Mary didn't waste a whole lot of time in unloading Victor, and then she turned around and married his older brother."

Ellen's eyes widened and Mike shook his head. "Well, at least she believes in keeping it in the family," he remarked with a bemused little smile.

"She certainly does. Now, as for Tony, Mary's present husband, he was at a presidential fund-raiser during the critical period. His then girlfriend verifies that he —"

I stopped dead.

Slowly — and at long last — the realization took root. I slapped the palm of my hand against my forehead.

How could I have been so stupid?

CHAPTER 35

Noting my expression, Ellen leaned across the table. "What's wrong?" she demanded, her voice unnaturally high-pitched.

"I have to leave." Which, in view of the meal I'd just packed away, was a lot more difficult than it sounds. For a minute there I thought it might require a crane to haul me to an upright position. But somehow I made it to my feet under my own steam. "I'm sorry. It was a fantastic dinner, and I should at least give you a hand with the dishes, but —"

"Aren't you feeling well, Dez?" Mike put in, starting to rise.

"Please. Don't get up. The truth is, all I'm feeling right now is stupid."

He obediently sat back down again. "I don't understand."

"Unless I'm very much mistaken, one of those 'airtight' alibis I referred to before has a hole in it. And it's my own damn fault — I'd been operating under an erroneous assumption. I have to go and check my notes to make certain that I finally have things straight."

"You'll let us know what's going on?" Ellen said.

"I'll call you as soon as I have anything substantial to report."

At the door, Mike admonished me. "I realize that in your profession dealing with killers is part of the territory, but you will be careful, won't you?"

My thoughts went immediately to the lethal little ally in my handbag, which these days was even more vital to my well-being than my makeup kit. "You don't have to worry about that."

This, of course, didn't do it for my niece. "You promise you won't take any unnecessary chances?"

I promised. And then, after some additional prodding from Ellen, I promised again.

The instant I got home — without even stopping to take off my coat — I grabbed the Pirrelli folder from my desk.

I read what Vicky had to say that day she came to my office. Then I skimmed through my notes until I located the interview with Philomena. It was there, all right, in black and white — the clue that should have hit me over the head. If I'd been empowered with a functioning brain, that is.

Lastly, I double-checked those portions of the file concerning my questioning of the four suspects.

Satisfied, I closed the folder.

Suddenly I was reminded of that wonderful old TV series *The Odd Couple*. In one episode Felix — or was it Oscar? . . . no, I'm sure it was Felix — lectures that when you "assume," it makes an "ass" out of "u" and "me." Something like that, anyway. *Boy*, I thought disgustedly, *was old Felix on the money.*

And here I cautioned myself. On the basis of that phony alibi, I was certainly justified in reinstating one of the names on my ridiculously fluid suspect list. But I had no business being so confident that this individual was Christina's killer. Especially in view of all the missteps I'd made in the past.

But I was. Confident, I mean.

CHAPTER 36

I called from home at ten o'clock on Tuesday morning, my hands so wet I could barely dial and my insides quivering like Jell-O.

What if my request for another meeting was refused? What if I didn't even get the opportunity to suggest one? I could almost hear the dreaded click in my ear — and nobody had lifted the receiver yet.

Then, on the fourth ring, George Gladstone answered the phone.

"Mr. Gladstone? This is Desiree Shapiro."

"Hold on a sec; I've got someone on the other line."

A sec, it wasn't. I must have hung on for almost ten minutes before he got back with me. "So what can I do for you this time, cupcake?" The sarcasm in his voice was about an inch thick.

"I need your advice, Mr. Gladstone. It appears —"

"Hey, what's with the 'Mr. Gladstone'? It's George, remember?"

"Er, yes, *George*. The thing is, a new fact has emerged and —"

"This is with regard to Christina Trent's murder, I'm guessing."

"That's right."

"And you'd like to come over here and discuss this new fact, correct?"

"I'd appreciate it. We can make it anytime that's convenient for you."

"You want to know what time is convenient for me? *No* time. You must be under the misconception that I'm in my dotage, that your pulling this 'new fact' craperoo on me before would have slipped my mind. Well, there's nothing wrong with my memory, little lady, and I'm not about to bite again." I was all set to jump in at this point when he added almost admiringly, "I'll say one thing for you, though: You've got chutzpah."

"I swear to you that I've just acquired some important information on the crime. And I thought you'd be interested in learning what it is."

"Why me, particularly?" George demanded, sounding suspicious.

"That's part of what I want to see you about. The other part being, as I told you, that I could use your advice."

"Forget it. What's that old saying? 'Fool me once, shame on you. Fool me twice, shame on me.' "

And now the phone did click in my ear.

I'd really figured there was a decent chance that George Gladstone — who had already shown himself to be a man with a generous helping of curiosity in his makeup — would be so anxious to find out what *I'd* found out that he wouldn't be able to resist our getting together.

But it seemed I'd been wrong.

I tried to console myself. It wasn't as if I'd reached the end of the line. I mean, there *were* alternate routes to the truth.

In fact I'd take another tack this morning and canvass the tenants in the building again — some of them must be home during the day. On this visit, however, I'd be posing a single question — one I hadn't asked before.

About an hour later I was more or less ready to face the world. I was in the process of slipping on my coat when the telephone rang.

"You win."

"George?"

"I just phoned your office; your secretary told me you wouldn't be in today," he grumbled, obviously perturbed at having to make a second call. "I've decided to go on the unlikely premise that there really is a goddam update. Which means you'll get another crack at me." He chuckled. (Cackled, really.) "As much as I despise myself for it, cupcake, it seems that I'm an old busybody after all. Understand this, though. I'm not *quite* foolish enough to believe you really want my advice on anything."

"But —"

George rode right over my attempt to protest. "I have something scheduled in Manhattan this afternoon at four thirty, and I'll allow you to take me to dinner afterward."

"My pleasure." I was so relieved I didn't even care that I wasn't on an expense account.

"Why don't you meet me at Daniel's at seven."

I gulped. While I've never broken bread there, just about everyone in New York has heard of Daniel's, one of the city's most famous and (they tell me) elegant restaurants. As you might expect, however, the prices are as haute as the cuisine.

"I'll take care of the reservation," George was saying.

"Uh, do you think there might be a problem getting a table for tonight?" I put to him, trying not to sound hopeful.

He scoffed at the notion. "Don't you

worry; I have my connections."

Well, so be it. After all, this was probably my one opportunity to confront the man. And it wasn't as if I'd have to fork over the cash immediately. Somehow I'd find the money to pay for our dinner by the time my American Express bill came in. (Although my pathetic bank account aside, Daniel's still didn't appear to be the ideal locale for extracting a confession from somebody.)

Moments later I was considering a couple of fund-raising ideas.

I could stand in front of Bloomingdale's in my oldest clothes, completely disguised, and beg for handouts. But it might be years before I collected enough for this evening's meal. Plus, there was always the chance that someone might recognize me. (With my luck, that someone would be Nick or, worse yet, Derek.)

I could sell my body. But how long would I have to wait to get any takers?

The phone rang as I was searching for a third, more realistic possibility.

"We'll have to forget Daniel's. I've got to head home after my appointment. A client of mine just phoned, and she insists on dropping by my office at six thirty. Which in her little pointed head translates to anywhere between seven and seven thirty. It shouldn't take long, though. So why don't you come over at eight?"

Thank you, God. "I'll be there," I told him.

CHAPTER 37

I was one giant goose bump.

It wasn't that I was afraid of being physically harmed (although adjectives like "brave" and "daring" have never been uttered in the same breath as "Desiree Shapiro"). I mean, it stood to reason that George wouldn't care to explain the presence of a dead body in his own apartment. And as for his moving my lifeless and well-padded torso to another location, I'd like to see him try it. The guy was a little pipsqueak, for heaven's sake!

My real fear, actually, was that I'd walk away from here tonight having accomplished absolutely zip. Which, I had to acknowledge, was an excellent possibility.

Still, as I pressed the buzzer to 1C I automatically patted my handbag, wherein lay my trusty and just-in-case .32.

The door swung open, and before I could move out of the way, I was practically upended by a buxom and heavily made-up blonde — I'm talking about a female who made Anna Nicole Smith look like the girl next door. Fortunately, however, while I tottered for a second, I was able to regain my balance. (See? There *is* something to be said for being built close to the ground.) "Sorry, doll," the blonde murmured through collagen-enhanced (I'm sure) lips. Then, turning to George, who stood in the doorway: "You *will* get my name in Page Six, won't you, Georgie?" she asked sweetly, the *New York Post*'s Page Six being where you find out which celebrity has been doing what to which other celebrity.

"Even if I have to murder you to accomplish it, cupcake," George responded amiably. This little joke was in particularly questionable taste, wouldn't you say? Since it appeared he'd already acquired bona fide credentials in that area.

At any rate, this other cupcake smiled uncertainly, then sashayed down the hall.

Once we were seated in his study — which, unbelievably, was dustier and more litter laden than during my previous visit — George plunged right in.

"Okay, I'm ready to be enlightened. So let's hear it. Exactly what is it you've learned?"

"It's really about a couple of things I finally realized."

"And just what would those be?"

I could feel my cheeks grow hot with embarrassment. "Um, when Victor Pirrelli's daughter first came to my office, she told me that the tragedy had taken place the night before her birthday — which was on March first. Well, it seems that somehow my overtaxed little brain translated this into Christina's having been fatally wounded on February twenty-eighth. And once I'd jumped to that conclusion, it stuck. But then a little more than a week ago I had a talk with Victor's mother, and she mentioned that in 1992 — the year her son got into his trouble is how she put it — William Jefferson Clinton was elected president."

George looked at me blankly. "So?"

"It took a while, but that's how I became aware of my mistake. During presidential election years there are twenty-nine — *not* twenty-eight — days in February."

I could almost see the lightbulb go on in the man's head. But he brazened it out. "And your point is — ?"

"That the restaurant slip you produced for me doesn't prove you were in California on the night of the stabbing."

"Hey, no one was attempting to put one over on you. I remember distinctly that you asked me about my whereabouts on the twenty-eighth, and I showed you a receipt confirming that I was in California then."

"You're right. I made an incredibly stupid error. Like I said, I just *assumed* . . . To set the record straight, though, would you mind telling me where you were on the *twenty-ninth?*"

"Here we go again. But all right, I'll play. I was still in California. As I informed you before, I didn't come home until the day *after* the murder."

"Do you happen to have any verification of that? Another receipt of some sort, maybe? Or how about your airline ticket stub? Or —"

Glowering, George cut me off. "I'm afraid you're going to have to take my word for it. This weekend I finally got around to purging my 1992 files."

How convenient! And was he kidding — take *his* word for it?

"Not," he made sure to put in, "that I have to prove a goddam thing to you."

Well, it didn't seem I had much choice. So I resorted to this little ploy I frequently press into service when fighting a losing battle — but which, admittedly, rarely does the trick. You never know, though — right? "I'm going to be honest with you," I lied.

"One of your neighbors has come forward, and this individual swears to having seen you in the building that day."

For perhaps two or three seconds George was plainly stunned. Then slowly, a smile spread over his face. "Oh, please," he said smugly. "You can think up a better bluff than that."

He was right about its not being a very good bluff. But, unfortunately, he was wrong about my ability to think up something better. I mean, if I could have, I would have.

I was struggling for some sort of response when I floored myself by suddenly blurting out, "Look, George, I know you were responsible for Christina Trent's death."

Now, I should mention here that — while I can't nail down exactly when it had occurred — sometime fairly recently I'd pretty much abandoned any hope of bringing Christina's assailant to justice. At present my one goal was to provide Vicky with evidence of Victor's innocence. And to that end, keeping the .32 company in my handbag at this moment was a tape recorder — and it was whirring away.

No, this wasn't why Vicky had come to see me; she was hiring me to clear her father's name, she'd said. But at this juncture I recognized that we'd both have to be satisfied with an admission from the real perpetrator — if I could inveigle one out of him, that is. At least it would erase any lingering doubts the girl might have with regard to Victor's involvement in the murder of his mistress. Doubts she would rather die than own up to, of course.

At any rate, George didn't so much as blink at my accusation; it was as if he hadn't even heard me.

"Look, I'm not a cop," I went on, "and I'm not interested in seeing you get sent to prison. Besides — and again I'm leveling with you" — (only this time I really meant it) — "I haven't been able to discover any tangible evidence to back up what I'm certain is a fact. The only thing I'm out to accomplish this evening is to persuade you that Victor's sixteen-year-old daughter has a right to the truth. Vicky Pirrelli is a lovely young girl, George, and she's been deprived of a father since Victor was arrested. By the way, that birthday she was about to celebrate? It was her sixth. Vicky grew up believing that her daddy was a killer. Think what it would mean to her if you were to confirm that he had nothing to do with the murder after all."

George shook his head from side to side.

Then he peered at me with an expression that could well have been grudging admiration. "You've really got brass ones, Desiree, you know that?"

"This would only be among the three of us," I persisted. "If you would just give me *something* I could pass on to Vicky . . . I mean, was it an accident? Did you have too much to drink? What really happened that night?"

He uttered a short, harsh laugh. "This is priceless! One thing I'd like you to tell me, though: By what misguided logic did you arrive at the ridiculous notion that it was George Gladstone who did the deed? And don't give me any more of your craperoo about some phantom tenant claiming I was back from the coast by then."

"You're the only person with a motive who doesn't have an alibi for that night," I said simply.

"*Motive?* What motive? I stuck a knife in that girl because she wouldn't have dinner with me? That's laughable! Christina's killer doesn't have to be either me *or* Victor Pirrelli. Did you ever stop to consider that she may have been stabbed to death by someone you've never even heard of?"

"You could be right." This reluctant admission was followed by silence, so it seemed as good a time as any to broach that other little matter I found so disturbing. "Incidentally, you must have been surprised to hear from me again."

"I wouldn't say *surprised. Irritated* would be more like it."

"Did you really think that threat would get me to drop the investigation?"

"What the hell are you talking about?"

"Are you denying you wrote me a threatening note and pinned it to my pillow?"

"Your *pillow!* When was the last time you asked this lonely old bachelor over for a home-cooked dinner, cupcake? And unless I really am in my dotage, you have yet to give me a key to your place. Listen, I've never set foot in your apartment, much less your bedroom." Then with a leer: "I'd venture to guess that somebody you're a lot more . . . shall we say *friendly* with . . . left you that message."

"I assure you that whoever was responsible was never invited to my home. And I don't go around handing out keys, either. He — or she — gained access by picking the lock."

"Well, get it out of your head that I'm your guy. I'll give you two reasons I wouldn't have done anything like that. One, I have nothing to hide, so as far as I'm concerned, you can investigate your little heart out. And two, I'm the laziest son of a bitch I know. Even if I were guilty as hell and determined to frighten you off, I wouldn't have gone to the trouble of breaking into your apartment. I'd have delivered that warning the easy way: by slipping it under your door."

"Not if you wanted it to have maximum effect," I pointed out. "To really scare the hell out of me by letting me know you could get to me where I live."

"I'd have settled for under the door regardless. As I said, I'm not one to exert myself."

At this moment George had me half-believing him — about the note, at least. "Well, it's possible I made a mistake. And if so, I apologize."

"You made *two* mistakes. I also didn't kill Christina Trent. About Pirrelli's daughter, though, I'm sorry I couldn't be of any help to you there. The truth is, underneath this crusty exterior is a very warm and fuzzy fellow — someone who actually happens to like kids, even teenagers. Only I don't like them enough to pretend I murdered somebody."

And now George got to his feet. "But listen," he suggested, a smirk on his face, "if you're that anxious to make things nice for little Vicky, why don't you just tell her *you* did it?"

CHAPTER 38

Driving home that evening, I got the feeling George really *was* innocent — but only of being the author of that chilling communication I'd found on my pillow.

Listen, Tony Pirrelli had pressured me to terminate my investigation even before all that wrath was heaped on him by both his wife and his mother. Well, how much more anxious he must be now to have this whole thing just disappear. He probably decided it would allow him to revert to being the adored husband and son he was prior to my entering his life. And it was conceivable, too, that he was right.

I had to put a question to myself, though. Could I really picture someone of the stature of this highly successful attorney breaking into an apartment? Damned right, I could. If Vicky's uncle/ stepfather was sufficiently motivated, I could envision him doing just about anything to accomplish his objective. I speculated then that he might have come over that night with the intention of threatening me in person again — only somewhat more forcefully this time. But on not finding me in, he had seized on a note as a still more effective way to deliver his warning. Anyhow, the longer I thought about it, the more I recognized that Tony, being the individual most impacted by my poking around, was also the one most determined to have me desist.

And, look, where was it written that the killer and the pillow pinner had to be one and the same person?

The first thing I did on entering my apartment was to play the messages on my answering machine. One was from my friend and next-door neighbor Barbara Gleason (we share a common wall), and the other was from Ellen. I got back to Barbara first, since this was likely to be the shorter phone call.

"I was hoping you'd come with me to the eight o'clock showing of *My Big Fat Greek Wedding*. Everyone keeps insisting I shouldn't miss it," she said. And then accusingly: "But since you weren't around, I wound up staying home. You *know* how I hate going to the movies alone."

"I was out on business. We can make it another time, though."

"Maybe," she responded tersely. Following which she added in a more generous tone: "Don't worry. I doubt if I would have enjoyed it. Sounds like it's a lot more your kind of film than mine." I figured the conversation was about over at this point when suddenly Barbara chuckled. "I just thought about how you insisted that that talking pig should have won the Oscar for best actor a few years ago."

Now, this was not precisely true. What I *thought* was that *Babe* deserved to win for best picture that year. And guess what. I still do.

Anyhow, a couple of minutes later I telephoned Ellen. Happily, the exchange was briefer than I'd anticipated.

She was calling to find out how I was, she told me. I assured her I was fine and inquired about the state of her health and Mike's. They, too, were fine. Then I thanked her again for the lovely dinner. And after this she asked if I'd been correct last night about one of the alibis not holding up. I had too much on my mind to go into any details at this juncture, so I said I was continuing to check into it. The call ended with Ellen's cautioning me to be very, very careful and, as usual, eliciting my promise — in duplicate — to this effect.

★ ★ ★

It was well past eleven when I sat myself down on the sofa to do some serious dissecting about tonight's get-together with George Gladstone.

While I had fervently hoped for some kind of admission from him, I wasn't exactly surprised that none had been forthcoming. Actually, I would have been more surprised if he'd owned up to his guilt. Not that the truth would have put him at risk, you understand. Even if it had been documented on my tape recorder (which, of course, George wasn't aware I was carrying), his confession wouldn't have meant diddly in the absence of evidence to back it up. Just think about all the crazies who confess to practically every major unsolved crime in the country. Plus, we're talking about a case the authorities had considered closed for more than a decade.

At any rate, my meeting with George certainly hadn't lessened my conviction that he'd murdered his young upstairs neighbor — not in the slightest. I was more confident than ever of his culpability.

For starters, the man could swear to high heaven that he'd merely extended a few harmless dinner invitations to the deceased. But I vividly remembered Alicia's remark that the way he looked at her sister used to give the girl the creeps.

And here's something else. George maintained that he was in California on the twenty-ninth. He wasn't able to substantiate this, though, because — according to him — he'd purged his 1992 expense file *that very weekend*. What a coincidence! And don't forget, this was a guy who lived in total disorder (I wish you could have seen his office!) and bragged, too, about what a lazy son of a bitch he was. I'd have bet my new Anne Klein silk blouse (acquired for sixty percent off at Bloomingdale's last month) that the file was still intact. And that it contained an airline ticket stub that could put a lie to George's claim of being across the country when Christina was killed.

Well, if I was right about his having returned to New York by then — and I was as close to certain as you can get — why try to hide it? I mean, assuming, naturally, that his feelings for Christina were as innocent as he portrayed them to be.

Moments later I contemplated my earlier visit with George — and the fact that he was the only one of my suspects who appeared to have difficulty recalling his whereabouts on the day Christina was killed. In retrospect I realized that right away this should have set off a little buzzer in my head. The thing is, most of us — fortunately — aren't touched by murder all that often. So if and when we are, it's apt to make a pretty indelible impression. I've heard I-don't-know-how-many-people say they can still pinpoint precisely what they were doing when President Kennedy was assassinated. And, in the strictest sense, this wasn't even a personal tragedy for these individuals. What's more, it occurred close to forty years ago. In the present instance, however, the victim was a girl just about everyone agreed George Gladstone was enamored with (except, that is, George Gladstone himself). So wouldn't you think he'd remember being in Hollywood or Hoboken or Timbuktu when the object of his lust was stabbed to death?

Finally, I examined the man's assertion that the murderer could be someone whose existence I wasn't aware of — a notion I had also wrestled with off and on. But while I can't say I was prepared to totally disregard the possibility of a Ms. or Mr. "X" having perpetrated the crime, after tonight's little tête-à-tête the likelihood seemed remote.

Of course, I'm the first to concede that

nothing I'd managed to uncover about George was *proof* of his guilt. But putting everything together, I had little doubt that I was barking up the right tree at last.

Still, if I should present my conclusion to my client — and without the support of any really tangible evidence — would she accept it? And would it be enough to satisfy her? (Keep in mind that I was not only unable to deliver what she'd hired me for, but I'd even failed in my attempted compromise: to induce the real killer to confess.)

Well, there was one last thing I hoped to accomplish before making my case to Vicky. I would do my utmost to at least establish that George had been in New York on February 29, 1992.

Now, I already knew how futile it would be to check out the airlines in order to establish the date of his return flight. You see, I'd been faced with a similar situation during the course of a prior investigation. At that time I was trying to obtain some information with regard to a trip that had been made seven years earlier. The records of most of the airlines I contacted, however, went back five years or less. Then, just when I was ready to call it quits, I came across an airline representative who actually said he might be able to help me. Only guess what. In addition to the name of the passenger and the date of travel, he would require *the flight number!*

And can you imagine how willing dear ole George would be to furnish me with *that?*

But there *was* another option. I'd begin ringing those doorbells again.

Yes, I recognized it was a long shot that anyone would recall seeing the man around that day. But you never can tell. Maybe — just maybe — I was about to get lucky.

CHAPTER 39

I was in Queens by eleven o'clock the following morning. While many of the building's occupants were undoubtedly at work at this time, I was anxious to put my one question to whoever was available.

I kicked off my canvassing with the Corey twins.

As soon as she saw me on the threshold, one of the women (I believe it was Rachel) wrapped her arms around me. "It's lovely —"

". . . to see you again," her sister (I believe it was Rosamond) finished for her as she, too, embraced me warmly.

I was touched by the welcome. Unfortunately, however, neither lady had the slightest idea whether George Gladstone had been in town on the day of the murder. "It was just so long ago," I was reminded.

I got pretty much the same response — only minus the hugs — from the five other residents who opened their doors to me that Wednesday. But I took heart in the knowledge that there were still twelve units to go — thirteen, counting Jamie's.

Actually, I was kind of glad to return to my apartment early. I was feeling a little drained, and this would give me a chance to relax before my dinner with Nick. Listen, I intended to be absolutely scintillating tonight — or, anyway, as close to scintillating as it was possible for me to get.

After a late lunch I turned on the television to watch a couple of afternoon judge shows — a fairly recent addiction and one I'm not often free to indulge. Then I treated myself to a long, luxurious bubble bath in Ivoire. I was in the process of choosing what to wear (for the third time since Nick had asked me out) when the phone rang.

"Hi, Dez," said a rather dispirited voice — *his* voice. "I hate to do this, but I'm afraid I have to postpone our date. I was really looking forward to it, too."

"Is something wrong?"

"Nothing serious — at least, I hope not. I just heard from Loretta, the woman who looks after Derek while I'm at work" — Nick owns a florist shop about six blocks from our mutual building. "She was calling to inform me that Derek's been throwing up since he got back from school this afternoon. Probably because he scarfed down one slice of pizza too many. But under the circumstances I'm just not comfortable leaving him with a sitter. It wouldn't be fair to you, either; I'm sure I'd be preoccupied all evening. Uh, you *do* understand?"

"Of course, I do. Please tell Derek I hope he feels better."

"I will. And that reminds me. When Loretta handed him the phone and I told him I'd be coming straight home, he had me promise to let you know how sorry he is about ruining our plans."

"That was very sweet of him." Somehow I was able to say it without gagging.

Throwing up, my whatchamacallit! Did Loretta actually see him toss his cookies?

Of course not! Derek's stomach was no doubt in A-1 condition. Certainly it was in a lot better shape than Nick's reasoning powers. I mean, didn't the man *get* it? One way or another, that little worm was determined to drum me out of his father's life. And it looked like he was succeeding, too.

Once again I pleaded with the absent Tiffany (my personal candidate for "mother of the year"): *Come home, lady, and pick up your damn kid.*

Now, immediately following Nick's call,

I had nothing more challenging in mind for the rest of the evening than to sit around cursing out a nine-year-old. But after about fifteen minutes of this, I figured I might as well use the unexpected free time for something slightly more productive. So I made up my face and got into some clothes, breaking any previous speed record in this regard, I might add.

It was still early — only a few minutes to eight — when I arrived at what I will always consider Christina's old apartment house.

This time I tried Jamie first.

No, he said, his voice appropriately regretful, he couldn't recall seeing George Gladstone that day. "I might even have exchanged a couple of words with him, though. It was more than ten years ago, you know." (Like I needed to hear this from him, too, right?)

I went on to question another six tenants — for all the good it did me. Nobody was able to confirm that George had been in town on that February twenty-ninth, one of the individuals — a plump, redheaded woman who was probably in her seventies — chiding me with, "Christ! What a thing to ask! I can't remember who I ran into yesterday, for crying out loud!"

It was time to go home by then anyway.

It was getting late, and I was tired.

On Thursday, at approximately eight p.m., I was back to ringing doorbells. But I only spoke with two of the residents — neither of whom was the least bit helpful — before scooting out of there.

Now, this hasty exit had nothing to do with my getting more and more discouraged after every buzzer I pressed in that building — although I don't deny this was true. The reason I called it a night was that I'd suddenly become extremely queasy. And I was kind of shaky, to boot.

But even though I hadn't gotten to see as many people as I'd hoped to, I assured myself it was no big deal. Tomorrow I'd pick up where I left off.

By the time I reached home, however, I was in pretty sad shape. And while it wasn't as if I'd contracted beriberi or any-thing, I'll tell you this: I felt really putrid.

I was burning up, which I guess can be expected when your thermometer reads 103 degrees. Plus, I didn't have the strength I was born with. What I did have were chills, body aches, and a stomach so untrustworthy that I'd have set up my bed in the bathroom — only it wouldn't fit.

On Friday morning I got in touch with

the doctor. He listened to my complaints, clucked his tongue, and informed me that I had a nice case of the flu. Well, I could have told *him* that. (Besides, what was so nice about it?) He advised me to drink plenty of fluids and to keep taking aspirin to bring down the fever. "Other than that, I want you to get lots of rest," he ordered. (Was he *kidding?* I mean, what choice did I have?) "And let me hear from you tomorrow."

At any rate, as you can see, I managed to survive — with some help from my friends.

Both Barbara in the next apartment and Harriet across the hall left chicken soup at my door, Harriet's being of the home-cooked variety and Barbara's the product of one of our better local delis.

Jackie insisted on doing some shopping for me. I told her I didn't need a thing — I'd visited D'Agostino's only Thursday morning before going to the office. Besides, this was one of those very rare instances when my appetite had taken a powder on me. But you know Jackie. Overriding my protests, she hopped a cab to my place on Saturday and deposited two full bags of groceries in the hall. The big problem after this was figuring out where to store everything. Still, I suppose that having all that fruit juice on hand wasn't really such a terrible thing.

As for Ellen, she was ready to rush right over and minister to me, going so far as to suggest that she might take a couple of days off from work. Now, while I love her dearly and realize that I risk sounding ungrateful, the last thing I needed was Ellen hovering over me. It required a great deal of exhausting back-and-forth, however, to persuade her to stay away. But I finally found the magic words. "Dr. Riccardi says I'm highly contagious" — actually, he didn't say anything of the sort, but I'm sure it was true nonetheless — "and you don't want to be sick for your wedding, do you?" Even though it was about two months until the big event, this was apparently a sobering thought — sobering enough, at least, to dissuade my niece from playing Florence Nightingale. We left it that if she could do something for me, I'd holler.

On Monday I heard from Nick. He'd just tried reaching me at the office, and according to Jackie, I was practically battling for my life. I responded with what I hoped he'd regard as a brave little laugh. "I'm slightly under the weather, that's all," I told him stoically. At any rate, Nick asked if I needed anything. And then that wonderful man offered to fix a meal for me! I thanked him profusely and assured him I was managing just fine. (I mean, God forbid he should get a look at me in this state.)

It was almost as an afterthought that he said in this remarkably casual tone, "By the way, Tiffany's flying back next week."

By the way? A good two or three seconds elapsed before he went on, during which interval I was close to hyperventilating. "Of course, Derek is thrilled. But, you know, Dez? I have mixed feelings. I've gotten kind of used to having him around. Anyhow, the important thing is that he couldn't be happier about his mother's coming home."

Oh, yes, he could, I retorted in my head. *He could be as happy about it as I am.*

"She said to expect her a week from Wednesday. So if you're up to it and have no other plans, maybe you and I can get together that weekend."

I'm convinced it was learning about Tiffany's imminent return that did the trick. I mean, I began to feel better the instant I put down the receiver. Then, later in the afternoon, I was all but railroaded into recovering — again, courtesy of Nick — when I opened the door to find a cheerful delivery guy and two-dozen roses staring me in the face! That night I was even able to finish my supper.

Vicky phoned on Tuesday.

She opened on a reproachful note. "I thought I'd hear from you — whether or not you, like, really had any news for me." I apologized, explaining that I'd been out of commission for almost a week. After which she apologized back and, like the good kid she is, proffered her services. "They make great stuff at Frank 'n' Burgers, where I waitress, and I could, like, drop something off at your apartment. It wouldn't be any trouble, honest."

Now, until yesterday, even the *words* "frank" and "burger" would have been tough for me to swallow. As it was, though, I merely gulped a couple of times prior to telling Vicky how much I appreciated her thoughtfulness.

"I don't suppose you were able, you know, to do much investigating before you, like, got sick."

"Actually, I was in the process of following up on something."

"Really? What kind of something?" she asked excitedly.

"Let's wait and see how things pan out. This may be just another wild goose chase, and I'd hate for you to get your hopes up."

"I won't. Can't we —"

"Please, Vicky. It would be better to hold off until I finish checking everything out. I'll be back at work next week, possibly sooner. Okay?"

"Okay," she agreed. I could tell she was trying her best not to make it sound reluctant. But it did.

After Vicky's call I attempted to estimate when I'd be able to resume my questioning of Christina's former neighbors.

Maybe Thursday, I thought optimistically. *Or Friday.* I ended with a more realistic, *Monday, at the latest.*

It didn't turn out to be any of those days, though.

The fact is, I never visited Christina's old apartment house again.

CHAPTER 40

By Thursday I'd made up my mind to return to the office the next day.

That night Ellen unmade it for me.

"If you don't take it easy until you're a hundred percent, you're liable to have a relapse," she warned. And then, to drive home her point, she borrowed the tactic I'd so recently employed on her (you know, to dissuade her from nursing me into a breakdown). "You wouldn't want to be forced to cancel your date with Nick, would you?"

Well, obviously I shouldn't have been so eager to tell her that Nick and I planned to spend some time together the weekend after this one. But who could figure she'd use it against me? Nevertheless, I caved.

Still, I had every intention of resuming my canvassing tomorrow morning. But on Friday it poured — and I mean *poured*. Also on Saturday and Sunday. And remembering Ellen's words, I rethought my agenda.

I finally went in to the office on Monday,

expecting to go to Queens that evening.

Jackie didn't bother to censor herself when I walked in. "You look like something out of a horror movie. There's not even a drop of color in your face. How do you feel, though?"

"Much better." *Until now, anyway.*

It wasn't more than ten minutes later, just as I'd begun to transcribe some long-neglected notes, that she buzzed me. "Some guy's here with a package for you, Dez. You have to sign for it, so I'm sending him in."

A package? What flashed through my mind was *Maybe another bouquet from Nick.* But I rejected the idea at once. Flowers aren't what you could consider "a package." Besides, he'd sent me those gorgeous roses only last week. I mean, how spoiled can you get?

At any rate, after obliging the messenger with my signature, he handed me this bulky brown parcel. Taped to the front was a white business-sized envelope with my name on it. The correspondence inside, dated November 1, 2002 — that past Friday — was typed on heavy white stock with an embossed letterhead reading, THE LAW OFFICES OF WARREN AND WARREN. There was a Wall Street area address.

Dear Ms. Shapiro: (it began)

It is with deep regret that I must inform you of the passing of our client George Gladstone on Monday, October 28.

Shortly before entering the hospital, Mr. Gladstone left a package with this firm, furnishing us with explicit instructions that it be forwarded to you in the event of his death. In accordance with Mr. Gladstone's wishes, the package is herewith enclosed.

If our offices can be of assistance to you in any way, Ms. Shapiro, please don't hesitate to contact me.

Sincerely,

Marcus J. Warren

Marcus J. Warren, Esquire

Now, I'm not claiming that I'd actually *liked* George Gladstone, especially since I was convinced he was a murderer and — what I considered even more reprehensible — had allowed someone else to pay for his crime. Nevertheless, the letter left me feeling not only stunned, but even a little saddened — although, for the life of me, I couldn't figure out why.

After a minute or so I tore open the package itself — curious, apprehensive, and hopeful all at the same time. Inside was a small packet that held an audiocassette. And along with that was a handwritten note:

10/23/02

Hi, cupcake,

If you're reading this, it means that I'm no longer among the living.

I'm having some surgery done this coming Monday to remove a pesky little tumor that I somehow managed to acquire. They tell me the operation isn't that serious, but who knows what can happen when they open you up, right?

I decided that in the event of the worst (meaning the worst from my point of view), it wouldn't be any skin off my nose if I finally came clean. I made this tape for Pirrelli's daughter, and I'm counting on you to see that she receives it, since I have no idea where to reach her.

Bet you didn't believe me when I told you I was fond of kids, did you? However, I must admit that I'm not motivated entirely by altruism. Maybe fessing up will get me some points with The Man Upstairs.

Be seeing you.

Your former sparring partner,

George

PS: I still say I had nothing to do with that threat on your pillow. And the way things stand now, I think you can take my word for it.

At last! It was as if I were reaching the end of a long and tortuous journey. I was so excited that it was a real challenge to contain myself.

I glanced at my watch: almost eleven. Vicky must be in class. Well, I'd leave a message on her cell phone; no doubt she checked it fairly regularly. "Get back to me as soon as you can, Vicky. I have some news for you."

And now I just sat there, glued to my seat. I mean, dynamite couldn't have moved me from that chair.

While I waited for my client to return my call, I reflected briefly on the PS to George's note. Even before this confirmation from him, I was 99.9% convinced that that nasty little epistle was Uncle Tony's contribution to my investigation. Not that I'd ever be able to prove it, of course. But who cared? With George's confession to Christina's murder, Tony no longer had anything to worry about from me — and vice-versa.

I heard from Vicky about fifteen minutes later.

"Hi, Dez. It's Vicky." She sounded breathless. "What's the news?"

The words tumbled out. "George Gladstone had surgery last Monday, and —"

"George Gladstone?"

"He's the older man who lived in Christina's building — the one who was so obsessed with her. And recently I'd pretty much determined that he was our killer."

"Thank God," Vicky whispered.

"He died on the day of his operation. But before entering the hospital, he'd made a tape for you — maybe he had some sort of premonition. At any rate, he didn't know your address, so he left the tape with his attorneys, instructing them to deliver it to my office in case something happened to him. I can send it on to your house, if you like," I offered halfheartedly. "Or are you still living with your grandmother?"

"No, I'm home again. It was, you know, too hard to commute to school from Grandmom's." And now there was an urgency in her voice. "Tell me. What's on the tape?"

"I didn't play it; it's for you."

"I'll be there in, like, half an hour."

"But what about the rest of your classes?"

"Uh, that's okay. I won't be, like, missing

anything important."

Of course, the responsible thing would have been to try to persuade her to come by after school. But if I couldn't wait to hear what George had to say, how could I expect that Vicky would be able to hold out?

I had seen my young client only once previously — when she came to the office to hire me. And she looked entirely different today.

On the positive side, this time Vicky wore a skirt that was only three or four inches above her knees. Which, going by our last meeting, was positively demure for her. Also, she no longer had green-and-orange hair.

On the less than positive side, however, the skirt was so tight that if she ate so much as a grape, it probably wouldn't fit anymore. Plus, while her hair was currently one color, that color was purple.

She bussed me on the cheek, then sat down on the chair alongside my desk. "I'm nervous," she informed me after she'd finished gnawing on her lower lip. "Do you think he's, like, confessing?"

"It appears that way." And here the nurturer in me took over for a couple of seconds. "Listen, are you hungry? Would you like me to order some lunch for you before we begin listening?"

"No, thank you. I just, you know, want to hear the tape."

I nodded. It was already sitting in my cassette recorder, so I pressed Play.

And George Gladstone's voice filled my tiny cubicle.

CHAPTER 41

Hello, Vicky, my name is George Gladstone, and I'm dead. How's that for a grabber of an opening? (Ask Desiree to explain — if she hasn't already.)

I've got something to tell you — something you've no doubt been waiting a long time to hear. Your dad didn't kill Christina Trent. I did. Worse yet, I let him take the rap for her murder. In fact, I set things up so he would.

I'm making this recording because I want you to know what really happened that night. As Desiree put it when she was here yesterday, you're entitled to the truth. Also, under the circumstances, I no longer have to worry about being thrown in the clink for my crime, do I? And if you're listening, Desiree, I imagine you're pleased that all of your yakking finally brought me to my knees. So to speak, that is.

Anyway, here goes . . .

I flew in from California late that Saturday — the day of the murder. And at about eleven o'clock, I went to this all-night convenience store a couple of blocks from my home to pick up the Sunday paper. On the way back I spotted your father on the other side of the street, heading in the opposite direction. (The neighborhood is fairly well lit. Besides, I used to see him around here wearing this red-and-blue parka, which was pretty hard to miss.) At any rate, when I entered the lobby of my building, I ran smack into one of the other tenants — a Ms. Borg — who was on her way out to walk her Yorkie, a ratty-looking creature named Scheherazade. Ms. Borg had a studio on the fifth floor at that time — Christina lived on six. Well, the woman asked if I'd heard the row that had been going on at Christina's. Of course, this was a ridiculous question, considering that my place is on the ground floor. Anyhow, when I answered in the negative, that yenta was only too eager to inform me that for the better part of the evening Christina and her boyfriend, your father — I'm sorry, Vicky — had been yelling their heads off at each other. According to Ms. Borg, the altercation was apparently over by then, but she claimed that at one point things were so heated that she felt someone ought to get in touch with the police. I recall wondering why it had never occurred to her that she could be this someone.

But to continue . . . I wanted to make certain Christina was okay, so I went up to her apartment. When she came to the door, her *eyes were red and her cheeks were all blotchy. She wasn't crying then, but it was obvious she'd been doing a lot of that very recently, and I could tell she was still pretty agitated. I explained that a neighbor had just mentioned that she might be having some trouble and that I wanted to find out if I could help in any way. She thanked me and insisted she was fine. I knew she was ready to say good night, and I didn't want that to happen. You see, Vicky, I can admit it now. I had kind of a crush on Christina, even though she was a little young for me.*

"*A little?*" I muttered.

She was very mature for her age, however, George was saying.

I put in my two cents again. "*Pu-leeze.*"

I had the absurd idea that if I could get my foot in the door — I'm talking both figuratively and *literally — Christina might turn to me. Wishful thinking, I know. But the way I looked at it, she and your dad had just split up — or so I assumed — and there'd probably never be a better time for me to make my pitch. Well, I could smell coffee brewing. And, like everyone else in public relations who's worth their salt, I'm a dyed-in-the-wool opportunist. So I put her on the spot. 'Now that I've made the trek all the way up to the sixth floor, aren't you at least going to invite me in for coffee?' I* asked her. Something like that, anyhow. Christina said sure, but it was obvious she was being victimized by her own good manners.

As soon as I walked in I noticed that she had a knife in her hand — she was holding it at her side. When she saw my eyes go to the knife, she smiled and told me — and these were pretty much her exact words, too — 'I've been trying to hack my way through a frozen coffee cake.' Incidentally, Vicky, just about everyone and their Aunt Tillie had a microwave even then, but this evidently didn't include Christina — or me, either, for that matter. At any rate, Christina motioned for me to have a seat. 'I'll be back in a couple of minutes,' she said — she was turning toward the kitchen. I grasped her hand, the one without the knife, of course — I'm not *that* much of a half-wit. I only wanted to make nice, to console her, but she started to pull away. So then I did something really, really dumb. I reached over and put my arm around her waist to draw her closer. My intention was nothing more lecherous than to give her a peck on the cheek — that's the honest-to-God truth. But Christina ordered me out of there; her boyfriend would be back any minute, she warned me. Naturally, I should have left. It wasn't that I didn't realize how distraught she was that evening — as I said before, it was apparent the instant she

*opened the door. Nevertheless, I was deter-
mined to plant that little kiss on her just to
show her that this was all I had in mind. It
seems to me I put my hand under her chin at
that point; I'm not really certain — everything
happened very quickly. Anyhow, she raised the
knife. Thinking about it afterward — as I
have at least a million times since that terrible
night — I concluded it was very likely she was
merely trying to get me to back off. At that
moment, however, I was afraid she was really
going to use that thing on me. So I grabbed
her wrist to take it from her, but Christina
twisted her body. And we struggled, and . . .
oh, God . . .* (A pause, then in a choked
voice:) *the knife wound up in Christina.*

*It was an accident, but who would believe
me? Half the people in the building appeared
to be aware of how interested I was in Christina and how disinterested she was in me.
Anyway, I stuck around just long enough to
determine that she was dead, and then I got
out of there as fast as I could. Incidentally, I
even left my* New York Times *on the coffee
table, where I'd deposited it when I first
walked into the apartment. And for weeks afterward I was worried sick that the newspaper
would be traced back to me. Ms. Borg — the
woman with the Yorkie — had seen me carrying it, you know. And suppose your father*

had also picked up the Sunday Times *that night, Vicky. The presence in Christina's apartment of two Sunday* Times *might have aroused suspicion. But it never came to that.*

(A pause) *Now, where was I? Oh, yes . . .*

I used the stairwell where there was very little chance anyone would see me — and no one did. And by the time I got to the first floor, I'd made up my mind to try and provide the police with a more likely suspect: the man Christina was known to have battled with only a short time earlier. Your father, of course.

Actually, I wasn't at all sure Christina was telling the truth when she said he'd be returning. But, just in case, I went outdoors and watched for him. After a few minutes I caught sight of him about halfway down the block. I dashed inside and sent that antique contraption that's charitably referred to as an elevator in this place up to the sixth floor. Then I put in an anonymous call to the cops. I figured that, with any luck, by the time that elevator came creeping down again and your father made it upstairs to Christina's, the police wouldn't be far behind him. And . . . well, you know the rest.

I can't tell you how sorry I am for this despicable thing I did to your father, Vicky. Naturally, I don't expect you to forgive me — how could you? I destroyed the life of your parent, and in so doing caused you what must have been unbearable pain, as well. In the event you're wondering, though, there were times over the years that I did consider going to the police and admitting everything. But that's all I ever did: consider *going to them. The sad truth is, I was too much of a coward to go through with it.*

So as it turns out, this tape is both the least and the most I can do for you, Vicky. Just be assured that not only wasn't your dad a murderer, but more than that, he must have had some pretty decent qualities. Otherwise, George concluded (and I'm not sure, but I thought I heard a sob in his voice here), *he wouldn't have had the affection of a lovely girl like Christina.*

Automatically, I pressed the Rewind button. Then I glanced at Vicky.

There was an expression on her face that was . . . well, "rapturous" would be the best way to describe it. Suddenly she jumped up and hollered, "I told you my dad didn't kill her!" And tears began to roll down her cheeks.

I leaned across my desk and grabbed a bunch of Kleenex. Then, hurrying over to her, I all but shoved the tissues into Vicky's midsection. "Yes, you did," I agreed.

"He was — like — *framed!*" she declared, wiping away the wetness. Following which she added, "And I don't think it was, you know, only because my dad was such a perfect patsy, either. I'll bet this George was, like, crazy jealous of him."

"I'll bet you're right, Vicky," I responded, impressed once again with how perceptive this young girl was. "But, listen, you told me you wanted your father's name cleared, and now there's an excellent chance of that. I have a feeling the newspapers would be very interested in this tape and —"

She was taken aback at the suggestion. "Oh, no! Did I say that? I didn't mean — The only thing that's, like, important to me is for my own family — *his* family — to see how wrong they were about my father. I can't wait to play the tape for them — you know, all of them: my mom, my grandmom, and my uncle Tony. *Especially* my uncle Tony."

"Well, it's all yours now," I said, handing her the cassette.

We hugged then. "Thank you, Desiree. Thank you, thank you, thank you." She stepped back, smiling broadly. A moment later she put her hand on my arm. "How much do I, like, owe you?"

"Oh, don't worry about that. I'll be mailing you a bill."

But, of course, I knew I never would.

Philomena Pirrelli sent me a short note a few days later. It said simply, *The Pirrelli family is most grateful to you for proving to us this which we should have accepted on faith.* Accompanying the note was a check for a fairly substantial amount.

Now, I'm not denying I was pleased — and quite surprised — to receive the check. But while you probably won't believe me — in fact, *I* hardly believe me — the money was sort of an added bonus.

I considered myself paid right after George Gladstone's tape ended — and I saw that look on Vicky's face.

Sweet Potato Casserole

About 2 lbs. sweet potatoes
4T sweet butter, softened
1/4 cup heavy cream
1T Kahlua
Salt and freshly ground pepper to taste
Miniature marshmallows

1. Scrub potatoes, then cut a small, deep slit in the top of each.
2. Bake on center rack of a preheated 375° oven for about 1 hr., or until potatoes are fork tender.
3. In food processor fitted with steel blade, combine flesh of potatoes, butter, and cream. Process until very smooth.
4. Add Kahlua and season to taste with salt and pepper. Process briefly to blend.
5. Bake in ovenproof dish in preheated 350° oven for approximately 25 minutes or until very hot. Dot with mini marshmallows and bake for 5 to 6 minutes or until golden.

Serves 4.

NOTE: Casserole can be prepared in advance and refrigerated overnight or frozen, then brought to room temperature and baked as above.

About the Author

SELMA EICHLER is a freelance writer who lives in New York with her husband, Lloyd.

We hope you have enjoyed this Large Print book. Other Thorndike, Wheeler or Chivers Press Large Print books are available at your library or directly from the publishers.

For more information about current and upcoming titles, please call or write, without obligation, to:

Publisher
Thorndike Press
295 Kennedy Memorial Drive
Waterville, ME   04901
Tel. (800) 223-1244

Or visit our Web site at:
www.gale.com/thorndike
www.gale.com/wheeler

OR

Chivers Large Print
published by BBC Audiobooks Ltd
St James House, The Square
Lower Bristol Road
Bath BA2 3SB
England
Tel. +44(0) 800 136919
email: bbcaudiobooks@bbc.co.uk
www.bbcaudiobooks.co.uk

All our Large Print titles are designed for easy reading, and all our books are made to last.